RED

on the

INSIDE

Elizabeth Kuligowski

Burton Mayers Books

To my husband, Sam, and to my children,

Runa & Ingrid.

Author's Note

Dear Reader,

Thank you for picking up Red On The Inside.

This story is personal to me, not only as my first novel but as a reflection of my own postpartum experience. Writing this book was my way of navigating the darker side of motherhood—those moments of paranoia, isolation, and disconnection that can creep in during a time when we're told we should feel nothing but joy. Crafting Red On The Inside gave me structure when I felt most at sea, and gave me a way to make sense of the unsettling emotions that come with the life-altering shift into motherhood.

Gothic fiction and horror have always been a source of comfort for me, like old friends who understand that the world isn't always as simple as it seems. There's something in the shadows, in the strange and the eerie, that has always felt strangely safe. It allowed me to confront my own ghosts with a sense of distance.

At its core, this novel is about identity, trauma, and survival—about what happens when the past we've tried to bury begins to surface. If this book leaves you feeling haunted, but maybe seen in some small way, then I hope I've done my job.

Thank you for letting me share this part of myself with you, and thank you for taking this journey with me.

With warmest regards,

Elizabeth Kuligowski

Elizabeth Kuligowski

Chapter 1.

The house had been white once, though it was faded now, and the old paint peeled in the cold. Shedding its skin, flake by flake. Something about the proportions, an architectural oversight, gave it a collapsed aspect. The house was at the top of a mountain road and if you climbed up onto the roof you'd have a view of the whole valley below, the whole town of Castor and the wide river that cut it in half. It was Lana's house, and she sometimes toyed with the idea of painting it periwinkle blue.

From the front, the house was a little single story with flaking shiplap, but there was a second floor below it, where the foundations dropped away down the mountainside, held up by struts that Lana put her whole trust in. The Kootenays were beautiful, but you had to make compromises if you wanted a level kitchen floor. The bedrooms were in the basement. The back yard was a side yard. When Lana sat in the bath and looked out of the window, she felt like she was on an airship, nothing but tree-covered mountaintops, rusty now with autumn leaves, and endless blue sky.

The neighbour on one side was more than a stone's throw away and, like every other house in town, it was straighter and tidier than Lana's house. On the other side was a trailhead, from which little pieces of gravel occasionally skittered across Lana's driveway. Her house was the last one before the mountain really started gaining altitude. There was a gate heading up to the mountain, with yellowed maps behind plexiglass, and sometimes it felt to Lana that the house would rather be on the other side of that gate. It didn't feel right for it to be on the civilised side anymore.

Lana willed herself toward the little house, her home for the last eight years. Her body wouldn't move. She leaned her neck back to look down at the sleeping baby strapped to her chest, nestled in an ergonomic carrier. She hoped to see some kind of affirmation in the tiny face, but the baby's red eyelids were closed, his lips parted, drool soaking into Lana's t-shirt. The house begged for attention, daring her to look, but she knew that the smallest curtain twitch or flickering shadow at the window would crumple her resolve.

It was supposed to be a fresh start when they moved in, her and Magnus, after her father had died. But fresh starts can sour, Lana had learned. Now she knew what was underneath, what was down the mountainside. It was a facade and nobody else knew it, not even her family; it was something to bear alone. She thought about painting the house periwinkle blue, as if that would solve anything other than the flaking exterior.

Or I could go to the hire shop, get a backhoe. She knew what a backhoe was, she'd looked at the different models online.

And push the whole fucking thing down the mountain.

Except I can't.

Lana reached the house, eyes down, and eased in the key. This was supposed to be the kind of place where you left your front door unlocked, she thought. Maybe it wasn't so much about keeping people out. Someone was listening to her on the other side of the door. The house held its breath. Behind her, the wind ruffled the leaves, distant chatter floated on the air, life made noise. But the air on the other side of the door was grave and waiting. The front door was painted red and had been scratched by the claws of long dead dogs she'd never known, and it was a barrier between worlds.

She brushed her lips against the baby's soft hair, not really sure if it was a simple habit or a good luck ritual that had become second nature. The baby breathed deeply, wearing a sleeping expression of utter contentment, utter ignorance, savouring the evergreen air blowing down from the peak.

Lana put the key in the lock, turning the handle of a jack-in-the-box, waiting for the surprise that was no longer a surprise. She steeled her heart for the drop she knew was coming. The ghost was waiting for her. Like always. Waiting to take her hostage again.

Chapter 2.

The last few normal days were the last few days of the summer. Lana had a feeling, brewing for a while but impossible to put a name to. It was a vague sense that something was out of place. She was always just about to pick something up, or just about to say something important.

For a while she considered the possibility that it was part of some rare medical syndrome, because the sense of vagueness coincided with the feeling that there was something under her eyelids. Something like a baby's cut fingernail, she kept thinking. She rubbed her eyes until eyelashes came away on her fingertips. She scrutinised her eye in the bathroom mirror, holding it open and staring straight past her own reflection. Nothing ever there. She blinked furiously, dripped lubricating drops into her eye. Lana hated the way she had no choice but to watch the quivering drop, closer to her eye than anything should really be, watching it grow bigger until it was all she could see, and then the cold of it, and then the only reason she couldn't see it any more was because it was all over her eyeball, and behind it and up around the edges. It made her nauseous. There was a blurriness, although she couldn't pinpoint exactly what was blurred. Everything looked clear to her, the same as it always had, but she was sure there was something she *couldn't* see, something hiding behind the invisible air. There was something underneath.

***

Lana sat in the bath, combing through her long dark hair with her hands, easing tangles into smaller tangles. She pulled strands loose and gathered them around her fingers into little loops she could leave on the side of the bath. She meant to collect them after she'd finished her bath, but she always forgot.

Why keep them though? It's not like they're going back in. They're biological waste. And crafting with human hair is a slippery slope. That way lies masks made of human skin.

She made herself believe the hairs would have fallen out soon enough anyway. They were already loosely moored. Hair loss hit her hard after her other two kids, and she thought just maybe she'd gotten away with it this time. Her hair stayed almost obscenely luxurious until it suddenly started shedding like an old Christmas tree, a few weeks in. Now her hairline was chipped and, without artful arranging, bald patches showed above her ears when she put her hair in a ponytail. A lot of stuff had fallen out of her body; hair, milk, sweat, calcium, blood, one whole organ plus a new human being. A whole life that would outlast her. She was spiralling again. Her breathing got fast when she started to spiral. *Clench fists, deep breaths, focus on reality.* Lana twisted the hair around her fingers, until her fingertips shone white and throbbed. *And release, and calm.*

The birth had been awful. The word 'traumatic' came to mind, although Lana would never say it out loud. Lana supposed they usually were traumatic, in the way that blunt force trauma is traumatic, but in the emotional trauma way too. Still the body has a handy way of making you forget. *The body wants to duplicate.* She had forgotten the details, like she was supposed to. *Pre-programmed memory loss.* But there was a sense of having forgotten something awful, and it sometimes jabbed at her from nowhere, like there was a nerve left on the outside. Sometimes it was a weight, sometimes a cloud, sometimes something unspecific and incomplete. Far away but attached, like a trailing kite. *Like something at the end of an umbilical cord. Like the thing you thought he would be.* She pushed the thought away. Cody was fine. She didn't want to make him otherwise by stewing in negative thoughts. Not that she was superstitious. But it did feel almost unbelievably lucky, that all three of her children were alive and well and happy. It didn't always go that way. *Luck always runs out, you know. Time to pay the piper.*

Whatever that means.

Lana worried about bad luck catching up to her. She worried about a vast and inscrutable system of metaphysical justice and the balancing of cosmic scales, and she read about horrible things happening to women just like her, with kids just like hers. And she thought, *why not me?*

She had sat in this same bathtub, just a few weeks prior, (*was it really just a few weeks?*) writhing in pain and bleeding and trying not to scream and terrify the kids. Sometimes Seb left his room in the night and crept halfway up the stairs from his basement bedroom, to see if people were talking about him. Lana prayed he would stay safely cocooned in a dream. She wasn't ready. There had been some miscalculation. *The cosmic scales.* Lana remembered her husband, Magnus, white-faced, shouting hysterically into a telephone clamped between his ear and shoulder. There was blood in his beard, and it looked like ketchup. *Why do they call it 'having a baby'? Like it's such a passive thing.*

Lana had taken a lot of baths since. Red baths, from the after-bleeding. Baths salted almost to seawater, to clean the abrasions that burned and wept. She could sit in there for hours, reading steam-swollen paperbacks and falling backwards into her own private mind-space, until all the warmth was gone.

"Lana." It was Magnus. He filled the doorway, like a huge blonde bear in a flannel shirt and carpenter pants. "It's gross in here. It's like a sauna."

"He likes it." Lana gestured to baby Cody, asleep in his bouncer, his left eye and lip corner twitching into an occasional smile. *Sure, now you sleep.*

Sometimes Lana felt like she had two babies, a cherub who mostly slept, and a demon who didn't want anyone to sleep. *No,* she thought, *that's not fair. He's doing his best.*

"I think the humidity is nice for his lungs. It's too dry at night with the radiators. That's why he fusses," she said.

Magnus considered this. Lana could almost see the thoughts inside his head. He was thinking about buying a humidifier, weighing pros and cons, the initial cost, the running cost, the fire risk. Magnus moved to the mirror, stepping gingerly over the sleeping baby. He made an effort to smooth down his wiry blonde hair and made a dissatisfied noise. He rummaged in the bathroom cabinet while Lana hoisted her body out of the tub and wrapped a towel around herself. Steam rose from her skin and curled toward the ceiling. She swooned, light-headed. *Too hot. Boiled myself again. Like a frog in a saucepan, or whatever it is they say.* She blinked it away.

Beads of moisture clung to the ceiling. They would drip back down later, ice cold. The trick was to not be underneath them when that happened. Magnus unearthed a small glass bottle of oil his mother had bought him any number of Christmases ago. He rubbed a little into his palms and ran his hands through his beard. It smelled too strongly of sandalwood and clashed horribly with Lana's lavender bath salts. She wrinkled her nose. The oil had no effect. Magnus had the unruly, thicket-like beard of a man who spends time outside, shaped by strong winds and biting cold. Which was ridiculous, Lana thought, because Magnus was a homebody if ever there was one – a soft centred, sentimental man who just happened to look very rough around the edges.

"We need to go soon," Magnus said. "We need to have gone already. I guess it doesn't much matter." He shrugged his broad shoulders. "But maybe it's time you got ready? I don't think that towel's quite gonna cut it. This is a semi-formal affair. There's gonna be dips and stuff."

Magnus didn't like to push her. He knew the suddenness and the speed of the birth had hit her hard. He was gentle and she was grateful. She knew she was wasting time though. They had a lunch date with Magnus's parents. Her, Magnus, all three of the kids, Grandpa John and Nanna Julie.

Lana padded down the hall, the deep carpet drying her feet as she went. It was snipped away here and there where the kids had stuck things to it, things that were impossible to clean, like wax or glitter glue. Lana didn't sweat the small things. It was easier to cut away a chunk of the carpet with the little razor she used to shape her eyebrows, problem solved, and keep going. It was her house, after all. If Magnus even noticed that she'd been harvesting little bits of the carpet, he never mentioned it.

The kids were yelling somewhere, probably the living room. *That means they're fine.* She headed away from their cacophony, down the creaking stairs to her bedroom and tried to find something to wear.

There was an unspoken agreement that she would cover the tattoos that peppered her shoulders and back, plus one on her hip, a couple on her arms. There was no ink below the elbow or below the knee, not thanks to any plan – it had just worked out like that, like most things. But she had worn a dress with spaghetti straps once to a family Christmas party and the sideways glances she had received from Magnus's parents had been almost unbearable. The whole evening had been so painfully awkward that Lana had wished she could slither out of her skin and into a storm drain, and only return to her human form when everyone who had attended the party was long dead. She spent a good amount of the evening entertaining that particular fantasy. On top of everything, Magnus had made a terrible attempt to convince her that she might be warmer if she put something around her shoulders. He winced as he said it, physically appalled by the sound of his own underhandedness. He was the worst liar Lana had ever met.

Lana sometimes had a nightmare that she had wandered back in time to that party, and that hundreds of pairs of eyes were raking her skin for evidence of moral inferiority. It was stupid, and she and Magnus would laugh about it when she woke up. He called it 'The Christmas

Party Imposter Dream', which Lana thought would be a good title for an esoteric music project. But it was a deep and often painful truth that she wasn't what John and Julie had wanted for their son. With her flaking, precarious little house and her tattoos that seemed to represent a kind of flaking and precariousness of mind to her in-laws. There was nothing she could do about it but smile and pretend it didn't bother her as much as it did, and think of clever retorts to their passive aggressive comments, and smirk to herself in the dark when she replayed their conversations late at night, where she said all the things she had wanted to.

Lana stood in front of the open closet for longer than she meant to, staring in at her clothes without really seeing them. She swung the door back and forth experimentally, watching her reflection in the inside mirror. There was something wrong with the latch.

It felt like everything she owned was just broken enough to be annoying, but not so broken that anything desperately needed replacing. They didn't have quite enough money to be replacing things. Or buying new baby clothes, when the ones they had were only a little stained and dryer-shrunken. The closet wouldn't stay fully closed. The smallest draft would blow it silently open, usually in the middle of the night. In the morning it would be open, and Lana would catch sight of herself in the mirror and jump out of her skin. Even when she knew what had happened, even when she expected it. She meant to put a blanket over it, but she could never remember.

They call it Baby Brain, she thought. *Baby brain, baby blues. Baby talk to make real stuff seem small. It's only a little baby depressive episode.*

The clothes hung lifelessly in the closet. A mischievous streak made her hand twitch as her eyes fell on the spaghetti strap dress she had worn to the Christmas party. She grinned to her mirror self, sharing the joke. *Imagine if we did.* She rifled through some t-shirts before landing on one with a picture of a jack o' lantern smoking a corncob pipe. It just about covered her tattoos, but it was absurd. It was playing by the rules, the unspoken rules of decorum that governed her in-laws' fastidious home, but it was also ghastly, and they would hate it. *A most judicious choice.*

***

Grandpa John and Nanna Julie, as they liked to be called whenever the children were present, lived in a house that embodied everything Lana's house had failed at. It was straight and white like a sugar cube, with all four corners on the actual ground, adorned with freshly painted trellises and orderly flowerbeds. John and Julie were the sort of people who lived in a house like that. They were small and tidy people. Lana had come to hate their small and tidy conversation, but she did her best to smile. She hoped they couldn't tell the difference between a real and a fake smile. They didn't know her very well, and they didn't seem to know their son very well either.

Magnus was nothing like his parents. He was warm and genuine. There was something careworn about him, in the way his eyes crinkled when he smiled. *Which is a compliment even if it doesn't really sound like one,* Lana added whenever this thought occurred to her. All the surface stuff had been slowly sanded away while they'd lived next to each other, although Lana had clung to her hard edges, so that his emotions were wholly transparent. That was Lana's favourite thing about him. He was a pane of glass, and she was a hard little shard of obsidian. That's what made it hurt so much when he gave her that look. Somewhere halfway between pity and panic. He'd been making that face a lot since baby Cody was born. The same face he had worn when Lana's blood was pooling on the bathroom floor. There was a rug there now, to cover the stain. That was the generally agreed upon method of dealing with stains, and it had been her father's before they had taken over the house. *Like they say, if it ain't broke, throw a rug over it.*

When they had renovated the property, she and Magnus had flipped coins to decide whose turn it was to move a strategically placed square of carpet. More often than not there was some questionable inkblot underneath. They had played a game finding meaningful shapes in the stains. "That one looks like a skull with a scorpion coming out of the eye hole," Lana would say. "It means we should tread carefully, and not let any scorpions get in our eyeholes." Or Magnus would say, "This one looks like a pizza. It means we should order a pizza." And he would grin like an idiot, and they would buy pizza from the renovation budget, like it was a necessary expense. But now Magnus' broad, bearded face with its wonky smirk was corrupted by that expression, *those sad shining fucking eyes.* It was faded now, nothing like the as sharp as it had been, but it was there. He had no idea he was doing it, which made Lana feel like crap for resenting it, for resenting something only she could see.

Lana sat in the passenger seat of their van, which was as scratched as their front door, just a minute too long. But it was enough time for Magnus to come around to her window and fix her with his pitying look. Lana writhed under the scrutiny but kept her face level. She unclicked her seatbelt and opened the door.

"Stop staring at me. What?" she snapped.

He didn't take it personally. "Are you sure you want to be here? Are you okay to do this?"

No, obviously I don't want to be here. I want to be at home, in my hovel, like a goblin. I want to be where all my DVDs are, and where my in-laws aren't. I do it though. For you.

Lana took a breath. She reached up to touch his cheek, running her fingers through the blonde thicket of his beard. She smiled a real smile. Something about Magnus was like gravity, and she could catch a little of his groundedness just by being near him.

"It's just lunch," she said.

That's how things were between them now. Still good, still close, but with other things in the way. Amorphous things that occupied a different amount of space every day. Like someone was coming in the night and rearranging the furniture of their relationship. And they kept bumping into sofas and little stools with cups of coffee balanced on them. Their stuff, but in wrong and unexpected places. Magnus in particular was always ready to apologise and to shuffle cautiously around these things. Lana was more like to trip over them, running, and crash to the ground, and then tell nobody what had happened.

She scooped Cody out of his car seat and balanced him on one hip as she grabbed his collapsible playpen from the trunk. She shrugged the strap of the playpen onto her shoulder and swung her backpack onto the other shoulder. It was a much-practised manoeuvre and she held everything in perfect equilibrium. She tilted her head at Magnus, asserting her okayness. He raised an eyebrow in acknowledgement and stopped probing. He yelled at Seb and Emmy to get the hell out of the flower beds and shepherded them towards the front door. There was a plastic Christmas wreath hanging on a hook. *It's September. And they think I'm the weirdo.*

It was always strange for Lana to see Magnus with his parents. It felt like there was a real possibility that he was secretly adopted, *although that's probably too interesting to be likely. That's giving John and Julie too much credit.* Magnus was big and bear-like, both tall and wide, and permanently a little dishevelled looking. John and Julie looked just like some little toy townspeople that Seb had owned as a baby; small, compact, smiling plastic people that fit into special little slots in their sold-separately bus or modest home. Magnus could not be smoothed into a Fisher Price person, not that he didn't make the effort. In their own home, Magnus was either exuberant; playing with the kids, effusing on the latest very specific thing he learned during a late-night Wikipedia binge, or else grizzly; scowling about some DIY fuck-up or the congestion caused by seasonal tourists. Sometimes there was almost no time at all in between these two moods. *He's got a lot of feelings. Some people just have a certain capacity for feelings. Nothing wrong with it.* But perched awkwardly on a low sofa in his parents' reception room, he became a mannered guest. He accepted tea and talked about the weather with his mother (cold), and the disadvantages of ceiling mouldings with his father (dusty). He was quiet, which was eerie, only breaking into his normal register to admonish the children for putting their dirty hands on the furniture. Julie shot disapproving glances at Lana, like it was her fault their hands were dirty, and not the chocolate brownies on the coffee table. Lana stood in the corner, holding Cody to her chest. The playpen was unfolded but Lana hung onto him. He smelled familiar amid the choking pot-pourri fumes, plus he was a shield against social interaction. *Your mission, should you choose to accept it, is to hold the baby.* Lana briefly handed him over, when Julie insisted on a closer look. But his perfect lower lip trembled and he burst into tears. Lana did her best not to laugh, and graciously accepted him back. *Good job, little buddy.* He calmed quickly.

Emmy was doing her part to draw focus away from Lana too. She was good in that regard. She was naturally sociable and extremely loud. Emmy was three, *nearly four,* and what people charitably described as 'a good talker.'

"Nanna I have a funny joke!" Emmy screamed at Julie, while surreptitiously wiping her hands on her grandma's skirt. *Oh god, here we go then.* Even Seb rolled his eyes.

"Knock knock," said Emmy.

"Who's there?" said Julie.

"Who's there?" repeated Emmy. *Wow, that fell apart fast.*

"What?" said Julie, visibly shaken by the creative direction of the joke. Lana swallowed a snort of laughter.

"No, Nanna. I said Who's There. So, you say . . . you say . . . Who's There who?"

"Who's There who?" said Julie, floundering.

"Who's there, what? No, Nanna. Who's There is his full name." Emmy beamed. Magnus and his parents and Seb shared a puzzled glance, wondering if they'd missed something. *As Emmy's jokes went, that was pretty good. Linear, had a conclusion, didn't get stuck in an infinite loop, didn't switch roles with the joke recipient halfway through. Solid eight out of ten.*

"Now laugh!" Emmy insisted, pleased with herself. Magnus and Lana gave a very false performance, which rang sharply off the walls, and Julie looked concerned for both their mental well-being.

"That didn't make sense," said Seb quietly.

The kids were quickly deployed to another room to watch TV. Seb, as an introspective six-year-old, wasn't contributing much. *He's the same as me,* Lana thought. *He's mine and Emmy is Magnus'. Seb always gets a raw deal.* Emmy tried to dominate everyone else's conversations, making it impossible to do anything other than be her captive audience. So, the kids were watching, inexplicably, The Young Indiana Jones Chronicles, which John and Julie had on VHS.

Then John had needed to show Magnus something in the garage. He had implemented a system of coloured stickers for the fuse box, something that could not be missed. Magnus went reluctantly, with a worried backwards glance.

"Magnus tells us you've got the blues," said Julie, as soon as Magnus was out of earshot. *Of course.* Lana knew immediately that the fuse box had been a diversion, planned in advance. She looked down at Cody. He was bigger than he'd been when they had last visited. Less a baby every day, but more himself. Sometimes Lana thought she could hold him forever and hang on to every age and every fractal version of him. Nobody else would have a turn, because they weren't owed it like she was. Then she remembered he belonged to Magnus and Seb and Emmy, and to himself too. His eyelids were beginning to droop, one eye more closed than the other. *There's nothing wrong with him, it's just the way his eyes are.* His lips suckled at nothing. Lana's eyes burned, before she remembered not to be sad.

"Alana?"

"Oh, sorry." *I wasn't listening.* "Uh..." it took her a second to remember the question, although it had hardly been a question. "Maybe a little bit. It's pretty common, they say. Probably just tiredness more than anything." *Please don't try and talk to me about this.*

Julie made a face that seemed to have been decided on before Lana had even replied. Pitying but also exasperated. If Lana would only decide not to be so self-indulgent, the expression said, it would be better for everyone. *Or am I reading too much into these expressions she does?* They were extremely annoying, all pursed lips and sanctimonious head tilt. But Lana was mindful of not making an enemy because of a look, *even a series of looks over many years.*

"Alana, dear, do you know what you should do?" said Julie, as if the answer was something very exciting. Julie always called her Alana, even after she had specified that Lana would do just fine.

"What should I do?"

"You should get out of the house. It's really the best thing to clear your head. And if you want to drop little Cody over here, and go somewhere by yourself, that's no problem at all. He's quiet enough. And very tidy when he's away in that little pen of his. You need some friends, dear."

Amid her mild annoyance, Lana was proud of herself for successfully predicting the next thing Julie said.

"What with your parents being no longer with us."

And there it is.

It was a strange turn of phrase. They were dead. *Spare me the euphemisms.* And her parents would not have been *with* them, even if they were alive. Her mother had died when Lana was nineteen; her father years later in a car

15

accident. If they had been alive, Lana's mother would be living in Vancouver and they would likely never speak. They had a volatile relationship at best. *Volatile like chemicals.* Although she never said it out loud. Lana's father had been a shut-in. When she and Magnus had gone through his possessions, they'd found stockpiled cans of beans, chilli, potatoes and other unappetising foodstuffs dating back years. Judging by his magazine subscriptions, some of which still came twice a year, he had a casual interest in most mainstream conspiracy theories, and a couple of others besides, usually reserved for the more discerning antisocial hoarder. He would not be sitting in John and Julie's living room either.

It would be easier, Lana decided, to let Julie have her way. She had been feeling difficult today, determined not to have an easy time. But she looked into Cody's small, tired face and decided not to have an argument. What Cody wanted was to sleep. Later he would have some milk, and maybe lay on the floor and play with something shiny or jingly. What the kids wanted was more brownies, and to chase each other in circles, screaming about ownership of particular crayons. They would want to show Lana their drawings and describe in excruciating detail how the other had sabotaged theirs. They would want to regale her with some interpretation of plot of The Young Indiana Jones Chronicles. What Magnus wanted was to get through lunch without drama. Lana wanted to turn over the coffee table and accuse Julie of secretly despising her, but that would ruin everyone else's chance of getting what they wanted. So she said the words Julie was fishing for.

"It's just so hard without them." *That's what you're looking for, right?* Her words came out a little choked, and that slight waver sold it. Lana's life had been ruined forever by being orphaned as an adult woman, and everything she did that was unacceptable was a symptom of her sub-par family life. Julie was reassured of her worldview, and everything was plain sailing from there. In no time at all, Lana reassured herself, she would be out of there, and Julie would be lint-rolling every fibre of her from the furniture.

***

Over a table laden with quiche, crackers and an assortment of pasty dips in scalloped tureens, Lana noticed Magnus was avoiding his mother's eye. She stared at him. He kept his eyes on his plate, shovelling bread rolls into his mouth with grim determination. He had told Julie that Lana had the blues. It was a rule between them, not quite unspoken but vaguely defined, that he not say anything about her blue days. Lana couldn't bear the scrutiny, and he knew it. It was her secret to keep. And he had said something. He had shone a light into her brain, for everyone to see. She felt the floor drop away, felt herself drawing close and everything else floating far away. She felt betrayed and small, but didn't dare cry. She swallowed dryly and squashed everything down, making a new solid floor of all the sharp feelings.

Lana picked the soft centre from a piece of bread and passed it to Cody, who was perched on her knee, wearing his mother's arm like a seatbelt. He peered at the wad of bread intensely, trying to make sense of it, then crushed it in his tiny starfish hand, butter squeezing out from between his fingers. He was delighted, and began to lick butter from his clenched fist. *At least someone's having a good time.*

Lana had gathered anything she thought Seb and Emmy might like from the table, and assembled an impromptu picnic in the TV room. She had asked them nicely to try not to get anything on the carpets, but she didn't really care. She wasn't going to scold them if they did. Maybe that was why all the food seemed to be beige, to save the beige carpets from stains. Julie was nothing if not pragmatic. It seemed suddenly like a stroke of genius to Lana, and she felt bad for hating her. She gave Julie a half smile as their eyes happened to catch each other over the salmon mousse. But then Julie fired back a terribly pitying look, dripping with condescension, and Lana withdrew her charitable concession.

***

In the days that followed, she was guarded with Magnus, wary of telling him the whole of anything. She knew he would never have deliberately betrayed her trust. He had been coaxed into saying something. *It was a set-up.* Lana believed that wholly. But as much as she loved him, there was a small dark space between them. He couldn't understand why she was so protective of her truth. Barely anything was fully hers anymore. The kids rifled through every drawer in the house, they touched everything, and broke half of the things they touched. *And it's fine. It's whatever. They're just things.* But her experiences, good or bad, were hers alone. She decided who could be permitted to know them, and Magnus' mother, *fucking Julie,* was not permitted. And in realising that, she did miss her own mother a little, because she would have understood that.

Chapter 3.

Lana's father, Mike, had died in an accident, and they had inherited his house. Just her and Magnus, newly married. The police said maybe he had swerved to avoid a deer. She wondered sometimes if they had made that up entirely, thinking a story about a deer would soften the blow for a young woman. They didn't know the things she'd already seen. The road had been icy. He had hit a tree, invisible beyond the headlights, and died in a second. Lana had never lived with him. She had moved to Castor, the town that had always been his home, but had never been hers, to be nearer to him after her mother had died. And she had fallen in love with the fresh air and the trees and the space.

Lana knew him as Mike. She called him Mike. To think of him as Dad, or anything close to that, felt unbearably creepy. She had never seen her parents in the same room, and she had known that Mike would not come to her mother's funeral. Lana only went herself to feel some conclusion to the whole thing. *To be certain it's over and done with.* But afterwards, feeling no sadness at all, only finality and perhaps guilt, she had built an acquaintanceship with her father. It was the relationship between estranged parent and adult child, distant but easy. They met up every two weeks for a pancake breakfast, and Lana told him about her new apartment and her bakery job, and how they sometimes let her decorate the birthday cakes. She told him about Magnus, the man she had met in the hardware store. Mike did come to their wedding, but he sat in the back, and did not dress for the occasion. That was his way. Magnus' parents hated him and pretended not to know who he was. Which, of course, they did. Because everybody knew who he was. Mike had no friends, and only spoke to people in passing at the post office or the bus stop. He was a drunk, people said. *There must have been a kinder way to say it, not that anybody ever tried.* And he'd never been quite right anyway, people said. He didn't have his head on straight, they said. Lana made a conscious effort always to appear as if her head was on straighter than anybody else's. But it was impossible to shake the reputation as the offspring of a damaged person.

Lana had never set foot in the house before she owned it. She would drop her father off sometimes and leave him on the curb. He had insisted. She had wondered whether he lived there at all, or if it was just a house he liked to be left in front of. After he was dead, she finally had the chance to get to know him properly, through the things he'd owned. She would discover unpainted areas behind furniture and would smile and sigh, as if this was typical behaviour of someone she had hardly known at all. *Classic Mike.* She imagined she could feel him through space and time, welcoming her home. It was unlikely, she knew. He would probably be irked that she was in his home, moving his things, but it was nice to imagine that he might have let it slide.

Mike had never redecorated, and every wall and carpet and linoleum tile was awful. Magnus had pulled up the carpet, expecting to find damp, and instead found honey blonde floorboards, perfectly preserved. There were surprises everywhere. They discovered hidden storage spaces in the walls and acceptable tiles under unacceptable linoleum. Another house waited patiently to be revealed. They pried off picture rails, steamed woodchip wallpaper loose, sanded down textured ceilings, until it resembled the kind of house Lana had always dreamed of. It had been too big for a couple, and their combined belongings looked desperately meagre in the space. Totally unintentionally, they became a family of four, and it became perfect. There was room to leave toys out, for blanket forts and craft projects and running inside. Every inch of the house became marked with evidence of family life. Everyday paintings stuck to the fridge, special paintings framed on the wall, next to awkward family photos. Crayon marks on skirting boards, scratches on the glass coffee table, stains ground in and irreversible. Seb would spill something, inevitably, and when it wouldn't scrub off Lana would say, "oh well, looks like the house got a new tattoo" and Seb would feel better. *Because a kid shouldn't be made to feel like crap over something so fucking trivial,* Lana would think, without examining that thought too deeply.

Baby Cody had changed something. *Not ruined, just changed.* He was a beautiful and mostly calm little boy, but the violence of the birth had dragged something dark behind it. Lana felt tired. She tried her usual remedies. She made spicy soups with garlic and ginger. She opened windows and drank strong lemony tea. But nothing helped. And as she nursed Cody, she sometimes felt like she was falling down a long dark hole. He seemed to draw her energy from her body. She didn't begrudge him, but she knew something was wrong. Magnus knew it too, and he made regular unsubtle suggestions that she talk to someone besides him. A professional. It was impossible for her not to feel insulted by that.

Lana wasn't sure that the something that was wrong, was something wrong with herself. She never told Magnus, but it felt like the house itself was twisting somehow. It felt different. Lana felt certain that her safe harbour didn't feel quite so safe nowadays because of Cody's birth. She had screamed and bled in the bathtub, and she had felt the shadow of death on her skin. She had felt a ghostly hand of coldness and eternity, and she could not forget it. It had worked out. An ambulance had arrived, followed by a hospital stay. She was sewn up and given new blood, and handed pain medication that she hadn't taken, and her new baby boy was placed into her waiting arms like the last piece of a puzzle. Her life had been saved, but it almost hadn't been. It was a strange thing, she thought, to blame a house for something that had happened within its walls. But that's what she had done, and there seemed to be no easy fix to the relationship.

The house did not seem cozy as the months drew colder. Now and then, Lana would feel a chill indoors or sense the air becoming close. Sometimes she thought she saw something move that shouldn't, or a shadow drift across a wall. Sometimes the plume of steam rising from the kettle would twist in an unusual way, or leaves would blow into the house and dance for a moment too long. Things lingered. The natural laws skewed. *Only inside the house*. Lana's attention was always called away by something more pressing, but she would later come to recall these things and wonder why, how, she had ignored them. She would worry how much she had overlooked that autumn, or maybe even before that. She could not say for sure when things had started to become amiss.

Before the ghost had appeared, on what promised to be the last warm day of the year, they had a family picnic in the garden. Everyone was actively ignoring the chill in the air and refusing to succumb to jackets just yet, trying to bargain for a little more summer. Lana and Magnus sat on a blanket. The baby slept in his pram, a knitted blanket hiding him from view. The kids had forgotten completely about their food, and were digging a hole in an empty flowerbed. Lana watched them, trying to create something solid to archive in her mind.

Lana felt something on the back of her neck, and she felt for a bug or loose hair. There was nothing. She looked behind her. Nothing. The house drew her eye. Something flickered just out of sight. Her bedroom window. She thought for a moment, barely even an instant, that she had seen somebody standing there, although it had been too quick to leave her with a lasting impression of a thing seen so fleetingly.

"What's up?" asked Magnus through a mouthful of potato salad.

She turned her face to him but kept her eyes on the window.

"Nothing. Heebie jeebies."

"Heebie jeebies, huh?" he said, smiling. He followed her line of sight, to the window. "Is it that coat stand in our bedroom? With your big coat? It looks like an old-timey funeral director? That's given me more than a few heebie jeebies. Coming in late, lights out, you get a cold shiver, you think someone's there watching you and then there's this big shadowy thing in the corner of the room like a murderer. No thank you."

"No. Nothing so ominous. It's a more general heebie jeebie. You know that feeling when you realize you're dreaming? I feel kind of like that." *Or the opposite, like I've just realised I'm not. Like I've touched a little bit of a dream on the wrong side of my eyelids. Like -*

Magnus was making the pitying face again. He erased it unsubtly. He shrugged off his sweater and threw it over Lana's shoulders in one quick, unfussy movement. It was so warm, irresistibly comforting. Magnus poured her a cup of coffee from a thermos. She knew she had seen something, *but that didn't mean there was something there.* She didn't say anything more to Magnus. *Seeing things is not a good sign.* He would fret over it. She needed to keep some things to herself. She needed to put this little omission, this slightly worrying thing, in one of the dark corners of her brain, with all the other things she kept to herself.

Chapter 4.

It happened a week after the picnic. The kids were at school, Magnus was at work. That was the time when things seemed the most perilous. Lana tried to be content with just Cody and herself for company. Sometimes it was fine, if the TV was loud and there were things to do. But sometimes it all went wrong, and she felt like crying. The diminished energy felt tragic somehow, and her voice echoed in the house. She expected to see people around every corner, the kids galloping down the hallway or hiding behind doors. She expected to see something. Something had responded to that expectation. It was one explanation.

Lana was always awake early. She liked to walk around the house by herself, knowing everyone else would soon be awake. Getting the jump on the day, Magnus sometimes said. That felt about right; Lana sneaking up on the morning and Magnus totally at its mercy, bleary eyed and sour and not to be bothered until he'd adjusted to the surprise of another day. Lana made a cup of coffee and sipped it. She savoured the heat of it, of something freshly hot; not forgotten on a counter-top for half an hour, not microwaved three times. *Did I put the milk in?* The memory, from just seconds prior, was missing. She remembered staring into steaming black coffee, like a vision of the future might present itself, but now it was white. *So, I must have.* That sort of thing was happening increasingly. Little details got pushed out.

Cody began to fret in the bedroom, his cry crackling through the baby monitor in her sweatshirt pocket. She went to him, gathered him up and nestled with him in the armchair she liked to nurse him in. As she fed him, taking the time to appreciate his fluttering eyelids and goofy expressions, she picked up her book, left splayed open on the table next to her. Lana read, and realised she was adrift in the story. She turned the page back, one-handed. She didn't recognise anything there either. She thumbed back a full chapter before she got her bearings. *Add it to the list.*

The morning blew past the same as always, with never enough time to avoid a rush, in a whirlwind of lost shoes and blueberry jam disasters that necessitated the changing of clothes. She all but pushed Magnus, laden with children's school bags, out of the door. The door closed, sealing her in. The silence was deafening. Lana's ears rang. And every time she placed a plate in the sink or closed a cabinet, the sound was jarring. Even the baby was quiet, his eyes roving around the room, content to watch invisible air currents. It was impossible to hear her own thoughts over the longing for sound. She had to´ go outside. Swapping her sweatshirt for her overcoat, the baby bundled up against the autumn chill in his pram, she headed down the mountain into town.

***

Castor was a small town, not lively but alive. There was a stone fountain at a crossroads, where people gathered to have lunch and kids sometimes sat with skateboards across their knees. There were tourists on vacation, staying in bed and breakfasts, or in the lake houses outside of town. It was undergoing something a revitalisation. There was now a gallery with artists in residence. There were stores that sold handmade wind-chimes and bohemian glassware that hadn't been there a year ago. Ten years ago, the way Magnus told it, Castor was the place to get a plate of remarkably good plum cobbler at a remarkably fair price. The Red & White Diner in the square now served a dragonfruit sorbet that was the colour of beet salad and didn't taste like much at all. It didn't feel like a big deal to Lana, but she knew it touched a nerve for Magnus. He ran a hardware store, the only hardware store. It had a conservative clientele, and too much change couldn't be good for business, she supposed. Or maybe he just missed the plum cobbler.

The sunlight sparkled on pavements, damp from the valley fog that blanketed Castor most mornings. In the summer it was like living in a terrarium. In the winter it was like a snow globe. Currently it was cold and astonishingly bright for a few hours a day, but mostly it was cold and dark, and the ground was always slick with semi-frozen leaves. Lana let her feet choose her path, wandering aimlessly, simultaneously enjoying her free time and trying to waste as much of it as possible before the house was full again.

She thought about work. Lana had a part time gig as an online transcriber, typing out the things people said at focus groups and employment tribunals and the occasional prison phone call. She'd been taking a break since Cody. Except she knew deep down that it wasn't a break. She had no co-workers, just a portal where she booked jobs and submitted Word documents. Nobody had reached out about her extended maternity leave. *Nobody even noticed. Maybe there's nobody to notice. Maybe it runs itself like the house in that Ray Bradbury story.* The thoughts organised themselves without much input, playing passively in her head like a tv left on in another room, because she didn't truly care what conclusion she reached. It was just noise, just a placeholder.

Lana bought bread from the bakery, leeks from the greengrocer, trialling recipes in her head for the soup she would make later. She felt a little sad for herself at the realisation that making soup was something she was looking forward to. *Jeez, what does that say about me?*

A storefront caught her eye. Vacant for months, since the shoe store went bust, it had been dark behind the glass front for so long Lana had stopped seeing it. There was a sheet of paper taped to the window now, so small that Lana had to go right up to the glass to read what was written. Scrawled in purple marker was the message:

"Coming Soon - Occult bookshop, spell-wares, oasis for urban witches. Homewares. Come along for coven meetings, social happenings, tarot readings, crystal yoga."

Puzzling over exactly how crystals might factor into yoga, and whether the witches of Castor could be considered urban in any way, Lana squinted over the notice into the dark beyond. Cardboard boxes, contents unpacked on the floor, candles, books and bunches of what looked like dried reeds filled the space. *Maybe basket-weaving factors into witchcraft somehow?* There was a cat too, curled up on one of the boxes. Lana had dismissed it as a piece of taxidermy until its tail twitched. She would have preferred it to be a black cat. *A witch's cat.* It was tortoiseshell and fluffy, if a little threadbare looking. The cat looked around blearily then fixed Lana with a judgemental stare. She had broken its sunbeam, she realised, and sidestepped apologetically. The cat was illuminated by the midday sun, like the first prize on a gameshow, and went back to sleep.

The shop stayed on Lana's mind, floating gently atop everything else, above the soup and the sting of being ignored by her anonymous coworkers. Lana thought, as she made her way back home, taking the incline at her own leisurely pace, that it wasn't so remarkable that the new ages had finally come to Castor. They already had a co-working space. They already had a cafe where you could make your own ceramics. Wicca felt like a natural continuation of the trend. *Or is that rude of me? I'm basing one hundred percent of this on '90s witch shows. There were a lot of '90s witch shows, now I think of it. What was that about?* Lana liked the idea of a coven in Castor, though she couldn't say for sure why, or how close she wanted to get to it. She had never thought of herself as superstitious or spiritual. She put her faith in the people around her, the people who were still there, and in everyday things. Introspection wasn't for her. She knew not to get dragged down by the past, by the what-ifs.

She pushed the pram through her front door and stabled it in its usual corner of the hall, leaving Cody sleeping. She glanced at the clock. The house was full of clocks. Magnus brought home broken ones he'd found at estate sales or, every once in a while, dumpsters. He fixed them, and it seemed to be the fixing that he was mostly interested in, but then he couldn't bear to part with them. They would all be home soon, Lana noted, brightening. She was tired from her walk, but now there were things to do. The routine, its inescapability, gave her energy. Its absence drained her. She knew it was supposed to be the other way around.

Something felt off though, something about the air in the room, like a window had been left open somewhere. The ether around her eyes and ears felt wrong. The atmosphere was too thick or too thin.

There was someone in the living room. A stranger.

Lana's heart leapt into her throat, choking her, like drowning in a dream. A cold sweat bloomed instantly, her arm hairs were lifted by an invisible static. *An electrical storm. Find cover.* Adrenaline flooded Lana's body with a hundred useless conflicting impulses.

Run! Fight! It's a dream. It isn't. I don't feel well. Cody. Run! Find a weapon. Get a knife from the kitchen and stab her right in the back. Wait, don't touch her! Just don't touch her! Lana didn't move. *Close your eyes, it'll all go away. No, keep her in sight! Don't let her get away!*

The intruder was facing the mirror over the fireplace, stock still. She was barefoot. Lana felt powerfully nauseous. She wanted to fall, needed for some inexplicable reason to be on the ground. Gravity sucked at her skin, her bones, drawing her toward the earth's core. *To the pearl at the centre of the mountain. But that's not how mountains work. That doesn't make sense.* It felt safer on the ground, although Lana could recognise the ridiculousness of that notion. She stayed upright, her body swaying in protest. The stranger turned slowly. Lana felt desperately that she did not want to see her face. But she looked all the same.

Oh, it's me. It's only me.

The stranger had Lana's own face. She was an exact reflection of herself, identical. Lana's body trembled. She clamped her jaw shut to keep her teeth from chattering.

Not identical, she realized.

The stranger had shorter hair. Lana's hand went nervously to her own hair to make sure it was as she remembered it, and just to make herself sure it wasn't some kind of trick. Thoughts were coming as pictures now – waxworks, mirrors, death masks, identical twins; her brain throwing out any relevant association, no matter how unhelpful.

It was only then that the stranger seemed to come alive, all at once, expression flooding the previously empty face. She became animate. The sick feeling was replaced with bewilderment. The fear, huge and irresistible, remained. Lana still couldn't move, couldn't speak, couldn't think. She could only stand stock still, completely dumbfounded, thinking the sorts of thoughts a deer thinks before it is crushed by the bright and thundering thing hurtling toward it.

"Don't panic," the doppelgänger insisted, daring Lana to panic.

That's my voice, was Lana's only coherent thought.

They stood in silence, looking at one another, unsure who should speak next. Lana noticed then that the stranger had no reflection in the hall mirror but shelved this concern for later. *No time for that now.* Clouds were rolling in from the edges of her vision, narrowing the scene in front of her to just the pale reflection of her own face staring her down.

A little awareness came back to Lana's legs. She took a few shaky steps back, bumping into the wall and sliding down it, keeping her eyes on the intruder. *Safer on the floor.* She thought for a second that it might make sense to go to sleep, right there on the ground. *It'll reset. Like a video game. It has to.* And then the urge dissipated. The fog cleared a little.

"What's happening?" Lana managed, swimming back to consciousness, finally slowing her panicked breathing enough to speak. She could feel sweat on her face, cooling as it evaporated. She could comprehend that something was wrong, but could not quite grasp what or why. "What is this?" She could only keep breathing and wait for a solution to present itself. "Am I dead?" She wasn't sure why she asked it.

"No, you're not dead. Why would you be dead? Everything's fine," said her double.

"Is it?" asked Lana.

It isn't.

The idea that she might be having some kind of medical emergency occurred to her, or that she might have been knocked unconscious somehow. Possibilities trickled in. She had seen something in the bedroom window, she remembered. This something and that something felt like parts of the same puzzle. She was hallucinating. She knew that hallucinations meant things were not going well, that she had failed to recover. Her depression, and she knew that was what it was although she would never admit it, had reached a tipping point and she had been flipped headlong into a different kind of messed up. *Postpartum psychosis.* She'd looked it up on her phone, panic-scrolling through symptoms while she nursed Cody in the pitch dark. *That's what this is.* But it didn't help her to know that. It didn't help her to know what to do.

"Everything's fine," said the stranger, seeing the thoughts spelled out on Lana's face. "But it's important not to panic. If you panic, you'll lose your grip. Now, I'm going to run you a bath. A nice relaxing bath. Doesn't that sound nice? And we can both calm down and have a conversation." The stranger backed out of the room slowly, keeping her eyes on Lana. And she was gone.

Lana was alone again. The sounds of the house returned; ticking clocks, Cody snoring and snuffling through winter congestion, the white noise hum of the furnace downstairs.

What just happened? It had been something horrible, and very real, but also complicated. She touched her face and looked around for further strangeness. Everything was normal. Maybe she was mistaken. Maybe nothing had happened. Or maybe her mind was broken now. It had snapped like a twig, and she couldn't trust anything her senses told her. But then she heard the unmistakable creak of the bath tap turning, and running water, and a different question presented itself. *Can a hallucination run a bath?* She crept toward the bathroom, still wearing her boots. Warm light and steam spilled from the open door, and a voice, her own voice, singing a song she'd never heard.

Lana stood in the doorway, leaning on the frame for support. The Other Her was there, perched on the side of the tub with her hand under the water. Her hand reacted strangely to the stream of water; completely solid, water parted, then suddenly insubstantial, water passing through. She seemed to be something halfway between a hallucination and real person. And she looked a little troubled, *understandably*, staring at her hand. She shut off the water, turning the faucet handle with palpable concentration.

"Come," said the duplicate. She reached up to the top shelf of the shower caddy and put her hand on a bath bomb. With an intense focus she coaxed it into her palm, whereupon it fell straight through her hand and into the bath, hitting the bottom with a dull thump. The bathwater hissed and turned a deep imperial purple. She knew about the bath bombs, Lana noted distantly. An intruder in her home was distressing, but an intruder knowing where she kept things was something else. Lana wasn't willing yet to commit herself to considering what this copy might be. For now, she was just an intruder that looked exactly like her. An intruder that was having some trouble with her corporeality. Lana could only confront the situation in fractions, unable to think ahead to the next little sliver of awfulness.

The front door banged open, hitting the wall behind it, ear-splittingly loud. Lana had waited all day for that sound and now it made her sick. She was defenceless, with no idea what to do. And now everyone was home, and she wished harder than she had ever wished before that they would leave. She heard Seb and Emmy's feet thundering along the hall, demanding peanut butter sandwiches and video games, and Cody protesting at the commotion, and Magnus shouting at the kids to stop being wild in the house.

Magnus called out to her, then he was suddenly in the doorway, cradling Cody with one arm. *Don't bring him in here!* But the words didn't manifest in time.

"Taking a bath?" asked Magnus, completely failing to notice his wife's spectral twin. "Fancy," he added, seeing the purple bathwater. "I still don't understand how you can get any cleaner though if the water is full of dye and bits of glitter and stuff. It's just more grime. Not that you're grimy," he added, grinning broadly.

Lana looked to the doppelgänger, who put her finger to her lips, inviting her to join a conspiracy.

Lana swallowed thickly and stammered, "Yeah. I thought I needed to just take some time. If... can you watch Cody? And feed the kids? There's some casserole in a box in the freezer. Don't let them have sandwiches."

"No problem. Maybe I'll just give them one sandwich to split or they'll destroy the house while I'm getting dinner on the table. I'll try and get them to keep it down. No promises though."

He walked away, humming a tune, untroubled.

Lana felt dazed and distant, and she could feel the seed of a migraine blooming behind her eyes, although some of the urgency had dissipated, and that almost felt like relief. Lana felt her blood tingling underneath her face and in her hands. But still, Magnus couldn't see the intruder. At least there was no intruder. Although Lana hadn't really thought that was a possibility. This was a projection, a ghost, something from inside her own mind, she was sure. She was reasonably sure. She felt suddenly so tired of scrabbling for explanations. The bath looked inviting. She thought about what the stranger had said. If she panicked, she would lose her grip.

That's probably good advice. And if I'm losing my mind I might as well have a nice bath. Why not? I'm probably going to wind up in the hospital eventually. And there won't be bath bombs there. The Other Her was watching with apprehension, waiting for her to join in the game. Lana began to undress. It didn't feel like an unusual thing to do. It was no stranger than undressing in front of a mirror. The double watched her, eyes lingering on the tattoos on Lana's shoulders and back, the illustrations that reminded her of things that needed remembering.

"Don't you?" Lana gestured at the inked areas of her skin.

"No, none." The ghost slowly removed her own t-shirt, held it for a moment then let it drop. It disappeared before it hit the floor, like a snowflake melting mid air. There were no tattoos. Really looking at her double made Lana's head ache. It strained her eyes as if she was looking into a bare lightbulb or a murky cellar. Both too bright and too dark. But still Lana searched her body for clues. The same appendectomy scar, like a secret brand. It was a club. A club for people who looked identical and weren't feeling mentally well. Lana and Other Lana were in it, Magnus and the kids weren't. They didn't even know there was a club.

A sound split Lana's reverie, a distant delighted shriek from baby Cody. The moment shattered as Lana's eyes darted to the door. The steam from the bath filled the air, fog obscuring the mirror. It was easy to forget there was anything outside of the warm, perfumed room. But it was real life outside. She looked back at the ghost. She was fully dressed again.

The bath water was perfectly hot as Lana slid into it,

and her mysterious new sister sat opposite, fully dressed in clothes that refused to take in water. Their legs touched, and Lana felt a faint electricity without temperature.

"Who are you?" Lana managed to ask eventually, starting with a question she knew the answer to.

"You. I thought that was obvious."

"But how? I don't understand this." Lana pressed.

Her reflection shrugged, declining to answer.

"Are you in my head? Did I imagine you? Am I seeing things?" asked Lana, feeling ridiculous. *Not that you'd tell me, right? Am I really asking a hallucination to confirm whether I've gone crazy?*

"No. How would I turn on the water if you dreamt me up? You know, I'm actually not so good at interacting with physical things. I think it's like a battery that runs down. I don't know the rules, not for sure. But I think that might have been the last little scrap of my energy, so you could have the good grace to be impressed," she smirked. "Why would you even think that anyway? Do you usually hallucinate things?" asked Other Lana.

"No," said Lana. *I don't think so.* "But it feels like a reasonable thing to assume, under the circumstances. What are you then? Why are you here?" Lana continued.

"Just visiting. Just, whaddyacall? Passing through," she flashed a self-deprecating smile.

"But what do you want?" Lana pressed, getting to the heart of it.

"To spend time with my sister, of course," Other Lana smiled, as if this were the most normal thing in the world. "To see what's going on with you. See how the other half lives. I wanted to see what it would have been like if... y'know. The road not taken."

"You're from a parallel reality?" asked Lana. *That's not so bad. I read comic books. I can accept a parallel reality.* A parallel reality was just science, something scientifically plausible, given her understanding of theoretical physics as presented by comic books.

"I don't know that parallel is the right word. Maybe more like adjacent. But sure."

"Okay. Okay, I can understand that as a concept." Lana tried to embrace a scenario where she wasn't mentally unstable. "But you can't just do that, you know. You can't just step into another reality for a vacation."

"Maybe *you* can't," the ghost snorted.

"Why aren't you... y'know, solid? Why can only I see you? Are you a hologram? Is the rest of you somewhere else?" asked Lana.

"No to the hologram thing. As for the other things; I'm not sure. It's not exactly apples to apples."

Whatever that means. This Other Lana, ghost, doppelgänger, whatever she was, smirked playfully, content to waste Lana's time. *Is it something else? Is this a trick?* Moments passed silently. Lana couldn't think of anything to say. The panic had burned itself out and what Lana mostly felt was tired. She had asked all the questions she could think of, and none had been answered fully.

"Is this right?" she said finally. "Is this okay, for us to see each other? It feels very wrong. No offence. I strongly feel like this isn't the sort of thing that should be happening. This isn't a normal occurrence and you're being very normal," said Lana.

"It's an unusual situation, I'll give you that. But so is everything, until it isn't."

"What if it's like in movies where the person can't meet their future self or the universe will implode, or explode, or whichever one it is? What if the fabric of reality is unravelling? Putting aside for a second how impossible this all is, I think it's at least... irresponsible," Lana concluded weakly.

"I think we're fine. We'd notice if the fabric of reality was unravelling." The ghost laughed at Lana's concerned expression. "I'm not you from the future, or the past. There's no timeline to disrupt. No paradox. I'm you from now. Just not the here and now."

They didn't speak about it again, about where she had come from. There had been a window for Lana to ask her questions, and the window had closed. They talked about other things. In one way they knew each other intimately, but in another way they were perfect strangers. There were little differences in their faces, their hair, their words. They had different names. Lana was Lana, and the other one was Allie. Lana wasn't sure if that was a genuine truth. Had she always been Allie? Or had she claimed the alternate nickname to make Lana more comfortable?

Lana had decided there were three possibilities. Firstly, Allie was a projection from a parallel dimension. She wasn't really here, but Lana could still see and hear her. Allie was only physically whole in her own dimension and so would go when she had seen what she wanted to see. Lana couldn't begin to guess how she had come here, but this theory was still the most likely, she decided, and the least frightening. Her second, less likely, less appealing, hypothesis was that her new house guest had magic powers. Lana doubted this was the case given her own decided lack of magic powers. Her final theory was that they were not the same person at all. This last theory was her least favourite because, if that was indeed the case, the visitor could be anyone or anything, and Lana had no way to get it to leave her house.

Chapter 5.

In the weeks before she revealed herself, or it could have been months, Allie wandered invisible around the house.

The first thing she saw was Lana, in the bathtub, screaming and writhing, with one hand pressed to her pregnant belly. She wore a bra and nothing else, save for the blood smeared here and there like finger-paintings. The water was red and roiling as Lana twisted like a speared eel. There was blood all over the carpet. There was a nice symmetry to that, Allie thought vaguely. It seemed immediately clear that she was watching the death of her parallel universe self. *I've gotten lost. I've gone in a circle somehow, or up a level or along a corridor. This is the wrong way.* She wondered, detached, whether another version would watch her die, whether death was a hall of mirrors with other selves looking into the next reality. *There's a hole here where there shouldn't be.*

Then she heard the name, *Lana.* The husband, *Magnus,* shouted it again and again, as Lana stopped screaming periodically to stare into space. Allie had known instinctively that nobody could see her. She had no place in this universe and the natural laws did what they could to support this. The physical stuff of that reality didn't acknowledge her in the slightest, being made of atoms as strange to her as she was to them. Allie did wonder though, when Lana stared in her general direction with a strange intensity, whether there was some connection between them.

An ambulance came. Allie watched for it through the kitchen window, like she was helping. As if she could run back to the bathroom and tell Magnus it was okay to let go of Lana's hand now, because help was here. *Help for Lana.* The lights turned all the raindrops on the kitchen windowpane blue. Allie stayed in the kitchen while Magnus wrapped Lana in a wet, bloody dressing gown. They limped past her and out of the house. Moments later a small, neatly dressed older woman let herself in. The small woman stared at the crime scene of a bathroom from the doorway, then closed the door silently. Allie followed her down the stairs, where the woman eased open the door of a bedroom. *A little boy and a little girl.* They were still somehow sleeping soundly.

The woman made a cup of tea and Allie sat across from her at the kitchen table, unnoticed. It certainly wasn't her mother, nor any version of her. It had to be the mother-in-law. She sat with her for a while, keeping a stoic vigil. *What else was there to do?* Eventually the phone rang, slicing the silence in half, and the woman made her first facial expression of the evening, one of exquisite relief. She sighed and gasped and thanked God, which felt to Allie like a poor taste thing to say. Allie could see that she loved Lana. She almost felt it. Allie doubted her own mother would have cared as much to hear that her child had not died horribly in childbirth.

She felt the first of many pangs of jealousy.

She had to wait now. She had to see the baby. It was inexplicable but all-consuming. *A baby who is worth so much suffering.* Eventually Lana came home, with the baby in her arms. Lana looked like a different person. She was smiling the small smile of someone who has sidestepped death. *Don't want to be too obviously happy, or you'll draw his eye again. She knows that.* The much-anticipated baby was extremely red and ugly but he was sweet tempered and quickly grew into a more conventional looking infant. Allie didn't have much experience with babies, but Cody seemed like a good example of one. He had a tiny candyfloss wisp of fair hair that Allie found quite impossible, given her own dark locks. She peered at him sometimes, when he was sleeping in his pram in the hallway and nobody else was around. Allie didn't like to think of herself as a voyeur, but she had little choice. She couldn't go back the way she came.

Lana seemed fine at first. Magnus scrubbed the carpet in the bathroom. The stain wouldn't budge but you couldn't really guess what it was. It could have been paint or hair dye or molasses. He took over the cooking for a while, switching between breakfast burritos and box macaroni cheese, until Lana respectfully insisted that he stop. She said she was fine and she made Magnus believe her. Allie did the same thing, every time. However bad things were, she hated for anyone to know it. They really were the same, underneath all the obvious situational differences. Their paths had diverged at some point, and Allie was consumed by the when and how, and if it was just one big decision or a combination of little things. But before those things, they had been the same. The pangs of empathy were real pangs: Allie felt for Lana.

When the house was empty, Allie made herself at home. She liked to open Lana's closet and look at all the things, like she was choosing her own clothes on any other morning. Like it was a normal day. Allie couldn't change her clothes. They were fixed, drawn on. And Lana's things were things Allie would never have bought anyway. Allie's real clothes were new, and crisp, and fitted well. It was an insult to her pride that the outfit she appeared in, although she appeared only to herself, was a t-shirt and grey sweatpants. Lana's closet consisted mainly of thinned denim from the thrift store, novelty t-shirts, and oatmeal-coloured knitted sweaters that made Allie think of attic insulation.

Allie had sat cross-legged on the bed while Lana and Magnus had taken the winter things out of storage. Clothes were strewn on the floor and ordered in piles. This was the stuff that drew Allie's curiosity, the way that families lived season to season. There was a continuity, with kids' clothes passed down. Everyone went toward the cold together. They would head into the summer together too and bring down the boxes of bathing suits and shorts that lurked behind the winter things. Allie would watch that too, if she was still around by summer, if she hadn't melted like a snowflake by then. She ran her hand over one of Magnus's thick sweaters. It seemed to breathe, no longer vacuum sealed and squashed flat. It expanded, acclimatised to the free-range air. Allie hadn't understood Magnus at first, but she was coming around to the idea of him. Everything he owned was somehow warm, even to her.

Magnus was tall and blonde, with a breadth of back and shoulder that made Allie think he might once have had an athlete's body, although he did not now. He was not the husband she would have picked for herself. She would have married someone clean shaven and lean, if she had gotten married at all. That was the kind of man she dated, on the rare occasion that she went on dates. Her usual fixation rolled around again, made her wonder what had diverged. What had happened in Lana's life that had made her choose Magnus, that had not happened in her own? She watched them together. Never when they were in bed, there was some things she didn't want to see. But she watched other little intimacies unfold between them. They would sprawl on the couch, intertwined. They held hands, or Magnus would absent-mindedly stroke Lana's hair, or she would put her feet on his lap. He had an easy smile. It was reassuring, in a way. Or it seemed to reassure Lana, at least. Stress visibly melted from her face when they were together. The little grasping muscle between her eyebrows relaxed its grip, the awkwardness in her limbs dissolved. She seemed to just exist easily. He was Lana's anchor. A grounding energy. He kept Lana on the right plane. Allie wondered once or twice, if maybe he could do the same for her. Now and then, during movie night, when the kids were arranged on blankets and Lana was busy with the baby on her knee, Allie would perch on the arm of the sofa next to Magnus and feel his warmth on her invisible skin.

After a time, she could never be sure how long, she felt less awkward being near them. She was behind them always. During chaotic breakfasts before school, in the darkened bedroom as Lana rocked Cody to sleep, often in the foggy bathroom with Lana. She daydreamed about revealing herself to Lana, if she could. She didn't want to scare her, she didn't want them to leave. Then she would be alone.

The idea came and went, and would come back whenever she was feeling sorry about her disembodied lot in life. And she felt for Lana and the kids in a real way. Or it seemed real. Sometimes it was hard to tell which feelings were real. And when Lana cried soundlessly in the night, when Magnus was sleeping, when everyone else was sleeping, Allie was certain that she wanted to help her. She could be the friend Lana needed. They shared a self-sufficiency. They were prideful and private. And watching Lana cry, just inches from her face in the darkness, Allie felt everything she had never cared to tell another soul. For all the life surrounding Lana, she was still the same stubborn child inside. Allie knew her loneliness intimately. Maybe she had found herself in this reality for a reason. Maybe they could complete each other somehow, and make a whole from two broken halves.

Chapter 6.

Thoughts gathered, resolve strengthened, Lana approached the red front door again, eyes down. She put the key in the lock, turning the handle of a jack-in-the-box, waiting for the surprise that was no longer a surprise. *Fuck, here we go.* She pushed the door open, wrapped one arm around Cody, hiding behind him, and stepped over the threshold. The ghost was waiting for her. She always was.

Allie stood in a doorway off the hall, as if she was just happening to pass between the rooms. But Lana knew she had been standing there, unmoving, since she had left hours ago. She had waited. Lana never got used to seeing her. It made her eyes hurt to see something so obviously unnatural. The strangeness of her appearance had been hard to pin down at first, but it was inescapable now. Small details were wrong and had become more wrong. Edges were blurred, skin gauzy. Her colours, her hair, eyes, clothes, were wrong. Faded, somehow. Her image was not pale, not insubstantial or translucent. Just wrong, and odd. A weak twilight illuminated her from within, like a dying night-light. Lana could feel her too. The air felt claustrophobic, unwilling to make room for the apparition. Lana sometimes felt her nearby when she could not see her, increasingly so. She was sure that the watched her sometimes, invisible. She worried that Allie could read her mind, although then she would certainly know that Lana had been thinking more and more about reaching out for help. She was thinking about going to the only place in town where someone might believe her.

Every time Lana came into the house she tried to brace herself against it, but every time she saw the ghost she startled, she felt a sickening little needle-sharp stab of fear she could not protect herself against. Sometimes the ghost would be standing in the hall, waiting for her. Sometimes it took a little longer for Allie to reveal herself. She might be standing in a corner of the bedroom, or in one of the kids' bedrooms. Lana didn't care for that. But every time was just as jarring as the first time she had seen a stranger standing in front of the living room mirror, with her back to her, a figure that definitely didn't belong in this or any other house. And here they were again.

"Don't scare me!" Lana breathed, exasperated, clutching Cody close and trying not to look the way she felt.

But it's too late for that now.

Chapter 7.

Lana saw the best in people, she thought. Or maybe it was that she saw the truth in people and didn't judge them too harshly for it. She tried to be charitable, because of how her relationship with her mother had been. Lana been unfair, she knew now, time and again. She could have given more. *You can always give more.* So, she had willed herself not to judge her father. She'd just let him be who he was, and tried to relate to him as best she could. It hadn't saved him in the end. *But maybe nobody gets saved in the end. That's why it's the end.* They'd had a good relationship. That was what really mattered.

Lana couldn't quite see the truth in Allie. It was buried somewhere within her like a splinter that inched further inward the more she tried to grasp it. It made it hard to know what to do with her. She was some kind of ghost, or projection, or manifestation. It didn't much matter what exactly. And now she was here. That was really all Lana had to go on. She had to believe Allie was benign because what else was there? She didn't know what she could do other than hope things turned out okay. She felt the impotence of the situation, but it was freeing too. There were no choices, and therefore no anxiety about choosing incorrectly. Being haunted wasn't the worst thing that could happen. *Maybe it could work out okay. Why shouldn't it? Why do things have to trend downwards? Is there some rule that things fall apart always? Can't they fall together? Fall into place?* But there was an anxiety underneath it, like a cold draft that Lana caught now and then. If things soured, Lana had no way to get rid of Allie. And she had no way to know what Allie could or would do to her if pushed. *So just don't push her.*

Lana had to admit that she did appreciate the company. The days were long and lonely, the early days always were. Magnus was at work, Seb was at school, Emmy was at preschool, Cody wasn't much for conversation. Allie was strange company, but now and then Lana forgot the weirdness of the situation and it was almost like being with a friend. Almost like being with a sister. Or what she could guess having a sister might be like. She'd never had much family outside of the one she'd created for herself so she had forged her own nuclear unit out of desperate need. She wondered if the same thing had happened with Allie. Maybe she had manifested her somehow to fill a particular void, dreamed her up and made her real. It was no less likely than her other theories, which ranged from insanity to time travel. She had considered also, for a time, whether Allie might be a guardian angel. But that theory was sliding down the list by the day.

"Let me help."

That's how it had started, with Allie insisting that she be allowed in, and Lana finding ways not to accept it. It felt like the other half of that bargain was too unclear. *I scratch your back, you scratch mine. Except I'm the only one with a back.* Allie said she didn't want anything in return. She just wanted to help Lana shoulder her blues, out of the goodness of her heart. *Sure.*

It was early afternoon, with a lot more day still to come, but so overcast that it might as well have been dusk. The whole morning had been like that. The sun hadn't really ever come up. Lana felt the same. She sat on the edge of her bed, a half-eaten and half-forgotten slice of toast on the nightstand. She was bone-tired and her nerves were frayed. Lana rubbed her temples, feeling every tight little sinew pressed against her skull. Cody had a tooth coming through and was spending hours of the day and night screaming inconsolably with a pain he couldn't understand. Lana had remembered finally the trick she had used with Emmy, teething gel on a toothbrush. She had done that. She had given him his special blanket, and he had clutched it tightly in his little fist, inhaled its horrible sweet-stale musk, and he had finally let sleep take him over. Lana stared at him, so small curled up in his bassinet.

She loved him more than anything in the world, more than the world itself, but if he started screaming again, she would start too. There was a pressure behind her eyeballs, the kind that signalled the coming of a sinus infection. Flu season was just around the corner.

"So sleep," said Allie, from just out of sight, floating on a shadow the way she sometimes did. "I'm here. There's no sense burning yourself out. Cody's asleep. If something happens, I'll wake you up. But nothing's gonna happen." It felt like the best idea anyone had ever had.

Lana felt her resolve weakening, but it seemed to her afterwards that she never completely agreed to the proposition. She was awake, her sinuses burning, her eyes watering, and then an obliterating sleep washed over her. For a second, she thought about the ice shelves in the Antarctic. The way glacier-sized chunks crack and slow-motion slide into the sea, like they're not incomprehensibly massive. There was something awful about it, something uncanny. They turned into floes. *Or did they? What the fuck is a floe? Is that the word? Did I imagine that?*

Lana realised she was dreaming. She dreamed the house was empty. It had been renovated. The layout was mostly the same, more accurate than any dream had a right to be, and the light coming through the leaves beyond the kitchen window was the same. But every wall was painted cold and bright eggshell white, plastered and sanded smooth, as clean and unexceptional as a hotel, or a snowfall. She looked for her sunglasses in the neck of her t-shirt. That's where she kept them when she was outside, when the snow was bright on the ground. *This is a dream, idiot. These aren't even your real eyes.* She wandered in and out of familiar rooms, not sure what she was looking for, occasionally forgetting and then remembering again that she was dreaming. She couldn't find the kids, and then it didn't matter at all. Because it was only a dream. And then the stab of uncertainty came again as she felt their absence.

She woke up coughing, and Allie was sitting on the

corner of the bed, where she had been before. It had been fine. Everything was fine. Lana turned over, wondered momentarily if she had swallowed a bug, decided she didn't care, and drifted off.

***

Lana didn't mean for it to happen again. It was supposed to be a one-time thing. Nothing had happened, just like Allie had said, and Lana was grateful for the rest. But it had made her uneasy all the same. Lana always felt awkward accepting help but, even though the person offering the help was technically her own self, this was somehow much worse than accepting a ride to the airport. She couldn't give Allie anything in return, which made her intentions hard to trust. So when Cody had a bad reaction to a routine jab, a week later, Lana could feel Allie's eyes on her. Cody was grumbling on his play mat in the living room, swiping ineffectually at the toys that hung from his mobile. Lana left him to it, baby-gates all secure, and went downstairs to fetch the sheets from the dryer. She took the basket to her bedroom and upended everything onto the bed. The sheets were still hot and smelled good. Lana briefly considered making a nest in them and resting her eyes for a moment. She settled for piling the warm linens onto her lap while she folded them, secretly luxuriating.

"You know, you don't look so good. Kind of pale, kind of weird around the eyes," Allie ventured, always right behind her. "No offence."

"Well... offence taken," Lana replied. "You can't tell people they look weird around the eyes. Who raised you?" She paused. *Oh yeah.* "Weird how?"

"Sort of grey, sort of sunken. Again, no offence."

Lana wondered if Allie knew what *she* looked like. Allie would glance into mirrors now and then as she passed then. It was natural to look at a mirror if you saw one in a room, Lana supposed. Like looking out of the window.

But it didn't seem like there was ever anything looking back at Allie.

She probably wouldn't want to see herself if she knew what she looked like. She was starting to appear a little strange in certain lights. In the evening, by the light of the mismatched candles on Lana's bathside, or in the glow of the kids' night-lights, Allie looked fine. But in the colder, harder light of Lana's bedroom, she looked off. Lana couldn't be sure if this was a recent development or if she'd just got more accustomed to actually looking at her. In the beginning it had hurt her eyes to really focus on Allie for more than five minutes. She'd had a couple of migraines resulting, she supposed, from the strange pressure it seemed to exert on her eyeballs. Now she could look at her just fine. Or she'd gotten used to the pressure. *Like a diver does a staggered descent so they don't get the bends. Is that what this is? Am I at the dark bottom of the sea? And what does that make her? One of those transparent fish with its guts on the outside?* Now Lana could see subtleties that she couldn't before. Little twitches of the mouth when Magnus said something funny, a slight glazing of the eyes when the kids told their long and rambling stories, small human things. But Allie's actual face was becoming somewhat less human. Unless Lana was imagining it. Unless it was just in her head, *some kind of paranoia.* Lana scolded herself for thinking it, for thinking of Allie as inhuman. She didn't mention Allie's appearance. No amount of "no offence" would make up for telling someone they look inhuman.

"I'm fine, trust me," Lana said. "I know I haven't gotten much sleep these last couple of days. I don't think it's even the jab itself at this point. He was fluey at the start and now he's just sour. I think his leg is sore where they poked him. He's not normally this tetchy though."

Allie always knew what she was talking about. Lana didn't have to say Cody's name. She always spoke her thoughts out loud, however far along she was in mulling them over. Allie always followed. Lana could easily believe there was some shared wavelength. It made sense. Or it made as much sense as anything else did now. Lana piled her freshly folded sheets into the closet. It was a shame Allie couldn't fold laundry, she thought, finding her trademark pragmatism despite everything.

"But you know, you could always just take a nap. I would watch him. You never let me do anything. I'm here to help you and you're so damn stubborn." Allie said it with love, smiling, but her jaw was set. It was a fair point, Lana knew. She *was* stubborn. Which meant so was Allie. They were equally matched, except Lana got tired. Lana faltered.

"I said I'm fine. Anyway, I want to start dinner soon," Lana said, throwing the laundry basket into a corner and heading for the bedroom door. Allie was close behind her. "I was thinking tortellini soup. I'm not sure the kids will go for soup but they can fish the tortellinis out and just eat those. Or more likely fish them out, peel them open, eat the tortellini filling, smush up the pasta like playdoh. Is it tortellinis? Tortellonis? Maybe it's just tortellini. Anyway…" she trailed off. She felt light-headed, like she'd stood up too fast.

"I think you should sit back down," came Allie's voice from nowhere in particular. "You really don't look good. Can you hear me?"

Lana could hear her distantly, through a thick fog. But Allie's voice was fading out, being replaced first by distorted watery sounds, then a sharp whine. *It's the ice sheet breaking,* Lana panicked. She braced herself against the sound, trying to hold the two halves of herself together, as her vision whited out. When the whine finally subsided, and things came back into focus, she was lying in her bed.

She felt her face, her forehead. The light-headedness had gone. She thought, with total certainty, for half a second, that it was morning, that it was time to get the kids ready for school. And then she realised the light was wrong, and Magnus wasn't beside her, and she was still wearing her clothes. And Allie was there. *Get away from me. No, that's not it.* She wasn't usually there in the morning. She waited downstairs for everyone to come down for breakfast. Lana was always grateful for that. It made her more like a normal roommate and less like something that was haunting her. She was never in the bedroom when Lana and Magnus were. Or Lana never saw her there anyway. She did sometimes worry that Allie could be invisible when she wanted to. But there was nothing she could do about that. It was better not to think about it.

Her mind was wandering, still sleepy. She sat up, trying to get her bearings, scraping clues together. She remembered a noise, blinding whiteness, then nothing. She looked at her watch. It was Magnus' old watch, huge and cracked, with extra holes poked in the leather wristband with a sewing needle. Almost half an hour had passed. She had left Cody for nearly half an hour. She needed to get him. *Now!* She swung her legs out of the bed, almost falling, and scrambled past Allie, up the stairs two at a time, into the living room.

Cody was fine, blinking sleepily. He had shuffled and wiggled his way over to the sofa. Relief flooded Lana's body, as well as a little nausea. *I left him alone. What if he'd died? What if he'd choked or suffocated? What if, what if. And what for? Because I'm tired? Because I'm too busy with Allie?* Lana gathered him up and sat down on the sofa with Cody in her lap, breathing him in and resisting the urge to cry. He smiled, pleased to have reached the sofa, pleased Lana was there to recognise his achievement. Allie drifted into the room. Lana looked at her, searching for some kind of explanation. Allie's face gave nothing away. She just returned Lana's gaze, statue-still.

"What happened? Did I pass out?" was all she could think to ask.

"I think you were close. You sort of stumbled, then you went to lie down. I think you would have passed out if you didn't. I guess it's kind of a fine line between fainting and taking a nap because you're about to faint. Sort of a pre-emptive faint. A controlled descent. Cody had a sleep on his mat. He kind of lost his temper at that little bendy mirror and wore himself out with righteous anger. It was pretty funny. It must be crazy to be a baby. I kept an eye on him."

Allie didn't seem distressed in the least. She seemed pleased with herself, like she wanted Lana to feel the same, to tell her well done. She seemed to have the situation under control, unlike Lana. Lana ransacked her immediate memory. She'd lost time, she'd lost track of the sequence of events. She wanted to believe Allie. She wanted someone to be in control of things. If it couldn't be her, Allie seemed like the next best option, the next most responsible person.

"I don't remember getting into the bed. I was by the door then it's blank."

"That's not great. I'm sure it'll come back. Maybe you were like half unconscious, just wandering around on autopilot? Have you never woken up with a hangover like 'where did these library books come from?' Or maybe you were sleepwalking? You didn't say anything to me even though I was calling your name, asking if you could hear me. I'm not sure you could."

Lana looked down at Cody. His eyes were bright, lips pursed in a curious little pout. There were creases on his soft cheek from the playmat. She brushed the pink indentations with her finger. He scrunched his face on one side and grinned.

"Sleepwalking?" asked Lana.

"Sure. Have you ever sleepwalked? Sleptwalk? No that's wrong. It's just sleepwalked."

"When I was a kid, yeah," said Lana.

"Me too," said Allie, eagerly. "But I wasn't sure if you … if that was the same. Because I still don't know where we, y'know, diverged. Anyway, maybe you should speak to a doctor or a therapist or something?"

"About where we diverged? How would they know something like that?" asked Lana, feeling lost. *She doesn't know. That's something.*

"No, you idiot," said Allie, laughing. "About the sleepwalking."

"Oh, yeah of course." Lana laughed too, awkwardly. The tension faded, turned into something slippery and uneasy, but something that could wait. Lana leaned over the arm of the sofa and flicked on the lamp beside it. The daylight outside was weak, and seemed to be fading by the minute even though it was much too early. Some huge dark cloud must be closing in. Not just one cloud. A deep grey blanket was settling in overhead. The lamplight helped, dispelling some of the weird shadows. Lana felt strangely that she might be less likely to fall back into unconsciousness if there were no shadows to trip over or into. She cuddled Cody close, putting her lips on his forehead, smelling his hair.

"Sorry, I'm feeling a little spacey. Maybe it's a blood sugar thing."

"There's some chocolate on the top shelf of the far-left kitchen cabinet. The kind with the little caramel pieces. I saw Magnus put it up there. I think he hides things in there because we're not tall enough. You'll need a chair. Oh, and also I think Cody might need to be changed. Before you get too comfy. He was doing that butt-shuffle thing he does."

"It's so weird that you see him do things that I don't," said Lana, getting tentatively to her feet, balancing Cody on her hip.

"You've seen him do that little butt dance thing. He does it all the time. He'll be moving in no time, y'know. That's something people say."

"No, I meant Magnus."

Allie thought about it, tilting her head on one side in a strangely robot-like gesture.

"Yeah, I guess. I know it must be creepy to you that

I'm around him and the kids when they can't see me. I get that it's creepy. I'm not a psychopath. But I don't have much choice. I'd rather not be invisible, obviously. Maybe I shouldn't nark on your husband."

"Well in this particular situation it benefits me to know about the chocolate. And that one time you told me about the brie wedges that Emmy pushed into the heating vent? That was essential information."

"You would've figured that one out sooner or later," said Allie, grinning.

It added up, *more or less*. But Lana couldn't recall getting from the doorway to the bed. That was something significant. She couldn't remember laying down or pulling the covers over herself. She couldn't remember kicking off her slippers, but they had been neatly paired beside the bed when she woke up, and she was almost sure she had been wearing them before. She had lost a little fragment of time, and it did not return over the days that followed. She told Magnus a version of events, feeling bad that she edited everything she told him recently, removing Allie from her day. *Fix it in post. Except changing the story doesn't change what actually happened. That'd be something actually useful.*

She told him she had felt she was about to pass out, then woken up in her bed. She didn't tell him how much time had passed, or that she'd left Cody alone upstairs. He suggested, like Allie, that it was something like sleepwalking. That she might have fallen asleep while standing up. *What if it's her? What if she can put an idea in his head? Or is that crazy?* Magnus knew, like Allie, that Lana had sleepwalked as a child. It wasn't a stretch. But he waved away the idea of speaking to a professional. Maybe he thought it was a trap, Lana guessed. He had made the suggestion before, and she had not taken it well. *He had learned.* And she felt guilty all over again, for being so adamant about refusing help. Now Magnus felt awkward to broach the subject, to suggest something he believed would help. He was only ever trying to help, and Lana had punished him for it. She hadn't wanted anybody to have access to her private thoughts, her personal space, her time. That seemed ridiculous now.

Chapter 8.

Lana's family doctor was a small-boned man with a smile too big for his face. He had a slightly manic quality and habitually glanced around the room like a bird, a quirk that had always made Lana feel ill at ease. He looked, to Lana, as if he had not slept in several years and had learned to do without, which made her feel that he was perhaps not the person to help her. She hadn't even opened her mouth yet, but she could feel that answers were not here, not from him. Lana had brought all her babies here as newborns and he had measured them, judged them acceptable, said "that's a fine baby you've got there" as if that was the only thing he knew to say when presented with a baby.

He sat across from Lana, a remarkably large and empty desk between them.

"So," he glanced at his notes, glanced at the door, glanced at the clock for good measure, "Alana. What can I do for you? How can I help you today?"

"I'm having trouble sleeping," she said.

He started writing on a pad, his eyes flicking back to her periodically, tapping his ballpoint on the desk between his note-taking.

"Getting to sleep or staying asleep?"

"Both. I can't fall asleep when I want to, I have nightmares, but I've been drifting off when I don't mean to. You know, I had a baby not too long ago, so I'm up to feed him a couple of times a night, often it's more, sometimes it's all night, and-"

"Of course. Well, having a baby is just about the worst thing for a healthy sleep pattern. Your bedtime routine is disrupted. You're breastfeeding?" He radiated anxious enthusiasm.

"Yeah," said Lana.

"Good, good. That's what's best, really. I'm not making a judgement, you understand? I'm sure people do what they have to do. And some people just aren't able to breastfeed, and some people … well."

You are making a judgement. Do a better job keeping stuff to yourself.

"Even just in terms of time management," he continued. "Which means more sleep for you. For both of you. It's so much easier to put the baby on the breast than prepare formula, warm it, make sure it's the right amount. And, of course, you'll always waste some. And there's the expense. Forgive me, I'm rambling on and on. You're anxious about the baby though, I'm sure. That's just how a mother's brain works. You're sleeping light. You don't choose to, it's just something that happens. The baby sleeps in your bedroom?" he was still scratching away on the notepad. It was impressive, Lana thought, that he could write so much and say so much and keep looking around like he feared some kind of assault was imminent. This was a man who could keep a lot of plates in the air, she thought grudgingly. It was difficult to know when she was supposed to reply.

"Yeah," she seized the opportunity to talk. It felt very much as though the doctor had made up his mind about the situation. He seemed to need very little input from her. "I'm worried I've been sleepwalking… maybe."

The doctor looked up, and fixed her with a genuine expression, genuine engagement. He left a space for her to elaborate.

"A few days ago, I was feeling pretty tired, I had this low-level headache I get sometimes. Quite a lot of the time if I really think about it." *All of the time?*

"And do you have this headache now?" the doctor asked, writing more slowly now, like maybe he'd only been pretending to write before.

"No," Lana admitted. *It's only in the house. And only since Allie. Don't say that.* "I was at home with the baby. He was playing in the living room. I felt faint and I thought maybe I fell, but then I woke up in my bed like I'd just taken a nap. But I couldn't remember taking a nap or deciding to take a nap. I felt like I was falling. And then nothing. And then I woke up. Like I lost a little bit of time."

The doctor looked concerned. He slowed a little, to match the speed of Lana's words and expressions.

"And was someone with you? Was someone looking after the baby? Because you really shouldn't let them be unsupervised if they're not secure."

"Yeah," said Lana. "My... uh... a friend was there with him." It was the first time she had ever admitted Allie to someone. Admitted that there was something to admit, anyway. *Why did I say that? What if he tells Magnus? No, why would he? As long as I seem normal. He wouldn't need to.*

"Did your friend see what happened?" he asked.

"She said I got into bed, went for a lie down. But, you know, she's not the most observant."

"That doesn't really sound like sleepwalking," said the doctor.

"I know. But I already talk in my sleep all the time. In the morning, my husband tells me all the crazy shit I said when I was dreaming. Sorry to swear. And I used to sleepwalk when I was a kid. Sometimes I would wake up outside in the street."

"Was that also during a stressful time?" he asked.

"Yes," Lana said. *Huh, maybe this wasn't a waste of time then.*

"So, then I think it's probably stress," he concluded, speeding back up again like a driver moving past a wrecked vehicle. "You don't think you might have postnatal depression, or anything like that? The baby blues?" He was looking at the notepad now, not at her.

"No, nothing like that," said Lana without pausing at all to consider the question. It was second nature, totally automatic, to lie. It was easier when someone's eyes weren't on her.

It felt strange to involve someone else in what was happening inside the house. Lana didn't mention Allie by name, but the events revolved around her, and her influence. Talking about it felt like a betrayal of trust, but she wasn't sure whose. It was weird to lie to him and pretend that she was looking for the cause of a problem that she was increasingly sure she already knew. *So why did I go? I knew a doctor wouldn't help. Because the headache comes from Allie.*

It wasn't a stretch to assume that whatever had happened, her lapse in consciousness, her lost time, had also been the result of Allie's presence. She answered the doctor's questions, about when she went to bed and how much sunlight she got, but half-heartedly, following a more likely line of inquiry in her head. *Allie had suggested sleepwalking. It's logical, I guess. I've got the history to back that up. Or it was stress, baby blues, anxiety, something like that. Maybe it reached some kind of breaking point. In which case, it's lucky Allie was there to watch out for Cody. Like the guy said, can't leave a baby alone.* But it also seemed possible that Allie knew she had done it, that it was some side-effect of her very existence. And if she knew, she had lied to Lana's face.

"Is that something you'd be interested in?" asked the doctor.

"Sorry, what? What did you say? I didn't catch that," said Lana.

The doctor wrote something down, probably that she wasn't listening to him.

"I could refer you to a sleep clinic, and they would be able to monitor the situation overnight, if you'd like? They'd hook you up to a machine and collect data and that would give us a clearer picture. Or, of course, it could just be stress. I don't know how useful that would be if your sleep problems are as the result of your current situation. You'd be surprised how often people just enjoy a peaceful night of sleep at the clinic, wires and all, because the problem is more environmental than anything else."

That wouldn't surprise me at all.

Lana knew he was talking about Cody, not Allie. But it was eerie, all the same, to have someone reference the toll her 'current situation' was taking. Her first instinct was to deny that there was any kind of situation at all. She knew he was right. The tests would show nothing. There wasn't a test for what was wrong with her.

"No, I don't want to do that. You're probably right. Stress. Waste of time. Thanks so much." Lana stood up and pulled on her coat.

"You might try the mother and baby group in town," said the doctor, standing abruptly and darting past her to the door. He opened it before she could reach it, as if he didn't like the idea of her touching his door handles.

Lana had been to the group before, with Seb for a few weeks, with Emmy for even fewer. She hadn't bothered to go at all with Cody. There was too much pressure to chat. She was not naturally sociable, and not good at faking it, particularly in the vulnerable and difficult few months after having a baby. She would prefer a group where new mothers could sit without talking and drink coffee.

"They've moved to a new venue. The ceiling fell down in the community centre," he said, smiling inappropriately. "It could be just the thing. Get a support network. That'll help with your stress."

That's your diagnosis? Loneliness? That's kinda funny if you think about it.

***

They were waiting for her when she got home. It was dark outside. Lana had lingered in town, getting her thoughts straight. She went to the fancy bakery, the one that was always too full to take the stroller inside. In the evening, by herself, it was no problem. It was fun, going places by herself, but it made her feel constantly that she had forgotten something. She wasn't sure what to do with her hands without the stroller, or the carrier, or a small hand in hers. She wasn't sure how to hold her arms when she was walking, or how to be a single body with just four limbs.

She was always an amalgam of one or more human beings. *That's weird to think about.*

She bought a chocolate brioche that was marked down, already going slightly stale but still good. That would make her popular when she got back, she thought. When she walked through the front door, Seb and Emmy were watching some terrible TV show, too loud and bright. They didn't turn to look at her. They were too tired and overstimulated. They got like that sometimes. She could tell all this from the backs of their heads. She knew them better than anyone and knew the minute details of their moods. So she knew how hysterical they would get if she presented them with chocolate cake now. She put the cellophane bag on a high shelf instead. She would make them French toast tomorrow.

Magnus was sprawled on the sofa, eating the kids' leftover fries. Allie was perched on the arm of the sofa beside him. They turned together greet her. It was eerie. The eeriness crawled on the back of Lana's neck. *Nope. Don't like that.*

Lana felt guilty that Magnus lived in such close proximity to Allie without knowing she was there. He had no privacy, like Lana, but he thought he did. *It's almost worse.* Allie didn't seem to have much interest in following Magnus. After all, he couldn't see her. *What would be the point?* She had never given much thought to the kids, or what they might think if they knew Allie was there, watching them. Allie had more interest in them than Magnus. They were the children she could have had. *They're genetically half her. How could she not be interested in them? How could she not love them a little bit?* They would be terrified beyond belief if they knew she was there. It was the kind of primal horror a child would never forget. Lana prayed they never became able to see her. She prayed they would never find out. She didn't like to think about how it might end, how this might play out.

Magnus beckoned her over with a drowsy head tilt and

turned down the TV a few clicks, bringing it to a tolerable volume. Seb and Emmy turned to protest and Lana saw that Emmy had coloured her whole foot green with a marker and there was a bunny rabbit sticker in her hair. Seb gave her a small polite wave, a dozy grin on his face. They returned their attention to their show, probably sensing that TV time would be over soon, that it was inevitably, as always, time for bed. Lana dropped onto the sofa beside Magnus, kicked off her shoes and swung her legs up over the arm rest. He pulled her close and she melted against his warmth. Allie was gone, Lana noted.

Magnus kissed her head, casual and proprietary, his beard tickling her face. It was a small thing, a little show of reassurance, that communicated a lot. He knew she didn't like to involve other people, to admit problems. To ask for help. He was proud of her for swallowing her pride. He wanted to show her, without making too much of a fuss. She put her head on his chest, listening to his booming heartbeat. She honed her hearing in on the reassuring noise of his insides, the pumping blood and the underwater sounds of human mechanisms.

"Cody's sleeping," said Magnus. "He's been a little monster. I tried to give him the frozen milk and he hated it. I heated it up first, obviously, but he wouldn't have it. It smelled like soap but I Googled it and that's just how it goes. I think that happened last time, with Emmy. Anyway he'll be glad you're back. You'll need to feed him before his big sleep. This is just a little nap. Anyway, how did it go?" His voice rumbled through his chest, sounding loud and far away at the same time.

"It was good. He said probably sleepwalking. Probably due to stress. With the baby and everything."

Magnus breathed a sigh of relief. Lana felt bad. *It wasn't a lie. He had said that.* She merely omitted the part where she knew it wasn't true.

"I'm sorry," he said. "I'm sorry if any of this was my fault. I know you're under pressure. I should be doing more. But work is such a fucking shit-show right now. I worry… Y'know, it doesn't matter."

Lana glanced at the kids, seeing if they noticed Magnus' swear.

"Oh they can't hear us. They're practically catatonic," he said dismissively.

"It's not you. You do lots. You're so much help with the kids. Even though I know you give them cookies and I know you let them watch more TV than they're allowed. But you know when I need space and you make it happen. I'm sorry I need to recharge, like a robot or something. So, if anyone's sorry, I'm sorry. I shouldn't count on you for so much. I should have friends. I feel like such a fuck-up that I don't have anyone else. I should have a support network. That's what the doctor said." It was true, but Lana only said it to make him feel better. "You're great. You're perfect," she said. *You poor idiot.*

Lana looked up at Magnus. He was doing the expression he did when he was trying not to cry. It was a sort of sneer tinged with confusion. It was the only way he could hold his face still. Lana had always thought it was funny.

"You don't have to cry, y'know. You're such a wuss," Lana laughed, and was surprised to find that a tear broke free from her own eye as she did so. *What's that about?*

"I wasn't going to cry," he choked.

"Why're you doing that face then?" she wiped away the tear, hoping he hadn't noticed.

"I'm just very invested in this show. It's an emotional journey," he said, staring hard at the TV.

On the screen, a purple cartoon octopus sang a song about vegetables.

"Yeah, these kids have really got great taste. Very discerning." She gave him a squeeze. He was solid and soft and so familiar. Lana had never really had a childhood home. She and her mother moved from place to place, and none of those places made a lasting impression. But there was a feeling when Magnus held her. It was nostalgia for all the times they'd shared and the other couples they'd been together. It was appreciation for everything they'd overcome and how much they had grown in each other's company. It felt like the feeling people described when they talked about their childhood homes, Lana thought. Magnus was the house she had grown up in, and every detail of his face had a special permanent place in her heart. *And that's one of those things too crazy to say out loud.* She knew she was a romantic to an embarrassing degree, deep down, and so was he. And they were both equally embarrassed by that fact. So she just grinned at him, and he did his best to return the favour.

"I should make us some dinner," Lana said, getting up from the sofa. "What do you want? I'll make you whatever you want."

Whatever you want, always. Just don't ask me to tell the truth.

Chapter 9.

When Allie had something important to say to Lana, she preferred everyone else to be out. On weekday mornings, Lana would wave goodbye to Magnus and the kids, sometimes with Cody on her hip, sometimes darting back into the house to grab someone's forgotten sweater or a banana for the car ride. She would close the door, and Allie would be behind it, waiting for her turn to speak. Lana knew she would be there. Lana barely startled any more.

"So how did it go?" Allie asked, following Lana as she went back into the kitchen to tidy up the breakfast things. "With the doctor? What did they say?"

"Just that it was probably just stress," said Lana, sweeping toast crumbs from the counter-tops into her cupped hand.

Allie nodded.

Stress is good. Stress works.

***

Lana took baby Cody for a walk down into town. She did that sometimes. There was a little path, just wide enough for the pram, flanked by overhanging trees that made it seem like a tunnel. The leaves were burnt orange and rust red now and so beautiful. That's what Lana had told her anyway. Cody was transfixed every time they walked down that way. Lana wasn't much of a storyteller, but Allie could guess how the light filtered through the leaves, scattering little sparkling bright sunbeams through the stained glass canopy. Cody would love that. Lana would pick a leaf, one that was either bright or big or interestingly shaped and press it in his squishy little hand to hold onto. He would stare at it, wide eyed and drooling, or scrunch it or occasionally try to taste it. He was amazed by everything, and that was Lana's favourite thing about her kids. She hadn't said that part out loud. That was just something Allie had noticed. That was something Allie liked about them too. Her own senses were dull now. She couldn't feel the world around her in any meaningful way. It cheered her to see Cody be so excited about mashed sweet potato that he covered his face in it, rubbing his hands in it until it was under his cuticles. That was what zest for life felt like. Lana could leave the house and watch Cody be amazed by things objectively more fascinating than pureed vegetables. The seasons were passing. The world kept turning, as if it could do anything else. But Allie stayed still. She could see a corner of that world through the window, in the back yard. She could see the crushed leaves and pinecones in the foot-well of the stroller when Lana returned from her walks. Sometimes she saw frost creeping up the windowpanes, in the night when Allie was alone in the pitch-dark living room, and it felt like winter was pressing its hand against the glass.

Last week, she had watched through the kitchen window as Magnus' car pulled into the driveway, bringing Seb back from junior hockey. It was dark outside but, by the porch light, she saw Magnus' hot breath linger in the air for a moment. Seb was ebullient. He had scored a goal against his long-time nemesis, a boy whose name he did not know. His fingers were red with cold, and Lana had made him a hot chocolate to sip while he effused about the crushing defeat he had inflicted. Seb was quiet most of the time, but when he got talking about something he loved, there was no stopping him. It was a nice evening. But it was the memory of Magnus' breath, floating in the glow of the porch light, which had stuck with Allie. It marked some turning point. There was no denying that things were headed in a certain direction.

It was getting colder, darker. It was time to fortify the house, stock up on pantry essentials in case of a sudden cold snap. Her life, or whatever it was, was a permanent state of shelter-in-place. It was always a cold snap. She couldn't leave. And she stayed the same. Her clothes stayed the same, while everyone else layered up in sweaters and winter coats. She thought she remembered the feeling of wind on her face, and feeling of cool salt waves breaking over her body, and grass and sand and the smell of cold air. She thought she remembered feeling pain, but she wasn't sure.

Allie wasn't stupid. She knew Lana left the house when she needed a break from her. She knew Lana was stressed because she was never really alone in her own house. They were both living in a perpetual state of being the last two guests at a party. But both of them felt like the host, just waiting for the other one to leave. And, of course, neither of them could. Even if they wanted to.

Lana had been a mess to begin with. Allie would have been content to leave, back when maybe she could have done. But she had stayed to watch Lana, then she had stayed to help Lana, then the window had closed for sure. The world had turned too far for her to catch up.

She had helped Lana, she was sure. Lana had seen a doctor. *I would never have done that. And she'd mentioned friends, the night before. She said something to Magnus about a support network.*

They were the same person. Allie never would have guessed that her own destructive, lone wolf tendencies could survive a husband and children. But Lana was proof that they could. Lana had thawed externally, sure. She cooked and cleaned and cuddled. But her core was still frozen, untouchable. Just like Allie was all the way through. Lana needed her. But still, Allie needed Lana more.

Lana didn't suspect anything. *She believed the doctor.* Allie had been anxious that he would reveal something else. *Although how could he possibly know?* There wasn't a scan or a blood test that would help reveal the truth. Lana was happy enough with the explanation she'd been given. It was stress. She was already falling apart when Allie got there. Probably something like this would have happened even if Allie had never intervened. She was lucky that Allie was there to keep an eye on Cody. *What if she had died? Fallen and hit her head? What then?* Lana hadn't looked good, that was true. She would have fainted anyway, without a doubt. But Allie knew, on some level, that she was pushing her. Lana rubbed her eyes when she looked at Allie, and complained of headaches all the time. Allie had put the puzzle together.

She exuded some kind of psychic pressure that bothered Lana. She didn't want to hurt her. But it was intoxicating to have an effect, any effect, on the physical world. She could talk to Lana, of course, but this was a measurable, perceptible effect. It felt like validation that she existed at all and wasn't just enduring some kind of personal purgatory.

Lana had escalated it by trying to push her away. She didn't want Allie to be alone with Cody while he was sleeping, or while Lana was sleeping. As if it mattered what Lana wanted or didn't want. Allie watched Cody while Lana was sleeping most nights. She didn't tell her because she knew how Lana would react. Lana's obsessive need for control was irritating, her stubbornness an unnecessary obstacle. She would rather suffer than let go of even a fraction of her responsibility. Even as it crushed her. She didn't trust Allie. And when Lana had turned away from her, increasing the distance between them, Allie had pushed her. She had reached out across the room with her mind, with whatever force hurt Lana's eyes and clouded her judgement. Allie felt the energy leave her body like a tendril, snake-like and twisting and imbued with her sustaining force, and touch Lana. A real touch. A physical touch. And Lana was on the floor.

Regret and delight fought for dominance. It was more emotion than Allie had felt since she had entered Lana's reality. The suddenly real stakes made her heart race, her actual heart. The fierce panic that she had reached a point of no return was overwhelming, sickening, fracturing. What was the next step? She needed Lana to wake up and be fine before things got out of hand. What had she even done to her? She needed to step back. Instead, she moved on instinct, something she thought she didn't do any more, and she reached out her hand to try and shake Lana awake. Allie's ghostly hand had gone through Lana's arm, like it always did. Of course it did. But it didn't come out again. Something in Lana, little hooks under her skin, had hold of her. Allie's body became sand and poured into Lana's.

And suddenly she was filling a different space. The other half of the hourglass. She was Lana. She was whole.

She was bombarded with stimulus. The dim room was suddenly blindingly bright. Nothing was making noise, but it was deafeningly loud. Every mote of dust landing on her skin felt like a sting. It was too much. Touch and sound and sight all blurring together into a hurricane. She wasn't prepared. She could only think to run, rip herself away, like an animal caught in a snare. She needed to extricate herself from Lana's body, and from responsibility and from blame.

She scrambled to form the most basic plan. If she could, she needed to get out and deny everything to Lana when she woke up, if she ever did wake up. If she was even still unconscious. She might well know and feel everything that was happening. If that was the case, Allie was fucked. She could only hope that two minds couldn't co-exist, that her consciousness necessitated Lana's unconsciousness. Her mind went suddenly clear. She hadn't been aware that her ghost awareness was lacking. But it felt now that her brain was running at double speed, now that she actually had one.

This could change everything. There could be a way out. There could be a way out for her.

Chapter 10.

Castor was perfect. The perfect place to start over. Not that Tess could fully start over. She had a baby for one thing. Thirty weeks old, as the baby books said. There were limits to how far she could reinvent herself. She couldn't make herself not a mother. Although her ex, Emily, had managed to do just that. And then there was the fact that Tess had started bursting into tears for no reason when little things reminded her of her ex-girlfriend. So it wasn't really for no reason. It just seemed that way to other people. Emily had been Tess's ex for a little bit longer than thirty weeks. But Tess had been so busy with the baby that getting over the excruciating implosion of her life's most significant relationship had been stored away somewhere until she'd had more free time. That time was now. So there was that.

The breakup had hit her all at once, resulting in a very public emotional breakdown in one of Vancouver's trendier coffee spots. She had planned the outing. A new cafe had opened near her apartment. She was wearing clean clothes, had put time into her make-up, and was wearing her baby in a chest carrier that had been a gift when she was still pregnant. He was sleeping, his cheek on her chest, clean and freshly dressed in a little teddy bear onesie, cute as a peanut.

Everything was going according to plan. She got a latte. She sat down at a little table, the perfect balance between rickety and charming. It was the kind of trendy place with a perfectly curated playlist of indie deep cuts, photogenic muffins and customers afflicted with just a touch of narcissism. Tess liked coffee shops. She had spent a good portion of her life working in them. She judged this one to be the kind of place that would attract the kind of parent that she wanted to be, the kind of friends she would want to have. The baby woke up when she sat down. He did not like to be in the carrier when she was sitting down. There didn't seem to be any reason for it, but he was adamant.

Tess took him out and sat him on her knee, breaking chunks off her walnut bread with one hand, sipping her coffee, batting away little baby hands as they tried to upend the cup.

***

The baby's name was Steve, and it didn't suit him. It probably didn't suit any baby, Tess thought. She and Emily had agonised over the name, even before Tess was pregnant, when an actual baby was just an abstract at the end of a long and arduous process, before they'd even looked at potential sperm donors, or which clinic they would use. They were equally invested in finding the perfect name. Of course, later, that investedness became more and more one-sided, until finally the baby replaced Emily entirely. Still, Tess was glad not to be totally alone. She had someone to be responsible for, and answerable to. Steve could be her break-up coach. Tess didn't really think of him as a baby so much as a partner-in-crime, a co-person. Maybe because it was just the two of them against the world now. But probably because he had a name like Steve. He seemed reliable. She could count on Steve.

They looked for a unique name first, one that nobody else would have, one inspired by nature or characters from classic novels or obscure songs that made them feel profound things. They had half-settled on Hallow. It was deep, but it was fun and quirky. It said Halloween, and The Legend of Sleepy Hollow, but also made Tess think of hawthorns and brambly, thistley things, and folklore about magical creatures that live in ancient hedgerows. And then Emily ran into an old friend in the health food store and, by some bizarre coincidence, that was the name she had chosen for her soon-to-be-born baby girl.

Or maybe, Tess thought, it wasn't so bizarre. Maybe

the kind of stuff they had grown up with, maybe the media that had shaped their name choice, had also steered Emily's friend in the same direction. How many other queer couples in Vancouver had arrived independently at that same name? It made Tess anxious about how much her thoughts were her own. They set about finding another perfect, unique, thoughtful name. But something about it still bothered Tess. Why did she even want a name that nobody else had? Why did it need to be unique? It was certainly more for herself than for the baby. Halfway through the pregnancy, the whole thing suddenly felt so hubristic and insane.

Steve, she decided alone. It had been her grandfather's name. He was a nice man. It was a nice name. She sold the idea to Emily by insisting that such a traditional, old-fashioned choice was the most unexpected thing to do. And that in a classroom where every kid had a name like Maverick or Western or Blythe, the unconventional choice was Steve. People always laughed when they told them. But maybe that was just the people they hung around with. Maybe they weren't nice people.

None of their shared friends had kids. Sometimes it felt to Tess that they were using her and Emily as some kind of trial run. They would see how difficult it was, how expensive it was, how much of a negative impact it had on their relationship. They probably felt it hadn't been worth it. "Those poor people," they were probably saying now. "God, poor Tess. Stuck with that baby. A single mother."

Sometimes when Tess couldn't sleep, she wondered if she had forced Emily to go through with the process. That's what Emily had said to her. She had said she'd been swept along by Tess' desire to have a baby. Tess specifically remembered her repeated use of the words 'manic' and 'obsession'. She wondered now and then, at inopportune moments, how much truth there was to Emily's accusations. Is there something wrong with me? Should I be in charge of a baby? But she was. That's all there was to it. Emily didn't even want a little part of him. It hurt to find out that someone she loved had a radically different view of their shared life. Every blood test, discussion, scan, every little piece of bureaucracy on the path to getting pregnant felt like a triumph to Tess. It turned out that it felt to Emily like a noose tightening.

They weren't married. But they had planned for a future. They were going to open a store together. They would sell new-age books and crystals and incense, what Emily called 'witchy shit'. That was pretty rude of her, Tess thought now. Tess believed in gods and folklore, and that there was magic in the earth and in people. She had been riding high on her own feminine energy when she had been pregnant. She felt close to something big, something bigger than any one person. Her faith had waned considerably in light of recent events.

They'd almost had the money together for the store. It was all planned out. But the baby had taken precedent. That dream was tabled with no discussion. A new dream was happening. Emily accused her of something that sounded worryingly close to abuse. She said Tess had gaslit her into her vision of a nuclear family that she never actually wanted. It was better for Tess not to think about the things she had been accused of. She was sure they weren't true. She was mostly sure. The best thing she could do for Emily was get away from her. At least they were on the same page there. But the self-doubt had been destructive. Tess could shelve it until after Steve was asleep, but it had to come down some time. She had to look at it.

**

She handed Steve a piece of her walnut bread, a piece with no big chunks of walnut in it. Things like that had become second nature very quickly. Tess didn't think of herself as someone who was good at taking care of things. She had never had a houseplant longer than a month. But she knew how to look after Steve. She knew how to love him. She tried to trust that was enough.

He made another attempt to knock her coffee cup, now almost empty, to the floor. She knew he was going to do it and shifted it just beyond his reach. She drained the cup and shuffled Steve back into the carrier, putting her arms through the straps. She reached behind her back to secure the buckle. She couldn't reach. She tried the other way, switching which arm was behind her back, and which was behind her neck. She tried both arms behind her back. She had hold of both halves of the buckle, but she couldn't get them to meet. Her spacial awareness was off. She had used a mirror to buckle it before she left the house, she realised, and there was not one here. The two pieces of plastic might be a millimetre apart, but she could not coordinate them.

She felt hot, her tear ducts prickling. She knew what was coming. Even as Steve looked up at her with his big gentle eyes, there was nothing she could do to avert it. Her eyeliner ran down her cheeks in two grey stripes. It was bad. She tried to keep quiet, but a couple of anxious breathy gulps escaped her mouth. Steve got spooked and he started crying too.

She realised afterwards that she could have asked a barista to help her buckle the carrier. It would have been no big deal. Instead she had a meltdown in a nice place, in front of other people. She could never go there again. She might as well leave town. It was an intrusive thought, that had been coming to her more and more over the last couple of months. It was difficult to get childcare. She was working now and then at a cafe, but she knew she was starting to eat into her savings, the money that had been for the store. So she might as well leave, get out to one of the cute little towns she and Emily had road-tripped through on vacation a couple of years back. She remembered one in particular, part-way between

Vancouver and Calgary, mountains on all sides, with a river running through. The mountains had been beautiful in the summer, with a kind of lushness in the trees and the air that barely seemed plausible. But the river was something really special, wide and smooth as a highway, and the colour of a perfect summer sky.

She looked it up, on a whim, after the incident in the coffee shop. Castor, she remembered, like the twins from Greek mythology. That would be a good name for a baby, she thought idly, and then felt a twinge of guilt for Steve's sake.

It was 200 miles from the nearest IKEA. Where else did furniture come from? She imagined them living in a barren cube of a home, brutalist architecture on the outside, sepulchre on the inside. Or just a leatherette beanbag and a flatscreen tv on the floor, like a tragic bachelor pad. She wondered how much a one bed apartment might cost her. She looked it up. It was cheap. It was astonishingly cheap. She knew Vancouver was expensive, but she could not have predicted that somewhere with an obviously thriving tourism industry and so much natural beauty would be within her budget.

There was a place available, right in the centre of town, a green and yellow wood-panelled building. It was a commercial property, an old shoe store with an apartment above it. She read more. She could go glade skiing in the winter, not that she knew how to ski or what glade skiing even was. She could learn. And hiking in the summer. She could buy one of those back carriers for Steve. There was a new zip-lining park. Would that be something she'd like?

She clicked on a picture of Castor in the autumn, what it must look like at that very moment, clad in vibrant hues of orange and brown. It looked like a cornucopia, a brimming basket of little red brick buildings and trees. People came for the outdoor activities, to take photos and to breathe the mountain air. But Tess could live there. It could be home.

Chapter 11.

"Do you want me to go to the unit and get the Halloween junk?" Magnus asked Lana one particularly cold evening, when they were all sat around the dinner table. It was oddly quiet, and the gentle humming of the furnace in the basement seemed louder than usual, reminding everyone of the coming cold. Baby Cody was sitting in Emmy's old highchair, which was also Seb's old highchair, with a little padded insert to support his uncoordinated body. He was grinning madly, happy to be included, and making little grunts and hand gestures for Magnus to pass him food. He wasn't especially interested in eating solid food, but he liked to squash soft things between his fingers. Magnus passed him a piece of bread to lick the butter off.

"Lana," Magnus said. "The Halloween junk? It's less than two weeks. It's very unspooky in here."

It's spooky enough for me.

"That cobweb up there is pretty spooky," she said pointedly.

"I'm not getting rid of that. I'd rather have spiders than flies. Spiders don't bother anyone. Anyway, I think one little cobweb and one spider that I honestly can't even see is a little more understated than I was hoping for. We need a few plastic pumpkin lanterns, and you know it. It's tradition," said Magnus. "For the kids too, I guess," he added unconvincingly.

"I'm gonna be a robot," said Seb, with his slight lisp. "Did you know I'm going to a Halloween party?" He was systematically removing the crispy cheese layer from the top of his lasagna.

"I did know," said Lana. "At school, right?"

"No, in the canteen," he said, suddenly worried that he and his mother weren't on the same page.

"That's at school. It's part of the school." Lana turned her attention back to Magnus, who was now trying to pry the lump of bread back out of Cody's buttery hands. "I'll get it," said Lana. "I'll get the stuff tomorrow. I haven't decided what I want yet. Some of it might not be appropriate for Cody."

"You think it might be too scary? I'm not sure how far he can even see," said Magnus.

"No, idiot, like what if he picks off those window sticker things and eats them?"

"He can't even crawl. He'll be fine," said Magnus, wiping his hands on Cody's bib. "You're not feeling it this year, huh?"

Lana felt an icy breath. A sudden drop in temperature. She couldn't see her, but she knew Allie was here. The same way Magnus couldn't see her thoughts, but he could feel them. Since she had told him that she was suffering from some kind of anxiety-induced sleep disturbance, Magnus was constantly on the lookout for potential stressors, or indicators that Lana's stress levels were becoming sub-par. It was kind of him. He was attentive and he cared. But it was also very annoying, mostly because it reminded Lana that she couldn't tell him the actual cause of her stress. *It must seem to him like I can't cope with normal stuff. Like keeping the kids fed and clean and clothed, cooking and cleaning and organising stuff is too much. He can't see the problem. It probably looks to him like there isn't one.* If that's what he thought, he was good at hiding it. But Lana didn't see how he could realistically think anything else.

"It's just a bit of seasonal affective disorder, I guess. You're right, I'll feel better once we get all the spooky shit up. It's time for the big skeleton to make his triumphant return," she smiled. The big skeleton was a 6ft tall, plastic, posable skeleton. It was one of the more bizarre and impulsive purchases they had made as a couple. It was meant for the front lawn, but somehow it always spent Halloween inside the house, usually sitting in a chair and wearing human clothes. Once they had left it on the front porch to hold a bowl of candy for trick or treaters, and it hadn't felt quite right. It was like part of Lana's extended family. They'd had it longer than they'd had Seb, which was always strange for Lana to consider.

"You said a bad word," said Seb, grinning.

"I did. I'm sorry," said Magnus.

"Don't like skettin," said Emmy, her tiny lower lip sticking out in a pout.

"You love the big skeleton!" said Magnus. "We'll dress him up. What would you like him to wear? He could be a wizard, or a bunny, or maybe a princess?"

"Princess," said Emmy, immediately cheered up. "Can I wear my princess dress now?" The skeleton was now totally forgotten.

"You can wear it after dinner, when you're not covered in sauce," said Magnus. "And Daddy's gonna put you guys in bed tonight because Mama is going to her group."

Seb and Emmy shared a conspiratorial smirk across the table, forming an unspoken plan to make things difficult for Magnus.

"They're not *my* group. They're *a* group," said Lana.

"They *could be* your group."

They won't be though. These things are always a bust. She had been to the mother and baby group before, and it hadn't quite clicked. Although things were a little different now. It was just the mothers for the foreseeable future, meeting just one evening a week in a store downtown, until the ceiling of the community centre was repaired. The group hadn't been able to find a space that was safe for babies to crawl around, but they hadn't wanted to completely pull the resource. *Because things could get desperate quickly*, Lana thought. It seemed like it would be a lot easier to talk to people without a baby in tow. But Cody was also useful in drawing focus away from her own awkwardness, which manifested as nervous grinning and talking just a little too quickly. These things were softened by the presence of a baby.

It wasn't really the prospect of grown-up social interaction that had persuaded Lana to go along. Part of it was wanting to be out of the house, but not the biggest part. She had looked it up online and discovered which store they were meeting in. It was the witch store.

She knew that it was a long shot that anything would come from it, but it felt too much like fate to waste. She had a supernatural predicament. She knew that people who called themselves 'witches' in the modern world were a totally disparate group of people with wildly varying beliefs and practices. Some of them kept the pagan feast days, which Lana had heard of but could only name one, Samhain, because it was also Halloween. It got a lot of play in folk horror movies, which made up most of her resources about the supernatural. She also had podcasts about the satanic panic, things she read on trashy websites about the new age lifestyle trends of celebrities, and old tv shows.

She knew there were people who made medicine from herbs or made star charts to divine their trajectory through life, or had blogs, or just wore a pentagram and left it at that. How much they resembled the kind of witch she was looking for was debatable. The kind of witch she was looking for was one from a movie. *But the kind with tarot cards and a crystal ball, not the kind that builds a wicker man.* She wanted to know what she was up against; what Allie really was and what she could really do to Lana. If anyone would know, it would be someone who sold occult books.

***

An hour later, Lana sat in her parked car, bundled up against the cold evening air. It was dark and she didn't have her kids with her. She kept glancing into the back seat, at the baby-shaped space in the padded car seat, expecting to see Cody cocooned in blankets and snoozing gently. But he was at home with Magnus. He was probably asleep by now. If Magnus had managed to put him down. Allie was there too, of course. Lana wasn't sure if this made her feel better or worse. Was it better that she had left behind an invisible ghost in the shape of herself, like a golem? Except that she couldn't control Allie. They were usually both at home. Lana felt better about that. Allie was like a reflection, and Lana felt that she couldn't push through if Lana was there to block her way. *The other side of the mirror is unguarded. There's just a me-shaped hole for her to fall through.* At least Allie couldn't meaningfully interfere with anything real, Lana decided. Or that was her hope.

There was a coldness now in Lana's bones, that sweaters and hot water bottles couldn't thaw, like the pain from an old fracture. She had noticed it growing, congealing, in the last week, since she had passed out and lost time. She was at the mercy of that cold. It felt like something of the ghost had made its way through her skin. Her body had been compromised, just like her home. Her brain was the only thing left that was really hers, and she was beginning to have some concerns about that too. It was time to do things.

Lana opened the car door, her heart jumping just a little when the roof light illuminated her reflection in the rear-view mirror. Her blood was on edge all the time, latent anxiety in every red cell. She pushed the feeling down and took deep breaths. She had to look normal. She had to do whatever she could to not seem crazy. Frazzled was okay, sleep-deprived was okay, but nothing more than that.

Lana composed her face into an easy smile, or what she hoped was an easy smile. She stepped out of the car, the cold air bypassing her skin and going right to her bones, straight through her. She pulled her coat tighter, over Magnus' thick hoodie that she had stolen because it smelled like home. Her plan wasn't a good one. It was barely any kind of plan at all. It felt futile, and the darkness around her and the cold under her skin made it worse. *At least I'm getting out of the house.*

The store had been in the back of her mind for a while. It seemed to appear at the same time Allie showed up.

Lana wasn't sure how much she believed in coincidences. Then again, she wasn't sure how much she believed in ghosts until a few weeks ago. Had it only been a few weeks?

The green and white storefront was pretty in a traditional way, save for the sign that hung over the door featuring the name, The Looking Glass, and a painting of the Cheshire Cat riding a broomstick. It was mostly old fashioned, with a scalloped striped awning and freshly painted window frames, like an old general store or a haberdashery – like something that didn't really exist anymore. But that was Castor in a nutshell. The husk of the heritage silver-rush town was still there, but the community it served was somewhat unexpected.

A dark curtain had been pulled across the shop front window, but there was a gap through which Lana could see a little of the room beyond. Lana had sneaked a peek inside once or twice since it had opened, never stopping long enough to let herself think about going inside. Two sofas from the reading area had been moved into the centre of the room, and a variety of mismatched dining chairs had been added, roughly in a circle. Tables that normally displayed books had been pushed to the edges of the room. People milled around, with awkwardly crossed arms and polite smiles, avoiding the space inside the circle of chairs.

Lana saw the group organizer, a woman in her fifties with close-cropped grey hair, Susan. A flood of memories returned to Lana of the woman she'd forgotten in a hurry. Susan was a local busybody. Anyone who met her would describe her as capable, a fantastic ally and a terrible enemy.

Susan had helped Lana after Seb was born. Lana couldn't get the hang of breastfeeding. A blocked milk duct became inflamed and blossomed into a hot red weal on her breast. One of her nipples was bloody all the time, and every time Seb latched, it felt like the nipple was being sheared off. The pain only lasted a second, before settling into more of an ache for the duration of the feed. But she couldn't help but wince at the pain when it came again, every couple of hours. She was supposed to switch breasts, one feed on the left, the next on the right. It made her feel like a machine that dispensed nutrients. A machine that had to be used in exactly the right way or tubes became blocked and the whole thing stopped working. She hadn't followed the operating instructions, she had stopped nursing Seb on one side, wary of the pain, and then her breast hurt more than anything she could imagine. It leaked constantly, seemingly not milk but acid. It was not a good feeling.

Lana had felt like she had no control over her body, which suddenly felt and did things it never had. Susan had told her what to do, even though Lana had not asked. Lana could have gotten the advice about hot compresses, massage, the application of cabbage leaves, from the internet. But Susan had also told her, with her kind eyes and a slight Irish accent, that it was normal. Millions of women had gone through the same. They'd been fine. Lana would be fine. Lana liked Susan, she remembered. But she was also embarrassed to have accepted her help. She felt the weight of a debt still owed.

Lana saw the witch too. She knew it was her. She'd seen her putting up flyers around town. But Lana was sure she would have known her even if she'd never set eyes on her before. She was soft, ethereal, obviously a witch. Her eyes were cloud grey and huge, with eyebrows so pale they were almost invisible. Her dirty blonde hair was in two long haphazard braids covered in flyaways. She wore a completely shapeless black dress that made it difficult to know what kind of shape her body was underneath.

Lana knew she had a judgemental streak, probably stemming from the fear that people were judging her. She was perhaps being uncharitable to the witch. *Is it harsh of me to call her 'the witch'? I guess that's what I need her to be.* Lana had a habit of making a snap judgement about someone, and then overcompensating for it by trying not to believe it.

When she had first met Magnus she had judged him as soft, fair-weather. He seemed like he would be terrible in a crisis. Like someone who gave up easily. Like someone who might cry. She hadn't thought he had the fortitude for a long-term relationship, especially not with her. Lana felt so terrible for thinking that about someone who'd been nothing but pleasant to her. He asked her on a date and she hadn't wanted to go. She was just finding her feet in Castor, and people talked about her, about her being the daughter of the local hoarder shut-in. She felt dark and knew her sharp edges would tear through someone like Magnus, who seemed so wholly good and nice. But she'd felt so bad about judging him that she'd said yes. And now she couldn't imagine life without him. Apart from being her husband, the father of her children, he was her only friend.

Lana didn't make friends easily. She had never managed anything more than trivial chit-chat with the other parents at the school. There had been events, school plays, parents' evenings, but it was too difficult to break past inconsequential chatter about the weather or the children's schedules. It wasn't entirely a result of her situation, she knew, because she didn't have many friends as a child either. She had learned to enjoy her own company and to be alone.

Her social circle consisted of her husband, two small children, a baby and an inscrutable doppelganger. She smiled to herself, unable to resist the twitching of her mouth corners, when the thought occurred to her. It was ridiculous, and it was impossible to ignore the fact. If she wanted to stay sane, she knew deep down, she needed to bring somebody else into the situation. *Not Magnus. He's too close to it. God knows what he would do.* But a stranger, someone whose mind was already open to that kind of thing, was fair game.

"Are you going to go in?" said a voice from behind her. A young woman with dyed black hair and heavy eyeshadow was smiling nervously at her. Lana realised she had been staring at the door as though she'd never seen one before.

"Sorry, I was just getting my thoughts together. Long day," Lana laughed.

"Just enjoying the quiet, eh? Is it your first time here?"

"It's my first time, this time. I mean, I've been before with my other kids. In the community centre, before it imploded or whatever happened. I've had another kid since then. He's at home, of course. I'm Lana, by the way."

That went well. I said my name, at least.

"Jen," said the woman. "It's okay to be nervous. But it's a really good group. I'm not sure about the choice of location though," she laughed. Lana laughed back automatically, in meaningless agreement. It was a habit. The woman gave Lana's shoulder a reassuring squeeze that was so overly familiar that Lana almost flinched. Instead she managed to smile and follow the woman through the door into the warm and fragrant candlelight beyond.

Chapter 12.

Tess had not been in Castor long. If she was being honest with herself she was feeling a little out of her depth. She and Emily had planned to open the store together, planned it down to the last detail. But it seemed now that most of the actually useful information had only existed inside Emily's head. Tess had been happy enough to let her deal with the less interesting side of things. Practicalities were not her strong suit, and the realities of inventory, redecorating, and tax forms meant that it took a little longer to open than she'd hoped.

She was still unpacking her boxes when an officious middle-aged woman came through the door with a proposition; let the local mother and baby group use the space temporarily, for free, in exchange for valuable word-of-mouth advertising. Apparently, an endorsement from this woman, Susan, could be the difference between sink and swim for a new business. Tess wasn't sure how much she believed that, but she couldn't be completely sure. Tess was a mother too, Susan pointed out. She could join the group.

It could be a good move, Tess thought, not so much to get advice but to feel out potential new customers. It was only a little bit morally dubious to gather a bunch of isolated, sleep-deprived women into her place of business and try to sell them candles. Anyway, she would need to be there to make sure they didn't break anything, she had concluded.

People filled the store, showing each other photos on their phones of their kids and their various achievements or rashes. Susan greeted each new person at the door, pointing occasionally at Tess. Tess wondered what she was saying about her. Probably just that she was the owner of the place. Hopefully that it was an exceptional business she had here. Hopefully not that she was a charlatan that was best avoided.

Tess could feel a case of imposter syndrome brewing. She was new in town, new to running a business, new to selling her beliefs. It was one thing to believe in tarot cards. It was quite another thing to sell tarot cards. It felt too personal. And her spirituality had taken a hit in the separation. She hadn't realised the depth of the insufficiency, or how much it was hurting her. She hadn't realised she had moved across the province to reinvigorate it. Not until after she'd done it.

She had felt so supported by the universe, by the fates, when she had gotten pregnant. She hadn't known it would destroy her relationship. She hadn't known she would be a single mother. It was what she'd prayed for, what she'd manifested, but it was also slightly wrong. That's how magic worked in movies, she thought. There's always a twist, just enough to put people off, to make it seem not worth bothering with.

Customers needed to believe in her to buy things. She couldn't admit to being burnt out. She had to keep smiling, keep the incense burning and keep wishing people a blessed day. Even though that felt slightly wrong too.

Tess was intuitive. It was her secret power. She wasn't sure if being a practising witch had made her more empathetic, or if her natural empathy had attracted her to witchcraft. It was difficult to disentangle the two. But she had an eye for people. She was always uncannily good at remembering the regulars in the various cafes she had worked in. She was good at reading them too, guessing what kind of non-dairy milk they wanted before they even said anything, feeling out things about them. Sometimes secret things. It didn't feel as magic as other things did. There was no ceremony, no special words or cards or crystals or candles. She just knew. Some people could read auras, but she wasn't really sure what that meant. What did an aura look like? Maybe it was more of a metaphor. Maybe that's what she did. Maybe people just wanted her to know. Maybe it wasn't so much her drawing information out of people, as them throwing it at her. For the right person, someone who really wanted Tess to understand them, little throwaway lines, little gestures and twitches, were like a code that she had no trouble deciphering.

She had seen Lana before, and she'd remember her like she remembered everybody. Lana was usually pushing her stroller around town, with a thousand-yard stare. Tess had seen her eyes darting to the window of the store. Tess was certain she would show up at some point. Tess had initially guessed she was a bored housewife, looking for something exciting, something to spice up her life. But she was re-evaluating that initial assessment. For one thing, she was wearing jeans. Faded sky blue with a small hole in the left knee, an actual genuine hole from kneeling on that knee more than the other, rather than a fashionable distressed aesthetic. Her hair was long and thick and dark, but it was twisted up behind her head with a functional clip. These weren't the choices of a woman seeking meaning in the supernatural. She wasn't trying to spice up anything. Maybe she wasn't here to covertly scope out the store. Maybe she was actually there for the mother and baby group.

There was a self-service coffee station next to the counter. The Looking Glass sold books, so Tess had put in a reading area and a coffee area. If she could keep people in the store longer, she reasoned, they would be more likely to buy things. It was proving very popular. Susan released her newest guest from her clutches, who then made her way to the coffee station, drawn there as if by a magnet. Tess could relate to that. She followed her.

"Hi," said Tess. Lana spilled her coffee just a little. A tad skittish, Tess noted.

"Hello," said Lana. She licked the spilled coffee from the side of her hand. "I know you. You're the owner, yeah? Of... here." She gestured vaguely at the room.

"That's me. Tess." She thought for a second about

initiating a handshake, before dismissing the idea as profoundly awkward.

"Alana. But call me Lana. Everyone does."

Tess nodded. A silence moved in, catching them both up in it. Tess wasn't quite sure what she wanted to say, or why she had even gone over to Lana in the first place. Luckily they were interrupted by Susan who, satisfied that nobody else was going to turn up, had closed the door and commanded everyone's attention.

"Well, hello everyone," Susan said, when she was satisfied everyone was listening. "I see some new faces today. A very good turnout at our new temporary venue."

"The community centre smelled like mildew," Lana whispered to Tess. "The candles are a massive improvement."

"I was worried they might be a bit overpowering. They're the only ones I have enough of. They make the cat sneeze," Tess whispered back.

"I'd like to propose a 'get to know one another' exercise," Susan continued, with the obvious glee of someone who likes to subject other people to awkward social encounters. "Pair up with the nearest person. I've prepared some questions, which I'll pass around." She made her way around the room, handing out small pieces of paper. She pressed one into Lana's hand and moved on.

"It's laminated," Lana said.

"If you told me one person in this room owned a laminator, I would have said it was her. No hesitation," said Tess. She dragged two spindle backed chairs over to where Lana stood with her coffee, frozen to the spot with the stress of choosing a partner.

"Yeah, no shit," Lana laughed. "Are you here? Are you part of this... mother and baby thing? Or are you just here to make sure we don't break stuff?"

"Both," said Tess, sitting down. She fished a baby monitor out of her dress pocket and showed Lana the sleeping baby on the screen. "He's upstairs. It's somewhere to go that I don't need to get a sitter."

Lana sat down too.

"He's cute," said Lana, although there was no way she could tell that from a grainy video feed. "We picked a good spot. I want to stay close to the coffee machine," she said with practised self-deprecation.

"I know, right? That should be question one on the card – on a scale of one to ten, how tired are you?"

"Let's add it. On a scale of one to ten, how tired are you?" asked Lana.

"I'll say five. It's not so bad at the moment. I'm still not getting a full night's sleep, but I can so barely remember the feeling of eight hours at this point that it almost feels like something I imagined. Does anyone get eight hours? How about you? One to ten."

Lana wanted to say ten. She wanted to say twelve. Tess could see it in her eyes.

"Maybe eight," Lana said. "It's not going well. I either can't sleep, or I can't stop sleeping."

"It can be like that though, right? Having a baby? Just ricocheting between narcolepsy and insomnia? I mean, it's crazy."

"You're not wrong," said Lana. But Tess could feel she really meant it. She wasn't feeling sorry for herself, she wasn't looking for pity. What was she looking for?

They went through the rest of the questions on the card, which ranged from oddly clinical topics like breastfeeding and sleep schedules, to deeply personal questions about postpartum sex. They answered the less mortifying ones as best they could. Some of them they agreed not to touch. They got onto the subject of the stupidest ways they'd accidentally woken a sleeping baby, and were laughing together when Susan gave them a two minute warning.

"I want to add my own final question," said Lana, who had loosened up considerably.

"Sure. Shoot."

"What music do you like?" Lana asked.

"That's a big question. I guess I like nineties grunge bands like Hole and The Smashing Pumpkins, and kind of lo-fi indie that could be emo music, but could also just be arty soft rock. And . . . it's actually quite hard to think of music genres. I like internet playlists of the soundtracks of cool tv shows. And Appalachian folk music, when the mood strikes me."

"That's a very specific answer," said Lana.

"It's a big question, like I said. So, what's your jam?" asked Tess.

"I like all kinds of music. But I guess if I'm being specific, I like sixties girl groups a lot. I like Elvis and Slim Whitman and old timey cowboy music. I like whatever genre Lana Del Rey is. Or maybe I've just got a soft spot for a fellow Lana. You know that kind of nostalgic mumbling music?"

"Sad music. All those things are sad music."

"And the Smashing Pumpkins are not sad music?" said Lana.

"Maybe all the best music is sad music. Appalachian folk music, in particular, is extremely sad. It's a lot of stuff about falling in love with someone you shouldn't, and then being murdered and, more often than you'd think, becoming a ghost whose full-time job is to be sad."

"Fuck that," said Lana, before hastily adding; "I have a follow up question."

"Okay, make it snappy because Susan is looking at her watch and then looking straight at me. She's trying to send me a coded message of some kind. Oh, she's actually coming over. What did I do?"

"Do you believe in ghosts?"

Tess paused for a second to consider it. She hadn't expected that. She thought Lana was trying to make friends with her. This was not the logical next question.

Tess' automatic response was to look for her most earnest answer. She believed in most things. She knew people who believed in ghosts. Her grandfather swore until his dying day that he'd lived briefly in a haunted house.

"Yeah, I think so," she said.

Now they were talking about the real stuff, life and death stuff. But their time was up, and Lana had casually tacked it on to the end, something she just had to know before the next organised activity. Maybe that was something she asked everyone, Tess thought. Maybe that was her go-to icebreaker. Lana was smiling, like Tess had passed the test. But when Tess looked closer, let her intuition get a good look at Lana, she saw that there was a sadness to the smile. She was glad Tess believed in ghosts, but also a little sorry for her sake. That sad smile sent a shiver up Tess' spine. But Susan was calling for quiet and all eyes were gradually turning to her, Lana's included.

Susan started speaking, over-projecting into the small space: "Now that we've got to know each other a little bit, which is so important you know, what with all the new faces here tonight, I'll get down to business. Jeanette over there; say hi Jeanette-"

A woman with mousey brown hair who didn't seem to know she'd be called upon, waved tensely to the room full of eyes.

"Well Jeanette is a qualified breastfeeding counsellor, so she'll be able to answer any questions you might have about breastfeeding. She'll help you troubleshoot whatever problems you might have been having. And it's important to remember this is a judgement free session. Don't be afraid to talk about any concerns you might be having, any hurdles you might be facing."

Tess was certain that Susan would end up knowing whatever confidential information was divulged to Jeanette, and also wondered what kind of deal had been struck that this woman had donate her professional time free of charge.

"I'll be here to talk to anyone about literally anything

else. Baby furniture, safe sleep, developmental milestones, baby blues. And again, I must stress that this is a judgement free space. And with that in mind, I will turn you over to our lovely host, Tess, to just tell you a little bit about this venue and about the services she offers here," Susan concluded, turning a patronising smile to Tess.

Tess stowed her coffee under her chair, making a mental note not to forget about it, stood up and cleared her throat.

Her own sudden nervousness caught her off guard. She was good at people. Lana's question had thrown her. She was off-balance now, and the people gathered here could well be her future customer base. She pushed the weird feeling down, right down through the soles of her feet and into the earth.

"Hi, hello everyone. So, welcome to The Looking Glass. Yes, I'm a big fan of Alice in Wonderland," Tess said to polite laughter. "A looking glass is another, slightly outdated, term for a mirror. We use mirrors a lot in our practice, not least for scrying. That means looking into the past, present or future and revealing secrets unknown."

She was performing, hamming it up for the audience, doing a bit that she had perfected. But it was important to seem a little unprepared, relatable. She noted that Susan was making a face somewhere between contempt and fascination, as if she couldn't believe the rubbish she was hearing, but also would quite like a mirror that revealed secrets unknown.

"And when I say 'we' I mean witches, wiccans, pagans, polytheists, and anyone even remotely spiritually inclined. If you feel like there's something out there," Tess paused to stare into the middle distance. A couple of people followed her gaze, that's how she knew she had them. "And I'm not talking about aliens, even we have to draw the line somewhere," pause for laughter, "then come along to one of our events or just swing by the shop for a chat. My door is always open, during regular business hours," she concluded, beaming around at everyone. Lana had moved away during her speech and been trapped in a corner by Susan.

The eyes gradually moved away from Tess as people resumed their conversations. Tess was sure she'd been holding a cup of coffee, just a moment ago. She looked around her, at the surfaces and shelves covered in crystals and sage bundles and books about manifesting through embroidery. It was gone. She shrugged and went to make another. She could admit to herself that she'd installed the coffee station for herself more than for customers.

Another woman, who had introduced herself to Tess earlier but who's name Tess had somehow since forgotten, was already there, repeatedly dipping a teabag into a cup of hot water. "Hi," the woman said. She had huge green eyes, glittering with earnestness. She would be easy to get on side, Tess thought. Those big green eyes were looking for something. She felt a little bad about her snap judgement. But she was good at reading people, and some people were easier to read than others. Some people wanted to be read.

The problem was that Tess didn't really *want* to read people. It made life boring. It made her think of other people as boring. It was unkind, but there wasn't much she could do about it.

"The stuff you said sounded really interesting," the woman said. Maya, Tess remembered. It always sounded interesting to people, because it was vague, and they filled in the gaps with what they wanted to hear.

"I'm glad," said Tess. "I've got some leaflets somewhere about our events. Make sure you take one before you leave, yeah?"

The woman nodded enthusiastically.

"Yeah, I'll come by. I think this is going to be really good for me. It's exactly the kind of thing I've been looking for, y'know?"

Tess did know.

"Oh and, by the way, your milk is expired," said the

woman cheerfully, before walking away.

Tess opened the milk jug. It was full of lumps and smelled acrid. She had just bought it that morning. She'd made a cup of coffee less than ten minutes ago, and it had been fine. She'd never known milk to sour in under ten minutes. Unless someone put something in it while she was talking, like lemon juice. No, that was ridiculous. Still, she shot a glance at Lana, who had been closest to it. No, that didn't happen, she told herself. That was crazy. Nobody is interfering with the milk.

Lana met her gaze, pulled herself away from Susan and came to stand beside Tess.

"Sorry, she wanted to tell me how much she'd missed me at the group. I don't think that's true at all. It's been years and I was never that invested in it. Why are you making that face? Did something happen?" Lana asked.

"The milk soured," said Tess.

"Do you have any more?"

"Yes, of course I do. Don't you think that's weird though?"

Lana was still holding the cup of coffee she had made previously. It was black. She stared into it for a moment then sipped it.

"Happens to me all the time. I drink black coffee now most of the time anyway. Milk barely lasts any time at all in our house. There's two kids and me and my husband, plus a baby. We get through a lot of cereal. Is that a witch thing maybe? Causing milk to sour? I feel like I've heard that," said Lana with a smirk.

"What? That's not witches, that's sprites or something. Pixies, I don't know. Some mythological creature that doesn't exist. I'd have noticed if my presence curdled milk. I used to work in a cafe. It'd have been pretty fucking inconvenient."

Lana nodded, unconvinced. "Maybe you should switch to oat milk."

"I didn't do it!"

"I just meant that it lasts longer. It's more stable at room temperature," Lana laughed, and Tess could feel it had all the hallmarks of a running joke that could follow them both for years if things went a particular way. Sometimes things felt like that, like a ball of yarn tumbling off into the future, trailing a thread that Tess could follow if she wanted.

There was a lull, that coincided with a lull in everyone else's conversation. There was no reason for it. Sometimes silences line up in a way that feels important, and everyone is reminded of how much they don't like the quiet.

Lana was first to break it. She liked silences the least, of the two of them.

"Is your little one still asleep?" Lana asked, then grimaced a little, like she knew it was weird to call a baby a 'little one'. That seemed to be the vibe of the mother and baby group. That was what you called them. Little ones.

Tess looked at the baby monitor.

"Yeah, looks like. He's a good baby. He sleeps like a champ. Although I don't want to jinx it."

"Can't you just un-jinx things? Being a witch and all?" said Lana.

"That's the kind of magic you can't do anything about, unfortunately. That's the old stuff," said Tess, chuckling, but only half joking.

"Yours?" Tess asked. She was there for the baby group as well even if it was a little tricky to transition from host to guest.

"He does his best," said Lana charitably. "Sometimes he won't let me put him down though, at all. And I know they say to do a controlled cry, and not to spoil them or whatever. But that's easier said than done, right? I have another son and a daughter too, and they don't want to be woken up. Magnus, that's my husband, doesn't want to be woken up. I figure what's the point of everyone being woken up and Cody being distraught and me feeling like a bitch anyway because it literally hurts my brain and it hurts my heart when he's screaming like that. So we go into the living room and pound espressos and watch Mad Men very quietly with the subtitles on. Or *we* don't. I do. Cody just sleeps on my lap like a cat, just smiling and having his happy little baby dreams."

"And when do you sleep?" asked Tess.

"If he drifts off, I'll sometimes try and put him back in his bassinet, but he often just wakes up again, and we start the whole thing over. Sometimes it's easier to just let him sleep on me. I sleep when there's the chance. Sometimes Magnus wakes up early and we switch. Sometimes I sleep when Cody naps. He's better at naps. Do you think I'm an idiot?" Lana asked.

"An idiot?"

"For spoiling him?"

"No way. You're not an idiot. You know," Tess hushed her voice to a whisper, "I overheard someone earlier say she pays a guy to assemble her flatpack furniture. Like, it's not that difficult. How are you gonna help your kid with their paper mache, or whatever it is that kids do, if you can't put together a dining chair? It's got four legs and a back. Figure it out."

Lana laughed but her eyes were wet, like if she hadn't laughed she would have cried instead.

They stared at each other for a moment. This was the closest they had stood to each other all evening. Close-up, Tess could see that Lana had dark freckles scattered over the bridge of her nose, and she looked tired. The concealer under her eyes was thick and slightly the wrong shade for her skin. Lana smelled curiously of woodshavings, perceptible even over the almost overpowering perfume of the room. And she seemed anxious somehow. There was something she wanted to say. Some question danced in her dark eyes. Tess could see the edges of something glinting deep down. She wanted to get at it. A thought came back to her, Emily's voice chastising her. *You always pick at people's secrets*, she had said, time and again.

"Did you want to ask me something else?" Tess ventured. A direct approach was probably best. People were milling around the room, talking and laughing and being dangerously close to delicate things on shelves, but Tess barely noticed any of it. The world narrowed. There was something important here in front of her. She had felt drawn before. She was drawn to have a baby. It was a calling, and it there was a particular way that callings pulled on her heart. But that was the last time she had felt called to anything.

Tess had felt Emily moving further away from her, as her baby's movements grew stronger. The more she knew the creature in her womb, the less she knew the woman beside her. The baby was supposed to call Emily his mother too. They had discussed what he would call her, what they would call each other in front of him, how he would know her. And they had never come to a conclusion. Emily shot down any suggestion. She didn't want to be Mom, or Mommy, or Mumma, or even Emily. Tess guessed what was happening but she didn't want to put it into words. Words had power. They were concrete. She put her faith in magic, in divine balance and planetary turnings, and hoped that things would work themselves out. That had always worked for her before.

But everything has its limitations, even the hand guiding the universe. Even as they held hands at the farmers market, even as they looked at their baby flickering in black and white at the ultrasound appointment, they moved further apart, their orbits diverging irreparably.

Tess hung onto her baby. The idea that he was almost here, almost in her arms, kept her going. Until that fell apart too. Something wasn't quite right. She got a phone call one day from the hospital. Her doctor had gone over the recent ultrasound and wanted her to come in for another, just to check something out. Emily had asked her who had called. Telemarketers, Tess replied, and said she had just remembered she needed condensed milk for a recipe.

She went to the appointment and was prodded and poked, inside and out. *Vasa previa*, the doctor had said. Some of the blood vessels of the umbilical cord were exposed. If she went into labour naturally, the baby would bleed out, or she would, or they both would. The baby could die, or she could, or they both could. It would be a caesarean. There was nothing to discuss. Emily had screamed at her for keeping it a secret, her eyes round with concern and rage and bafflement.

The caesarean went the way caesareans do, with the crunching and rustling of paper hairnets and plastic sheeting. The main thing she remembered was trembling uncontrollably, feeling cold and out of control and like she just wanted it to be over. Emily held her hand, and it was reassuring, even though Tess could tell she didn't really want to be there either. They had that much in common, at least.

It took a while for Tess to fall back in love with the baby, Steve as he was by then, and she never fell back in love with Emily. They opened her up and all her love for Emily, their future together, their family, just floated away through the bright ceiling of the operating room. Tess felt like a stranger to herself, in those first few days, and like an intruder in her own life. She felt unloved by the universe, as pitiful as it was to accept. She had just pulled off her greatest feat of magic, she had created something so beautiful. But she also felt forgotten. Things had not gone to plan. The birth she envisioned was taken away from her.

Steve was supposed to be born at home, with a doula guiding her through a natural birth, the way it had been done for centuries. And Tess and Emily were going to cocoon themselves at home with him for the first few weeks, just breathing him in and creating unbreakable bonds. Instead he was cut from her body, two months early, sitting under a little blue light for his jaundice, having his measurements taken and being assessed infinitely like he was some bizarre new species. And when he came home, he belonged only to Tess. It was just them now. There was no guiding hand.

But now, staring at Lana's freckled and serious face, Tess was starting to get a creeping feeling. There was a fluttering in her chest, that felt uncannily like the universe was trying to tell her something, like her intuition was coming alive. An ember, long in a state of imperceptible smoulder, was growing hot. She could swear she almost felt like a witch again.

"If I were to ask you something," Lana began tentatively, "not about the shop or the stuff you do here, but just more of a general witchcraft-based question, is that something you'd be able to help me with?"

"Sure, that's fine. Is there something you're looking to explore further? I can certainly offer more... spiritual guidance. Is that the kind of thing you mean?" Tess was intrigued. Lana didn't seem like the kind of person who would be interested in witchcraft. It wasn't that she'd seemed close-minded, it just didn't fit her. To some extent, magic had to believe in you before you believed in it. It didn't feel like magic believed in Lana. She felt lonely, in a huge and vague way.

"And would there, by any chance, be some kind of customer confidentiality? Like a priest can't tell people your confessions. What's the ethics here?"

Tess' skin prickled with intrigue, but she stayed as outwardly calm as she could, like this happened all the time. She didn't want to spook her.

"Yeah, of course. I don't know that it's legally binding, as such. Maybe don't tell me if you've done bunches of murders. But you can count on me not to talk. Secrets are a big part of a witch's trade, you know. I've heard it all."

Lana snorted and grinned anxiously. She snapped the fingers on her right hand a couple of times, then clenched both her fists. A nervous tick. She opened her mouth but didn't speak. Tess could feel the energy of the secret, evaporating off Lana's skin.

A crackling cry pierced through the moment, and the tension broke like an icicle crashing to the ground. Tess thought for a horrible moment that the sound had come from Lana somehow, before she remembered the baby monitor. It hissed static, punctuated by Steve's fearful shrieks. One of his nightmares, Tess thought. He needed to be shushed and cosseted and he needed Tess to gently stroke his face, from his forehead to the tip of his nose. He needed this to happen before he realised he was actually awake.

"I need to go get him. Don't go anywhere," she said, scurrying through a curtained off doorway at the back of the room, and up a flight of stairs.

Chapter 13.

Lana found other people to talk to. The reason she had come, to ask Tess about her ghost problem, was on the back burner. She couldn't ask her if she wasn't actually there. Not that Lana begrudged her having to go to her baby. The cry from the baby monitor had thrown Lana off somewhat. Her body seemed to have suddenly realised that her own baby was nowhere to be seen, and she was feeling unreasonably melancholy. A hot feeling was welling up in her breasts, that made her extremely glad she had put absorbent pads in her bra. She lingered on the fringes of groups already in the throes of lively conversation, nodding and smiling, but contributing nothing. She was ready only for light socialising.

Tess reappeared almost an hour later, squinting against the ambient light, with the semi-bewildered expression of someone who has been close to sleep. Lana guessed she had been rocking her baby in the dark, waiting for him to sleep. Lana knew how difficult it could be to return to being awake after singing lullabies in the pitch darkness, holding a baby who is tiny and warm and snoring. It was easier to be pulled down by their gravity.

Things had wrapped up gradually, naturally. The candles had burned low, and lipstick smeared coffee cups littered every available flat surface. The guests had already pulled on coats and swapped phone numbers. Susan stood closest to the door, squeezing people's shoulders as she offered them a last piece of unsolicited advice. Tess wandered over to stand next to her, finishing up her duties as co-host, wrapping a blanket around her shoulders to ward off the chill that blew into the shop as each person left. Tess pressed leaflets into people's hands, wished them warm farewells and come-agains, while yawning unabashedly.

Lana took a leaflet and glanced at it. It detailed upcoming events at The Looking Glass, celebrating key dates on the pagan wheel of the year, of which there was a helpful diagram, beginning with a Samhain blessing and drinks evening. *I knew that one, at least.* There would be a regular book club, full moon manifestations and one to one psychic readings. *None of those things are gonna help me.* She lingered, pretending to read the leaflet, hoping that Susan would leave and she could talk to Tess in private. That didn't happen. They'd missed their moment.

Lana opened the door and was halfway through it, the wind biting, before Tess thought to say, "Hey, you should come to our Halloween party. It's on the leaflet." She jabbed a finger at the paper in Lana's hand. "Or, you know, if you wanted to talk about anything before then, you're welcome to stop by whenever."

Susan was pretending not to listen to then, but Lana could feel her joining their conversation, becoming attuned to their wavelength as only a practised eavesdropper can. Susan was harmless enough, but Lana knew she had been partly responsible for the rumours about her parents that seemed to resurface now and then. The rumours that she worried would make their way down to her children, to the parents at their school. She needed to be careful.

"Totally," she said, keeping her tone light. "See you then. I'd better get going before this turns into a hurricane! It was great to meet you. Take care." She shut the door behind her without a backwards glance. It was freezing, with a fierce wind that picked at her ears and cheeks. She made a mental note to ask Magnus about winter tyres. Surely it was too early, although you never could be sure. The evening wasn't quite what she had hoped for, but Tess could help her.

I could feel it, and I think she could feel it too.

Chapter 14.

Lana was away. It didn't happen often that Allie was alone in the house with Magnus. Mostly it was her and Lana and Cody, sometimes the other kids. Occasionally it was just Allie and the kids, but that was only ever for a few minutes, while Lana stewed in the bath with Cody in his bassinet beside her, or rested her eyes in the easy chair, or folded herself away in some corner of her brain. Allie saw her Lana sometimes, becoming distant, falling into a thought, eyes glazing.

It felt almost awkward to be alone with Magnus, without the usual buffer of Lana.

Lana didn't seem to have anything resembling a social life, which Allie understood. She was the same. Lana had mentioned that she was thinking of going to the baby group she'd been to when Seb and Emmy were born, at some new homewares store in town. Magnus had seized on it, and insisted she go. For her to even mention something like that, to entertain the possibility of a new social endeavour, seemed like a big deal. Bigger than it should have been. There was some old, oft-visited conversation there, she could tell.

Lana was a loner. Her only friends were her children and her husband, and Magnus thought it was bad for her. *He's probably right.* It did seem sometimes to Allie that Lana didn't seem completely well. He had practically pushed her out of the door, promising he would survive without her and that she would have a good time, as Lana found reasons to linger on the doorstep and needless questions to ask. The children ran around his legs, honking like geese, knowing there would be numerous opportunities for anarchy without their mother. Just before the door shut, Lana shared the smallest glance with Allie. It was difficult to read, but there was some kind of sadness in it, or anxiety. Lana wasn't doing well, Allie knew it. She felt a little guilty about it.

Allie had been home alone many times, and home when Lana and Magnus were both sleeping. This wasn't so different from that. It felt like the time before Lana had seen her. The house around her looked warm and lively and soothing, but going unnoticed made her feel small and sad. It made her feel like a ghost. Magnus had warmed milk for Cody, cradled him on the edge of the bed as Cody drank it in slow sips, dressed him and kissed him and lay him down in his cot. Magnus had allowed the other two to stay up an hour later than was customary, and allowed more cookies than Lana would have.

Seb and Emmy blew around the living room like a tornado, while Magnus read a paperback and half-heartedly shushed them. There had been a falling out over particular plastic bricks that were needed for their respective projects, there had been time-outs at opposite ends of the room, followed by tearful apologies. And then it was bedtime, with two stories and a barrage of nonsensical fragments from Emmy that were either questions or jokes, Allie wasn't quite sure which. Magnus lingered in the doorway, responding to her as best he could. Seb was asleep the moment his head touched the pillow. Magnus closed the door on Emmy while she was still chattering, said "goodnight peanut". And then it was silent, just Allie and Magnus.

He heated up a slab of lasagna in the microwave and ate it alone at the kitchen table. It was too hot, audibly sizzling, but he ate it anyway, using just the edges of his teeth and breathing steam. He scrolled through a news site on his phone and Allie sat across from him, watching him. It was interesting to watch people be alone. *A little bit creepy, but interesting.* They were so different from the people they were when they were interacting. Magnus was rarely alone. Or Allie supposed he was often alone at work, in his office above the hardware store, but what happened outside the house didn't really interest her. When he was at home he was usually reflecting something from Lana or the kids. Now he was just himself. His face was hard to read. Mostly peaceful, but with an occasional furrowed brow or frown in response to the bad news he was reading. *Penny for your thoughts*, Allie thought idly. Except that she couldn't pick up a penny, and he couldn't see her anyway.

He put his plate in the sink, made a cup of coffee and took it through to the living room. He sat down heavily on the sofa but didn't spill the coffee somehow. Allie moved into the space beside him that Lana usually occupied. He couldn't feel her. Lana was the only person who could feel her presence, and she wasn't sure that it was a function of her semi-physical body or whether Lana's soul or psyche or whatever recognised itself and translated that into feeling. Maybe to Lana, Allie felt like an extension of her own self, on some kind of molecular scale. She had thought about the physics of her situation a lot, but she didn't know enough about the theory of it all to differentiate it from philosophy or magic. What seemed to her like sound science was probably just meaningless speculation. Although what use was physics if it couldn't explain what was happening to her? She would have known if something like this had ever been observed, documented, studied. It hadn't been. And yet it was happening now.

At any rate, Lana seemed to have a sense when Allie was there, even if she made herself unseen, and when their hands touched there was some kind of feedback, faintly electrical but definitely there. But nobody else could feel her. If she didn't focus, she would pass through things, including people. But she had enough energy, enough patience, to sit beside Magnus, to lean on him a little, displacing nothing.

Maybe some people were more solid than others, she guessed. The children ran straight through her. Lana was here and there. Often-times they would end up occupying the same space, but it felt like something, like pins and needles, if Allie was remembering correctly how pins and needles had felt. Magnus required less energy to remain separate from. More than once she had bumped into him in the corridor, and although he never noticed, she was consistently knocked on her ass, totally astonished every time it happened. It was almost exciting, for her body to just react to something, like a normal person.

Sometimes she wished she could appear to Magnus the way she appeared to Lana. But it felt like it would be a hollow victory. He wouldn't be able to touch her. *Do I want him to touch me?* And she wouldn't be able to convince him to accept her, like she had done Lana. He couldn't be bent. He didn't have that personal stake, that inexplicable guilt that made Lana tolerate her. She could see it in her mind's eye.

He would know something was wrong straight away, as nobody was more used to looking at Lana, at wondering what was going on with her. He would reach out to touch her, already knowing his fingers wouldn't make contact, but needing confirmation that she wasn't real. He would scramble backwards, as if she hadn't spent evenings sat beside him, sat on the end of their bed. He didn't know her like she knew him. He would take the kids and leave. He was decisive like that, reckless. He didn't have a lot of opportunity to be reckless, but she could tell that he would be if he was pushed. He wouldn't care about the money or the house. And she would never see him or Seb or Emmy or Cody again. He would sell the house without ever stepping foot in it again. Or burn it down. And who knows what would happen to her then. There was an emptiness at the end of every scenario and time was running out to choose one. She felt herself becoming uncoiled, unspooled.

But here and now was cozy. The light was low and orange, and she could almost feel the warmth radiating from Magnus. She was willing to bet he ran hot. The light of the TV shone and sparkled in his blue eyes, which were the only thing about him that seemed cold. They were pale like ice, and a little at odds with the smile-worn creases that framed them. He was plainly not watching the show, some quasi-medieval fantasy thing that Allie had no interest in. He was far away. Allie wanted him to look at her, for that thousand-yard stare to break against her face like the gentle tide.

She wanted to take his face in her hands. She imagined how his wiry, blonde beard would feel under her fingertips, how he would smell and the warmth of his body. *It's the warmth, more than anything else. Life-giving, comforting warmth. Campfire warmth.* He was wearing the blanket that usually hung on the back of the couch. When he watched movies with Lana, they arranged themselves under it. Sometimes Lana lay her head on one arm of the sofa, with her blanketed legs over Magnus's lap. Sometimes Magnus lay on the sofa, and Lana did her best to fit her body between him and the cushions, laying partly on him, finding little spaces to fit herself, and the blanket over them both.

But now Magnus was by himself, and he wore the blanket like a cape, cocooning himself, one hand free to reach occasionally for his cup of coffee. He drank coffee at all hours of the day or night, with cream and sugar. Allie knew more things about him than she cared to admit to Lana. She wanted to know the textures and little details of him, things her ghostly form could not pick up. And she wanted to be under the blanket with him.

Chapter 15.

Lana was used to feeling disappointed with herself, but anger was something new. She found herself scowling unconsciously, bitter and venomous. It was sharp and strong and almost good. She hadn't felt anything as clear as this for a long time. In comparison, the past few weeks, maybe months, felt washed out. The feelings she'd felt had been blurred and bland. She had a shapeless anxiety about Allie all the time, but that was something gentle and draped over all her other thoughts. The worry was lukewarm and this anger was hot. It was the fire under her feet that she needed to spur action.

I couldn't tell her.

Before their meeting at The Looking Glass Lana had painstakingly workshopped what she was going to do, what she was going to say, when she got her alone. *The Witch. Tess.* But she had lost her nerve, and she couldn't let it go.

Lana was careful not to think too much about it when she was at home and Allie was all around her. *Just in case.* But when she was on her walks with Cody, or driving the kids to school, her failure played on a loop in her head. Every hesitation, every babbling waste of time. But then Tess hadn't been quite what she was expecting either. It had thrown off Lana's meticulous script. She hadn't seemed like someone who could perform an exorcism. *Although is that a service a witch provides? Isn't that a priest? I haven't got a priest though. Not the Gothic cathedral, world-weary priest with emotional baggage you see in films, anyway. I've got a witch, which will have to do. No which way about it.*

Lana had become more comfortable with the word. Exorcism. She hadn't wanted to acknowledge it. It seemed absurdly dramatic. But she'd decided to call a spade a spade, and to call a ghost a ghost. *And an exorcism is what it's called when you evict a ghost.* It was what came afterwards that worried Lana now. Not the actual getting rid of Allie but where she went next. They were still the same person. They were still tied together in some real way, perhaps more now than ever before. The energy that kept Allie's atoms from collapsing had wormed its way into Lana's bones. She could feel it vibrating in her back teeth. And that connection made it difficult to think of banishing Allie to some place unknown. She didn't want to risk being sucked into that same invisible portal into the beyond. *Would she disappear? Blinked out of a reality she never belonged to? Would she move back to wherever she came from, and be a flesh and blood person? Is the afterlife beckoning? Heaven? Doesn't seem likely.*

It made Lana's head ache and filled her with guilt. The two of them were entangled, and it didn't seem there was a way to fix it. But at the same time, Lana saw the way that Allie watched the children playing. Lana couldn't exactly stop her from watching them, or from watching her. She saw her own self from a distance, seeing her own children. She wasn't any kind of threat to them, at least. She loved them. She couldn't really do anything, except to Lana, maybe.

Lana had other things on her mind too. Real life, everyday things. *Like Halloween.* Lana wasn't feeling the Halloween spirit this year, something she would never have thought she'd admit. She had always loved it. She had a sizeable collection of novelty Halloween t-shirts that had become part of her year-round wardrobe, even if some of them were such poor quality that the designs melted in the washing machine, or the glow-in-the-dark appliqués expired and turned brown. It was probably something to do with the fact that a real ghost was drifting around the house. Lana thought about her Halloween decorations, still in a box in their storage unit across town. There was a packet of window decals of classic white-sheet-ghosts. It felt like poor taste to stick them up.

She and Magnus always did something on Halloween, even before the kids. Not necessarily parties, but they always made an effort. They went to the movies, mostly, to soak in the seasonal cheer with other b-movie cinephiles. Then, after Seb, they moved their movie marathons to the living room. Last year, they had woken up on the sofa on November 1st, squinting in the autumn sunlight, limbs entangled. They had only made it through a couple of films before they'd fallen asleep. Lana's legs had lost feeling, scrunched against the arm rest. But they had laughed all the same, wincing against pins and needles. Magnus scrambled out from around her and helped her to her feet. He brushed bits of popcorn out of his beard and put a pot of coffee on. *Only a year ago.*

It felt like nothing at the time, like just another day. But she remembered it clearly, like it was something worth remembering. *We were alone then.* Something like that was impossible now. The beauty of times like that was that they seemed totally unexceptional to everyone except the two people sharing the moment. *It had to be two people.* A moment like that is too small to be cut into thirds. But somehow two halves of something mundane become precious. It was in seeing the other half of it in someone else's eyes. Lana was never really alone now, so she could never really be with Magnus.

***

Allie was watching the kids watch TV. Lana was in the bath, trying to melt the anxiety out of her skin, trying to bring warmth to her insides. She wished sometimes that she could live in the bath, constantly immersed in hot water like a worm in amber. Cody snored beside her in his basket. He understood. He loved the bathroom and the steamy air and the sleepy colour of the ceiling light. It felt okay to let Allie watch the other two, but Lana really didn't care for her watching Cody. He was so small. He was still nursing. He had only recently become separate from Lana. He was still part of her, and that made him seem vulnerable somehow.

Lana found a crumpled towel beside the bath, dried her hands, and picked up her phone. Emmy's birthday wasn't far away. A few weeks could seem like a long time but it would be over in a flash. Lana hadn't decided what they were doing or when they were doing it or what birthday present Emmy was getting. These were her duties. They had talked about a bike, one with handlebar tassels and a basket, like the ones Emmy drew pictures of. Seb didn't have one to pass down. He was too uncoordinated to be trusted with something like that. Lana looked through some tabs she'd left open on her phone, brightly coloured bicycles modelled by laughing blonde children. She tried to make sense of measurements and weights and shipping costs. Her heart wasn't really in it. It was just something she needed to do, and it felt like she was working on it by just reading the same information again and again. To an outside observer, it probably looked like something an organized mother might do.

Allie drifted back into the room silently.

"They're still watching TV," she said, sounding bored but competent. "I'll be honest, they've seen a lot of toy ads. There was one about a doll that shits glitter. I swear I'm not making that up. You put actual non-biodegradable cartridges of non-biodegradable glitter inside the doll. Kids are gross. And Seb is sort of half doing his homework. It's going pretty slowly. It's just a poster. I don't really know how it's taking so long. He's been holding the glue stick for like twenty minutes without the lid. It's probably dried out." She glanced in the mirror, like she always did. It was a difficult habit to break, Lana figured. She seemed to expect to see her own reflection, but she never did. She moved to the bath and perched on the edge.

"What are you looking at?" Allie asked, gesturing to the phone.

"Present for Emmy's birthday. She's going to be four," said Lana. It was weird to say it out loud. It didn't seem possible that Emmy could be four. She was just a little baby, it seemed. But Cody had replaced her as the baby. Suddenly she'd grown up so fast, like she was waiting for permission.

"I know. Magnus was talking to her about it. About what she wants."

"Well I'm sure she'd be glad to know I'm on it. I'm looking at kid bikes."

"She probably wants a doll that shits glitter," said Allie, laughing. "You know it's probably not a good idea to use your phone in the bath. What if you drop it and it electrocutes you? You'd be dead."

"Better not drop it then," said Lana without looking up. "I think it only electrocutes you if the charger is still in the wall. Most likely it'd just break." Lana still hadn't looked up at Allie. She was busy pretending to be absorbed in her task.

"Are you okay? You seem more deadpan than usual," said Allie.

Lana put the phone down beside the bath. She didn't want to break it. All her photos were on there.

"I'm fine. I have a thing about birthdays. I feel like she was only just born, and now she's four."

"Don't be sad about that. She's gonna love being four. Four is so much better than three. She can get a little bicycle now. She can ... reach slightly higher cabinets. I don't really know what things are available to a four-year-old that aren't to a three-year-old, but I'm sure it'll be great," said Allie. She reached out her hand to stroke Lana's hair. But it didn't quite work. It went straight through, with the pins and needles sensation of having crossed the boundary.

"I think maybe she can bounce unsupervised at the trampoline park," said Lana.

"Well there you go. That sounds great."

Lana sighed. That wasn't it.

"You're thinking about your own fourth birthday," said

Allie, with the uncanny accuracy that made Lana sure she could read her mind. "You're thinking about all your kid birthdays and that nobody bought you a bicycle or baked you a cake or gave a fuck that it was your special day."

"Kind of," said Lana. "It's so stupid. I don't even know who I feel sad for. I don't feel sad for myself. Maybe I feel sad for myself as a kid. I didn't need that crap. But also, it happened, and I'm fine. I've had good birthdays since then."

"I think you might feel sorry for mom," Allie suggested. "For our mother."

Lana snorted. She didn't.

"She was shitty to me. She forgot my birthday more often than she didn't," said Lana. "And when she remembered, I'd always wish she hadn't. I don't really want to talk about it."

Or even think about it.

"Well luckily you don't have to, because I already know," said Allie, smiling in a grim, set way.

It was true. They sat in silence for a while.

"I don't remember if I loved her, you know?" said Lana. "I don't know if I ever did. It feels like the worst thing in the world because I think about how much I love the kids. Could they forget whether they loved me? And maybe that's selfish because I guess I don't really *need* them to love me. I would still love them. I don't think Cody even really likes me, but it doesn't really matter. But still… am I a bad person?"

"No," said Allie, sounding more certain than Lana had ever heard her sound. All her usual jaunty, unserious tone gone. "I *do* remember. You don't need to be so hard on yourself. It's got nothing to do with your kids. You'd be better to forget her. Just move on and break the cycle. I give you official permission. Because once you get sucked into that orbit, you'll never get out."

Chapter 16.

Saturday morning was Lana's. That's the way it had always been. It was her day to lay in bed an extra half hour. Recently it was more like an hour. Emmy started knocking at the bedroom door early, every day, itching to burst in and jump on her sleeping parents. But on Saturday it was Magnus' turn to answer it.

Emmy couldn't make sense of the week or the order of the days. Saturday was always a surprise and always a good one. Once she realised it was the weekend, she knew that daddy would make pancakes and fail to properly notice her mischief in his groggy state. She could draw on the floorboards just a little, put things in the freezer that weren't meant to be frozen, bring all her stuffed animals into the kitchen and get lingonberry jam on them.

Lana would sit up in bed to nurse Cody, then Magnus would come back for him, and sit with all three kids in the living room watching cartoons. It was almost quiet, the giggles and whoops of the kids far away and officially not her responsibility, just for a little while. The bed was cool and warm at the same time, and all hers. It was the closest thing to a hobby she had. Saturday mornings were a cornerstone of her well-being.

Lana lay tangled in the duvet, staring up at the ceiling, thinking about her storage unit. She needed to go there to collect the Halloween things. She may as well put some things in there. *Maybe some clothes that are too small for Emmy but too big for Cody? That might fill a big box.* There seemed to be a lot of clutter around recently. She idly wondered if she might be able to put Allie in the storage unit. That would be perfect, if she could just tidy her away. Not remove her from reality, just remove her from the house. Maybe she could haunt the storage unit instead, and sit on their old sofa and read Lana's old diaries to pass the time. Except Lana knew she would probably never return to the unit, if she knew Allie was in there. She'd bury the key. All her old furniture and picture frames and bicycles be damned.

Even in the time she was completely alone, Lana couldn't be completely idle. There were things to organise, little tasks to take the opulence out of the alone time, to legitimise it. She wanted to switch up the home décor. She'd been thinking about it for a while but couldn't remember specifically what she wanted to swap out. *Allie had said something about it. What did she say?* Allie wasn't there now. She respected Lana's alone time, or at least it seemed that way. Lana couldn't see her, couldn't feel her. She was probably in the living room with the kids.

Or she was nowhere. Sometimes it did seem like she wasn't anywhere specific in the house. Maybe she went back where she came from now and then. Lana wasn't sure. It felt somehow wrong to ask. Or like something Lana didn't want to know.

Allie didn't like the mirror in the bathroom. Now that Lana thought about it, she had walked in on Allie more than once, just staring at the mirror. She did that sometimes, just looked into mirrors, unhappy with what she saw or what she didn't see. But there was something particular about this one. It seemed to bother her.

"What are you looking at?" Lana had asked her once.

"This doesn't go with the room, does it? I have the same mirror. Where did it come from? Was it here when we moved in? I can't remember."

"Yeah, it was dad's mirror, I think. I don't think he put too much thought into choosing it. Maybe it came with the house when he bought it. Who knows? It didn't feel urgent to replace it. It wasn't broken or anything, so we just painted the frame and put it back up. I guess it doesn't match the décor as such. We didn't have much money when we moved here, and then I think it just became part of the wall, like a window. I suppose you look more at the reflection than the mirror itself," said Lana, looking at the mirror for what felt like the first time.

It didn't match, not now that she was really looking at

it. When they moved in, it had a very tacky ornate frame, with flaky gold paint. They had taped off the mirror, caked paint remover onto the frame, scraped and scoured, repainted it a darker gold. It was a weird mirror for a bathroom. Bathroom mirrors were supposed to be frameless and have integrated LEDs or be on the front of medicine cabinets. That was the kind of mirror Lana saw in the magazines she read in waiting rooms.

"When did you move in here?" Allie asked suddenly. She rarely asked things like that. She never seemed interested in prying.

"Oh, well it was after we got married but before Seb was born. Maybe seven years ago. I think. Maybe eight. Fuck that's a long time. What about you? The same?"

"No, not really. You moved here after your dad died?" Allie seemed to have forgotten about the mirror.

"*My* dad? He was your dad too."

They never spoke like this. It felt strangely exhilarating. The possibility of answers to things Lana had wondered since Allie showed up.

"I guess. He died before I got the chance to know him," said Allie. "Not that I had any specific plans to. It was some kind of car accident. But it wasn't eight or nine years ago. It was maybe one year ago, then I find out I've inherited this house."

They weren't the same people, Lana had noticed. They didn't do what each other would do in certain situations. They'd been in the exact same situations and had made different choices. Lana had gone looking for her father, feeling the loss of family after her mother died. Feeling a little guilty, if she was honest. It hadn't been good at the end. It hadn't been the way she wanted, and her mother's death was a dark memory she hated to touch. It had made her better though, in a way. It had made her kind to her father, more understanding than maybe she would have been otherwise. It had made her determined not to be her mother.

"When did your mother die?" said Lana, without meaning to. The words just fell into her mouth, surprising her.

"*My* mother? She was your mother too," said Allie, smiling in a strangely sinister way. Lana didn't reply. "I can't remember. I was maybe twenty-six."

"Shit. I was nineteen."

"Oh, I'm sorry. I didn't know. Wow, so you were just a kid really. I remember being nineteen. Things weren't good with her then. Or with us. You and me, I mean. Not us and her. Or..." Allie floundered, "You know what I mean. It was a bad situation. I had more time with her." Allie paused to really consider this. "And when you lost her, your 'her', when you were nineteen, those years were the worst of it," she said, slowly working through it. "I managed to build something with her after that, but it wasn't what that relationship was supposed to be. I guess we accepted each other, in the end. But it was never more than that."

There was no reason for it, but Lana's eyes suddenly burned, she felt the buds of tears beginning to bloom.

"Hey, I'm sorry. I didn't mean to pry. That's the problem with being each other, isn't it? We know all the sore spots. All the secrets," and Allie's eyes lingered on Lana longer than she would have liked, and Lana felt something creeping under her face, something boring in or something twisting to get out.

"I don't like to think about it," said Lana. "Talk to me about this mirror."

"Not a problem." Allie turned back to the mirror. "I was thinking instead maybe a nice rattan frame. Something less baroque, less gothic," she suggested.

The sound of Seb and Emmy yelling distantly brought Lana's awareness back to the present, still laying in bed, eyes closed now, drifting slightly. Emmy was insisting that Magnus crack her back, the way he did for Lana. He was telling her she was too small, and she was insisting through fits of giggles that her back was stiff. If her back was so stiff, Magnus said in the dramatic voice he reserved for playtime, she wouldn't be able to play aeroplanes, which was too bad. Emmy screamed, something between fury and delight, and then squealed as Lana assumed she was whirled into the air.

And Lana was in bed, maintaining her distance, thinking about home décor. She felt bad. Even though she was with the kids near constantly, she felt her own absence when she was missing from their happy memories. She wanted to go to them, to do the things that delighted them while they were still little enough to want her to do them. The joy that Emmy felt when Lana held up her little foot to her ear and pretended that it was a telephone always made Lana beam ear to ear with sympathetic giddiness. Seb was a little more sophisticated. But he would laugh so hard that he cried if Lana read him a story he knew well, replacing the odd word with random nonsense, and performing incredulity when he pointed out her mistake.

She noticed she was grinning just thinking about their particular laughs, the wheezing snickering they both collapsed into when something was so funny they could no longer function. It must be nice to be a kid, thought Lana, not for the first time. She sometimes felt like she had never been one. She experienced it vicariously through her own children, playing with Lego and making up rambling scenarios for the extensive court of little toy cars to enact. It was her job to make sure the kids continued to enjoy being kids for as long as possible.

Lana was vaguely aware that she could see the room around her, although she knew her eyes were closed, on the edge of a dream. Except it was the wrong room. She could not see the ceiling above her, but the mirror she had been thinking about moments before. She could see herself in the mirror, and she looked as confused as she felt. Nothing was in the right place. She caught the weight of it, just in time.

"You wanna hand me that then?" Magnus asked, right beside her.

She was awake, and dressed, and standing up in the living room holding the bathroom mirror. Everything between now and before was missing.

She'd fallen out of time and place, again. Fallen out of her own body.

Or been pushed out.

She scanned the room for Allie, not too obviously as Magnus was watching her. She was nowhere to be seen. Lana felt equally angry and afraid, wanting to give Allie a piece of her mind but anxious that she shouldn't. She had to deal with the here and now first. She was awake, she was in control and Magnus was waiting for her to do something. He hadn't noticed anything was wrong.

How could he not notice?

"What?" said Lana, trying desperately to catch up, without seeming frantic. She was clutching the mirror, but it was getting heavier. She put it down, leaning it against the wall.

The front door was open. The door of her car, parked on the driveway, was open. Magnus was standing in the doorway and looking at her curiously. Lana put the situation together. She was going to the storage unit today. Magnus was helping her load up the car.

"I've changed my mind. I want to leave it until I've got a new one to take its place. Otherwise we won't have a bathroom mirror. It'll be too annoying. I do my makeup in there," she said, trying to seem casual.

"Doesn't bother me," said Magnus, stepping out to close up the car. He came back and shut the door. "I think it's fine anyway."

He picked up the big mirror as if it was weightless, and took it back into the bathroom. Lana followed. The space where the mirror had been was paler than the rest of the wall. The space looked huge and naked without the mirror to break it up. Magnus put it up, covering the faded square.

"Hey, where are the kids?" asked Lana.

"Still in the yard I think," said Magnus, stepping back from the mirror to assess its levelness. "I don't know about Cody. Is he still sleeping? You're the one who checked on him last." A little worry was creeping into his face, as Lana stared back at him nonplussed.

"Yeah," she said. "Of course, yeah I checked on him. He's still sleeping. So I will wait until he wakes up, and I will take him with me to the unit. And you can stay here with the other two and work on your projects if they're happy to play by themselves. I picked up a new puzzle for Seb in town. It's in the towels closet. Feel free to break it out if he gets too bored. And in the meantime, I'm gonna make a cup of coffee."

"Like that coffee over there?" said Magnus. Lana's favourite mug sat on the edge of the sink, still steaming.

"Of course. I forgot." She considered taking a risk and thanking him for making it. But it was always possible she made it herself. Or that her body had made it, at least. On some kind of autopilot. She floated the possibility to herself, but she knew it was wrong. The sleepwalking hypothesis, which still came to her now and then, was just a way to protect her from the scarier truth. It was Allie. She knew now that it was Allie.

Allie had spent the morning walking around Lana's house, in her body, playing with her kids and touching her espresso machine. Maybe she thought she was doing Lana a favour, she thought, as she was already half asleep. Maybe Allie thought she might like to sleep longer.

Lana shivered, and the hot coffee did nothing to help.

"You okay?" said Magnus.

Lana shook her head before she could stop herself.

"My brain's all messed up. I think it's the breastfeeding maybe. Or some kind of nutrient deficiency. Potassium or magnesium or something totally random. Or it could be seasonal affective disorder. Maybe I'm seasonally affected," said Lana, smiling in a way she knew probably wouldn't convince him. "And I'm kind of cold."

Glad of a problem he could actually solve, Magnus shrugged off his cardigan. It was thick and grey and smelled faintly of things he'd cooked while wearing it. He draped it over Lana's shoulders, and she thought of the day they'd had a picnic in the garden and he'd done the same thing.

"Deja vu," she said, pulling the huge cardigan close around her. He held her by the shoulders, wanting her to meet his earnest gaze, to pour his eyes into hers. She couldn't do it. She kissed him instead, then pulled away to check for anything destined for the unit, anything she might have overlooked.

Chapter 17.

Steve was an easy baby, as far as Tess could tell. She didn't have much to compare him to, aside from the stories other parents told her, the things she'd read on motherhood websites and in parenting books she'd never finished. There was no need to finish them. Because Steve was easy.

Tess lay in her bed beside him, watching his little belly rise and fall, watching dreams bring tiny smiles and frowns. He was fascinating to her. He slept in later in Castor than he ever had in Vancouver. It must be something about the energy of the place, the drop in hustle and bustle. He could sense it. Maybe all babies could sense things like that. Or maybe he was just particularly attuned. His mother was a witch after all. What did that make him?

Tess felt freer in Castor too. Nobody knew her. Nobody knew it was her custom to get up early. She had to be at work excruciatingly early before Steve had been born, before she moved. She had to open up the cafe, often before the sun rose, clean the coffee machines, get everything ready to run seamlessly for hours, from horribly early to horribly late. But she was her own boss now.

The shop opened at 10am. But if it didn't, nobody would complain. Most of her customers were tourists, like she'd been once before. Her 'regulars' came for the events, or to lean on the counter and chat to her about the weather, about their various intuitions. It wasn't astonishingly profitable, but she made up most of her revenue in online sales anyway.

She spent her evenings listening to music, Steve nestled into the corner of the couch, working her way through order forms, packing things up ready to ship. And when the tourist season rolled around she would see a windfall, she was sure. For now, it was nice to chat and relax and watch the motes of dust spiralling on their sunbeams.

They had a cat now too. His name was Jasper. He'd shown up one day out of the blue. His face was frozen in a scowl and Tess was still finding new scars on his body when he curled up on her knee in the evenings. He looked straight through her, but was content to occasionally be petted very gently and respectfully. Jasper had a totally different set of rules for Steve, whom he allowed to squeeze him tight like a teddy bear. He would nip Tess if she was too familiar with him, but he seemed to recognise that Steve was just a baby. Steve got a free pass.

She wondered whether the last tenant had left Jasper behind, if he had always lived here and thought of Tess as his new tenant. He did have that entitled air. Then again, so do all cats, thought Tess. Or had he seen her moving in, known she was coming, and spied an easy mark? That idea made her smile. If so, he had been right. She could never have turned him away. She had felt very generous since the move, extending her largesse to anyone and everyone.

Jasper yowled, low and sustained, barely loud enough to hear. He wanted breakfast but wanted Tess to think she'd thought of it on her own. He wasn't begging, he was just helping her reach the right conclusion. Tess pulled her gaze away from Steve's tiny face.

She lay on her back for a moment, getting her bearings, remembering the rest of the room. It still wasn't properly fixed in her mind. She couldn't walk around the house in the dark yet without bumping into the boxes she still hadn't unpacked. There was old water stain on the ceiling that was shaped like a monster with two heads. She needed to paint over it, and all the other miscellaneous marks and blotches that covered the walls in her new apartment. That was the kind of thing that happened when you moved in without viewing first.

There were things that hadn't been in the listing. Things like drafts and weird sounds. It was only a handful of rooms, over the store, and it was decidedly imperfect. The pipes groaned, the wood floors were splintered, the carpets were moth-ravaged and full of tiny holes. Tess had smoothed down the floors with a scrap of sandpaper, thrown away the carpets.

The landlord let her do what she liked. He was an elderly man whose primary concern was remaining undisturbed by tenants. He had spoken to her once, when he had given her the keys. He had said only that he didn't want to hear from her until she was ready to move out, which he hoped wouldn't be for a long time, and that she could carry out any renovations she wanted. He had added, as an afterthought, that he didn't want to hear that any additional tenants had moved in on the sly, like a boyfriend. And then he had looked down at Steve in his pushchair, and smirked as if nobody would want to shack up with a single mother. Tess felt her face turn hot, and bit down on the first response that came to mind. His judgemental smirk came back to her occasionally. She was worried he was right. But the rent was cheap, and she didn't like to be bothered either, so she let him go and hoped not to speak to him for a long time. Maybe he would die before she was ready to move out, and then she'd never speak to him again. Although bitter men tended to live a very long time in her experience.

She went to the kitchen, still in her pyjamas, and opened a tin of cat food for Jasper. She wasn't sure what he liked yet and she hadn't figured out the most cost-effective way to get it for him. She'd never had a pet before. Most people get a cat or a dog first, as a trial run for a baby, she thought. She'd worked backwards. That was something that tended to happen.

Tess made a cup of tea. She had a range of herbal teas on hand downstairs, in the little tea and coffee station next to the reading area. She recommended invigorating morning blends with turmeric or matcha or red ginseng, and soothing evening ones with fennel and valerian root. It felt like a betrayal of sorts that she hated all herbal teas. They were too aromatic and too flavourless at the same time. A drink shouldn't smell better than it tastes, she felt. And because she never actually drank them, she couldn't be sure whether herbal teas actually did anything, or whether it was, like so many other things, more about the energy you invested in believing in it. To her, herbal tea was just good-smelling bits of dried plant in hot water, but for some people it was the only thing that could facilitate a good night's sleep. And if it worked for some people, who was she to discredit it? It didn't pay to be judgemental in her line of work.

Tess made a cup of English breakfast tea, brewed strong, with oat milk. She wanted coffee, but coffee in the morning made her sweat profusely and talk too quickly. It used to be fine. Maybe it was something about getting older, climbing up through her thirties. Her father had insisted that he couldn't have coffee after 5pm or he'd be up all night. And he'd said it with such conviction, and such ruefulness, that Tess fully believed this. She would probably get that way eventually, and a single cup of coffee would hit her with the same force as hard drugs. Tea was fine.

She opened the fridge. It was empty, except for half a brick of unseasoned tofu, a cube of instant curry roux wrapped in beeswax paper, and a jar of tomato jam. It looked bad. It didn't look like the fridge of a together, organised person. There was always a little pocket of self-doubt at the back of her mind that she wasn't a proper mother to Steve. She wasn't organised. She wasn't even sure how this hypothetical organisation should look. But this wasn't it. Something was lacking. It didn't much matter at the moment though.

Steve was still mostly breastfeeding, which saved on money and time and the need to keep the fridge stocked with suitable things. But soon that part of their journey would be over, and he would be a person, a child rather than a baby. And he would need a variety of colourful vegetables to be already cooked and portioned and stored in aesthetically pleasing containers. He would need cheese cubes and cucumber sticks and little sandwiches cut into whimsical shapes. These things would have to be pre-prepared so that she could throw them into a bag and hand them to the babysitter when she came to look after Steve.

She would need to buy more containers, that was for sure. She caught herself before her thoughts spiralled too far into the future, too far away from her. Jasper was staring at her. His bowl, with its pungent cat food, was still on the table. He made the face of someone who has received poor customer service and is writing a scathing review in their head.

"I'm so sorry, sir. I'll just get that for you," said Tess, only half joking. She could swear he sighed with exasperation.

She returned to the bedroom for Steve, who had woken up and was chewing a corner of the pillowcase. She put on a pair of overalls over her pyjama top, and picked up the baby carrier from the floor. She buckled it around her waist, looped the straps over her arms and settled Steve into the seat, facing outward. His back arched against Tess' body, as he settled into a comfortable position. Tess shrugged on her coat, put a little knitted hat on Steve's head, and stuffed a handful of crochet produce bags into her pocket.

It was Saturday. Wednesday and Saturday were market days. It was better to go on Wednesday because it was less busy, she had quickly learned, but it always seemed to happen that she went on Saturday. Maybe that was just the nature of Saturday, she thought. People just ended up going places and doing things. That's why they didn't make another day Saturday instead.

Jasper ran past her when she opened the front door. She needed to get a cat flap so he could come and go on his own schedule. He needed Tess sometimes, but he needed his own space too. She could respect that. That's how she had been before Steve. Now there was no being alone. It was fine. She didn't need to be alone now.

Chapter 18.

Lana pulled open the metal door of her storage unit, shoving it upwards. It twisted around its spool on the ceiling and Lana wondered why all doors weren't like that. Even her garage door at home, which was the same size, wasn't like that. It just flipped up overhead. She got caught up in the small things sometimes. She liked their ability to distract her from the other things, that were less whimsical and more distressing.

It smelled cold and stale in the unit. The coldness and staleness blew past her into the corridor, and she breathed in air that tasted both sterile and wretchedly dirty. The things inside had been removed from human touch and from daily life for too long. She didn't like to come here, but it seemed to affect Magnus even worse, so going to the unit had become Lana's job. It made Magnus morose and sentimental. It brought too many sad things to the forefront, and he was not good at compartmentalising.

Compartmentalising was Lana's speciality. She didn't like to think of it as bottling up her feelings, because that's something people say not to do. It was more like emotional pantrying. Storing her hopes and fears away in cute little jam jars and tiny, interesting containers from an apothecary's shop. Her dreams sat on shelves, floating in brine and oil for when she might need them. She liked the idea of that. Maybe her brain was its own storage unit, she thought.

The things in the unit were things they vaguely wanted to keep, but things they could live without. If there was a fire at the unit, or the damp got in and mould started, it wouldn't be the end of the world. Really important things like Lana's wedding dress, special baby clothes, sacred mementos, were sealed in plastic and stored in the attic at their house. The things in here were lesser things. And they were things Lana didn't want to look at or think about until they were needed.

Lana tapped the pram brake with her foot, and left Cody stabled in the hallway. He was totally absorbed in the rail of little toys across his pram. There were beads to slide around a plastic ring, things that beeped and jingled, an elephant with crinkly fabric ears. They would keep him entertained for a time. She didn't want to take him into the unit. He was a precious thing and he didn't belong in there.

Lana collected the vacuum-sealed bag of last season's clothes from the basket under the pram and took it into the unit. The lights flickered on automatically and dust swirled. She felt it in her lungs and eyes and on her fingertips. She wasn't feeling well, if she was being honest with herself. She was colder than she had any right to be in all her winter layers, and the roots of her teeth had recently started to ache in a way that she knew couldn't be fixed by any dentist.

The first bed that she and Magnus had bought was dissembled in a corner, next to a meticulously organised plastic crate of clothes that didn't currently fit any of the children. There were books that were too ugly to display and not worth re-reading, but not ready to be given away. There were VHS tapes from when Magnus was a kid, a pressure washer for cleaning the patio, small kitchen appliances they'd been given by Magnus' parents, and a glass coffee table that didn't match their décor. Lana picked her way through all these things to the boxes of seasonal items. She moved the Easter things – a cardboard box of bunnies and papier mâché eggs and little wicker baskets for egg hunts. She nudged a partially disassembled Christmas tree out of the way with her foot, spying the box she was looking for.

She hefted the Halloween box up onto the glass coffee table and peeked inside - plastic pumpkins and black and orange paper garlands. She moved it to the door, balanced it on her hip and found the tangle of keys in her pocket.

She wondered suddenly if Allie had a storage unit, and

how many of the things from her unit were also in Allie's. Certainly none of the detritus from her life with Magnus, and from the kids' lives. But there were other things here too, things from before that.

There was a smaller box, burnished walnut and still lustrous in spite of years of negligence, on the row of metal shelving that lined one wall. Every time she came into the unit, she made a special effort not to look at it, to seem outwardly as if she hadn't noticed it, even though there was nobody else there. She knew exactly where it was though, and exactly what it looked like. She could picture it in her mind so precisely that it was as if she was looking right at it. That was one of the things from before, something that was wholly hers, and something that was probably Allie's too. Lana felt it begging to be looked at, like it always did. She complied.

She couldn't say why she hadn't got rid of the little wooden box. Someone she didn't know had given it to her after her mother's funeral. "Something you might like to have," they had said. And Lana hadn't really known what to make of that. She couldn't remember the face of the woman who gave it to her, which made it worse somehow.

It was a trinket box, full of little pieces of crystals and stones and stray pendants from necklaces, odd earrings and charms. A little magpie's collection of rocks and broken costume jewellery. Lana had tipped it all out on the grass in the graveyard. It had been a sunny day and she was glad of something to do other than attend the wake. She inspected pieces of smoky quartz in the sunlight, holding them up and watching rainbows form in the chambers inside.

There was a mirror on the inside of the box, tarnished and silver backed. It was loose, the glue having long since turned brittle, and it had fallen out into Lana's hand when she'd turned the box over. She pressed it back into place, the wrong way round, not wanting to look into the mirror that her mother had looked into maybe only days before.

Call it superstition, she had thought, but there was something too private about looking into someone's mirror almost on top of their grave. She had closed the box, and she had opened it only a handful of times since. But it suddenly occurred to her, for the first time, that it was a very strange thing for her mother to have owned. She was not a sentimental woman. She hadn't seemed to care for pretty things or useless things. She was utilitarian, to Lana at any rate. And Lana's mind went back to The Looking Glass, and the thick aroma of burning sage and lavender, and the crystals glinting in the candlelight. That was the smell of her mother's house, of her clothes and hair.

There was a lot about her mother that she didn't know, Lana had always known that to be the case, but had never felt inclined to remedy that. Who would she even have asked? She didn't know anyone else who knew her mother. Anyone that was still alive anyway. Except now she did, she realised. Now she had a sister.

Chapter 19.

There was snow on the ground, only a little, and mostly trodden flat by now. There were a few untouched patches left though, and Tess walked out of her way to be the first to tamp down the fresh fall.

The market vendors breathed hot air into chapped hands and nursed steaming cups, wrapped up in scarves and hats. Tess waved at people she knew. She put her cheek against Steve's head and relished being close to him, feeling his feet kicking with excitement now and then. These were the weekends she'd imagined before she'd moved.

She bought cheese and vegetables and fresh bread, not having any particular intention for the things she chose. She just picked what looked good, the things that called to her. She talked to the vendors about the weather, and their shared calling of selling quality items to the people of Castor. She was one of them already, she could feel it. It was like there had been a spot waiting for her, and she'd fallen easily right into place.

Tess stared at the display of a confectionery stall, at jewel-toned Turkish delight and almond-studded nougat, none of which she intended to buy. She felt a prickling at the back of her neck. It felt like eyes, and she turned sharply. There were no eyes on her, but she saw someone she knew, a familiar cascade of black hair surrounding a pale and freckled face, across the street. She was pushing a red stroller, laden with bags threaded through carabiners on the handlebar. Tess wasn't sure what compelled her, or what she was going to say, but she hurried over.

"Lana!" she called. Lana whipped round, immediately anxious, then smiled on meeting Tess' eye. "Fancy seeing you here," Tess said.

"Yes, in the very small town where we both live, on market day." Lana smirked.

Lana had a quality about her, Tess thought. It was

easier to see here in the sunshine, in the naked light of a cold and bright morning. There was something warm and self-deprecating and open. Up to a point, Tess remembered. Because there was that other something. The thing that made her eyes go opaque. That was the thing Tess wanted to unpick, entirely to sate her own curiosity. But she had a feeling that the rest of Lana, the surface part, was compelling enough on its own. Her hair was dark, but in the sun certain strands here and there shone with deep red colour of horse chestnuts. It was quite lovely.

"Yeah what a crazy coincidence."

"What did you get?" Lana pointed with a mittened hand to Tess' tangle of string market bags.

"Stuff. Nothing very interesting. Pastries. Cheese. You?"

"Beets," said Lana, and beamed with such earnestness that Tess almost laughed. "I'm gonna make a stew. The secret is spice. You gotta add heat to balance the sweetness of the root vegetables or it's gross. I don't know why I'm telling you this. You didn't ask."

"No, it's good to know, I'm sure. Although I'm not much of a cook," said Tess.

Steve suddenly flung his arms into the air, smacking Tess in the face. She had forgotten he was there. Lana smiled hugely and involuntary. Not the performative smile most people give babies to make them feel at ease. She gave him a tiny, ridiculous wave.

"And this is your little guy, huh?" Tess looked into the pram. A very nonchalant baby with wind-chapped cheeks stared back at her.

"That's Cody. Most people think he's a girl," said Lana distantly. "I let them have it. It's too awkward to insist he's a boy. Makes it seem like I'm trying to trick people or something."

Tess crouched down awkwardly to let Steve get a look at Cody. He was fascinated by other babies, and particularly by ones smaller than him. They existed in a realm between person and doll, which Steve seemed to enjoy contemplating.

The infants stared at each other, Cody with an expression somewhere between total blankness and disdain, Steve with one of pure joy.

"Could it maybe be his little bear hat?" Tess asked. The hat in question was fluffy and pastel pink with little round animal ears.

"It's a hand-me-down. He's warm. He doesn't know it's a girl's hat. It's not like he can even see it. It's on top of his head. People think I'm weird anyway, so it doesn't really matter," Lana shrugged.

"That's the spirit," said Tess, standing back up and adjusting the straps of her baby carrier. It wasn't really built for any movement more complicated than standing up straight and walking at a sensible pace. Any bend or twist sent it into chaos.

The sun was getting higher now, the light bouncing off the snow and into Tess' eyes. She squinted against it.

"What's up?" said Lana.

"Just bright," said Tess. "And this carrier is a pain in the ass. My shirt's all tangled up in the strap ad the velcro part isn't laying right. Ugh." She writhed fruitlessly. "I'm thinking it's time to switch to a stroller. But then it's so big. That feels like its own set of problems. I like your set-up, by the way." Tess pointed at Lana's stroller. "Very utilitarian. With all your carabiners and whatever. Functional."

"Thanks. I have three kids. Without caribiners, I lose all ability to function."

They looked at each other awkwardly for a moment. Lana started walking, a vague hand-gesture indicating that she was headed somewhere. Tess ambled along beside her. It felt like they took up a huge amount of the sidewalk with the stroller. Tess didn't know what to say, not because she had nothing to say, but because there was only one thing she wanted to say, but she was trying to wait for it to come up naturally.

"This is weird, but do you want to come over for a coffee? Like, right now? I'd love to stay and chat in the street but I forgot my sunglasses and also it's really busy. I'm only five minutes that way. Is that weird? If it's too weird you can say no."

Lana stared into the distance for a moment, lost in a thought. She snapped the fingers of her right hand idly. Tess had seen her do that before. She returned, shifting gears in a very visible way.

"Yeah, actually. That'd be nice. Let me get the changing bag from my car first and throw the stroller in."

***

Lana's car was full of crumbs, Tess observed, peering through the window while Lana collapsed the stroller. It was impressive how she was able to balance Cody on one hip and break down the stroller with the spare hand. She hauled it up and nudged it into the trunk with her leg, refusing Tess' offer of help. Tess turned her attention back to the crumbs.

She had initially thought it was some kind of horribly outdated decorative trim on the seats. Three kids' car seats were inelegantly jammed into the back of the car. One modest booster seat and two enormous thrones that swivelled on mounts. All covered in crumbs. The floor was littered with packets and Tupperware lids and Barbies with matted hair. Tess hoped she was not looking into her own future, and then felt bad.

Lana locked the car and reappeared with Cody still balanced on one hip, and a little wooden box in her other hand. The box was instantly intriguing.

"I know my car is full of crap," said Lana. "It can't really be helped most of the time. And I lost the pointy vacuum attachment. I wish I could just turn the whole car on its side and shake out all the crumbs. Or that it had a

133

tray, like the toaster. Sadly it's not that easy. This is for you, by the way," she said, catching Tess' eyes on the box. "Let's get to your place. This baby's getting heavy."

Tess wasn't used to having people in her space. Everyone was welcome in the shop downstairs, of course. But her own private home just above it had become like something sacred. It for her and Steve and Jasper the cat. If Steve wasn't with her in the shop, he was with Hannah, his babysitter. And she occasionally sat down with Tess for a cup of tea. She was twenty years old and described herself as "in-between things" so she wasn't too interested in chatting. She was very blonde and always smiling and flushed. She kayaked at the weekend, whatever the weather. Tess felt she could let Hannah into her family. But that was it. Her people were only three people, and one was a baby, and one was a cat. Lana was her first proper guest, and she hadn't even cleaned.

Steve was only a little older than Cody but he seemed so much bigger somehow. Had he been that small just a few months ago? Steve sat, more or less, on his playmat, which was just an old patchwork quilt Tess had bought from a local thrift store. She didn't have any proper baby things, except for the carrier, and none of her things matched. She wondered if Lana had noticed. Cody lay beside Steve, just watching him patiently, transfixed. He seemed to have realised this was not one of his siblings and was therefore a little suspicious. He was waiting for Steve to make his move.

Tess found a good plate, one with gold edges and painted flowers, and put a chunk of pecan loaf cake on it, that she'd just bought from the market. It seemed like a strange thing to buy at the time but it had turned out well. She needed to learn to trust her intuition more.

She put the cake in the centre of the kitchen table, with a knife, and put a pot of coffee on. Lana sat awkwardly at the table while Tess busied herself with the coffee and hastily washed cups. Lana had about as much recent experience being a guest as Tess had being a host, she could tell. Eventually Tess sat down beside her, setting down two cups of coffee. Lana murmured something that sounded like she had tried to say "thanks" and perhaps "great" at the same time, and smiled in a small, embarrassed way.

They had talked before, but it had been by the low candlelight of the shop downstairs, with other people around and the ambient noise of their chatter as a conversation buffer. Aside from the distant noise of birds and the bustling market outside, it was quiet. They could hear each other breathing. Tess sipped her coffee and it sounded grotesquely loud. They watched the babies rolling on the floor. Tess sliced the cake, Lana accepted a slice and informed her that it was good.

Lana broke the silence, surprising Tess.

"Oh, I forgot. This." Lana pulled the wooden box out of the huge tote bag by her feet and set it down on the table between them. Tess opened it tentatively, like it might explode. It contained an assortment of little crystals and charms, as well as a small pearl handled letter opener. The mirror had been turned back to front. She rummaged through the crystals, recognising most, naming them in her head.

"It's fairly random, but I want you to have this," said Lana. "It was my mother's. Someone gave it to me after she died. I don't actually remember who exactly gave it to me. It was a long time ago. Anyway I thought you might like it. It seemed like the kind of thing a witch might like."

She said the word 'witch' without stressing it. Usually if people said it outright, they added a slight ironic lilt to the word, as if it was silly and they needed to acknowledge the silliness of it in order to say it. There was something campy and amusing about it to most people. Lana just said it. It was a small thing, but it felt like something.

"I can't take this," Tess said. "It was your mother's. It like an heirloom." She very much wanted to take it.

"No, it's fine. I really don't want it. I keep it in my storage unit with all my old junk. But even in there it's like it takes up space in my brain. And I went there today and it was basically screaming 'pick me up' so I did. And then I ran into you and I figure maybe that's where it wanted to go. Does that sound crazy?" said Lana, her eyes pleading with Tess not to say yes.

"No." Lana looked relieved, and took another bite of her cake. "Things can be like that sometimes," Tess continued. "So did your mother practice witchcraft? Or was she spiritual or what's the situation there?"

Lana actually laughed.

"No, that would be so ridiculous. No, I don't think it was anything like that. This is a bit of an outlier. As far as I remember, she never had anything like this. Pretty stuff, I mean. Stuff without a clear purpose. I never saw this until after she was dead."

Tess nodded, feeling certain it wasn't quite as purposeless as Lana thought, and turned her attention to the letter opener. There was something crusty on the blade that Tess hoped was rust. She didn't really want to touch it, for fear of tetanus or worse. She scooped up the pendants instead, inspecting the largest one. It was white and smooth as glass, with a face carved into either side.

"I think this might be ivory," Tess said.

The other possibility was that it was bone. She didn't say that out loud. It didn't feel like the thing to say over coffee and cake.

"And this guy carved into it looks Greek or Roman to me." The rest were an assortment of faces or animals. "In my professional opinion, this looks like witch crap to me. We do like to collect little trinkets, like magpies or octopuses. Octopi?"

"Do octopuses collect things?" said Lana, not looking at her.

"Yeah, they make gardens," said Tess, not completely sure whether that was actually true. "Is that what you wanted me to tell you? Is that why you thought I might like this stuff?"

"I, uh... When we met before, there was a smell in the store."

"Oh, sorry. Was it a bad smell? I feel like there's this fog of baby shit and maybe I'm immune to smelling it now so I've been known to overcompensate with the incense."

"No, it's not that. Well maybe it's that. I think it was sage, and maybe a couple of other things mixed in. I'm not totally sure. I'm more familiar with cooked sage, as opposed to burnt. But it took me back, y'know. It hit me right in the nostalgia cortex. Smells are like that. I remember that smell from my mother's house. My house, I guess. When I was a kid. So, even though it seems so incredibly ridiculous, I could maybe see my way to believing that she was into this kind of thing."

Tess nodded, letting Lana process it in her own time.

"And, to be clear, I'm not saying that you're ridiculous!" said Lana, looking suddenly panicked. "It's just ridiculous that I would not know something like this about my mother. And a ridiculous thing for her to spend any time thinking about, it feels like. Because she was not somebody who enjoyed frivolous things or whimsical things. Not that witches are frivolous and whimsical!"

Tess laughed. "It's fair. There's a certain amount of whimsy."

On the patchwork quilt, Cody looked up at Lana, his face wet with drool. Steve was eyeing the cake still in Tess's hand.

"Is that why you were asking about ghosts?" asked Tess. "Sorry if that feels like it's come out of nowhere. It just felt like that was something."

"How did you..?" Lana was staring at her now, her brow furrowed, her tired eyes suddenly suspicious. Tess had seen that expression before.

"Yeah I can tell I hit something there."

"Do you, like, actually have magic powers? Sorry, there

was no good way to ask that. How do you *do* that?" asked Lana, her head tilted as if that might afford her some protection against Tess' intuition, or allow her to see the trick.

Tess smiled disarmingly and sipped her coffee.

"I don't have magic powers. I don't think. Or no more than anybody else has magic powers. There's magic in the universe, in little particles of time and light drifting around us. There's magic in nature and in dreams and in other things. I don't think that's a controversial opinion. I mean, there's magic in those babies, right? They're special things," said Tess.

"Sure," said Lana, studying the babies, squinting to see the magic in them. "I can get behind that."

"I have good intuition. I used to joke that I just had extensive customer service experience. But it's something I've always had, I think. I'm not psychic. But then again, what does it mean to be psychic? Is there really a difference between extra sensory perception and just being very perceptive? I can tell when something is 'something'. Someone will say something, just a small something. And it has a different colour to it, a different taste. It's hard to describe. You asked if I believed in ghosts. It felt like a 'something'," said Tess.

"I think that might actually be a magic power. That sounds paranormal to me. Or not paranormal, that sounds rude. Extra-normal. Anyway, remind me never to let you read my palm," she laughed.

That was something too.

"Why? What skeletons have you got buried?" Tess said it like a joke, and Lana laughed. But Tess would have put serious money on at least one skeleton.

Cody began to fuss, kicking his legs in frustration and making little squeaking snorts like a piglet. Steve had stopped making that sound, Tess realised. She couldn't remember the last time he had made those little baby bleats. She missed them.

Lana scooped Cody up onto her knee, where he cheerfully surveyed the world from his new vantage point. The cake on the plate was of particular interest to him, but he couldn't quite coordinate his limbs to obtain it. He made strange faces at the cake instead, seemingly hopeful that it might just spontaneously move closer to him.

"So magic is real? But not in the Harry Potter sense?" Lana asked.

"More or less," said Tess with a shrug.

"And ghosts?"

"That's a difficult question. I personally think that ghosts are projections of our internal selves. They're memories and hopes and fears, congealed into something whole. A feeling of being 'haunted' can often be an emotional wound of some kind. People used to say ghosts were souls with unfinished business on earth. But I think it's more likely that if you see a ghost, you're the one with the unfinished business."

Lana was grimacing, but nodding as if she didn't know she was doing it.

"You said yourself that this box was calling to you, urging you to do something. Do you have something unresolved about your mother? You're feeling her presence for some reason. How did she die? If you don't mind me asking?" She didn't need to know, exactly, but Tess very much wanted to. The more pieces of the puzzle, the more complete a picture she could get.

Lana was frowning.

"It's difficult to say," she said. "It's in that grey area between accidental death and suicide. I don't really want to get into it." She hugged Cody close, as he wriggled happily on her lap, and kissed the top of his head. Her eyes were shining.

"Are you okay? I'm sorry if I upset you. That's the downside to being intuitive, I guess. I don't have much in the way of tact. That's something Emily used to say, my ex. She said I knew *about* people, but I didn't know people.

I guess that's accurate."

Tess knew she was prying. Peering into Lana's eyes like she was trying to climb inside them. Emily had asked Tess not to look at her like that. She had said she could feel it, like the gentle pulling of a thread somewhere deep in her being. It was small but it was significant, like Tess was trying to get her nail under something. Whether it was magic or something else, it was a violation. She said that Tess had a way of breaking in and finding things. It sent a shiver up Tess' spine to remember Emily's words. This was before they had broken up. It had always been a problem for Emily. And Tess had hated to be characterised as some kind of villain, as some kind of trespasser.

"No, it's fine. It's just a lot. Man, I really really don't want any more of this crap in my house." Lana gestured to the box. She sniffed. "Will you take it?"

"Sure," said Tess. "Do you want a tissue?"

"Please."

Tess handed her one, crumpled and disintegrating, from her pocket. Lana sniffed and cleared her throat, trying to draw a line under something.

"Sorry. I don't know what I'm even saying half the time. My brain's all scrambled up. Cody was only born five months ago, which sounds like a long time, but it really isn't. I mean, you know. I've basically only just stopped bleeding. That's probably not right, but I just really don't want to go back to the hospital. Basically, I'm okay, I'm functioning. It was all very traumatic. The birth, that is," said Lana. There was something overly casual in her tone, at odds with what she was saying, like it was an excuse she'd relied on time and again. Maybe something she told herself a lot.

"I'm sure it was. Isn't it always? I had a planned caesarian, had to, so maybe I don't know. I was sort of hiding out in my head behind a plastic sheet, and the doctors were in charge of the rest of me. It was... not good. But in a way that's hard to explain. What happened to you?" Tess asked.

"I don't really know. You forget things. But something went wrong, I guess. I have two older kids, so you'd think I'd know what to expect. But something was different this time. I think it just broke me in some way. That sounds bad. Obviously it could have been worse. I just haven't been sleeping right and everything still hurts a little bit."

The winter sunlight sparkled on the window pane, cheerful and cold at the same time.

"I know what you mean. It's probably a bit of burnout, newborn sleep stuff, plus you're still healing. Maybe a bit of seasonal affective disorder? I get that," said Tess.

"I was thinking it felt like something . . . more than the usual bullshit. Sure, I'm probably anaemic and I sometimes wonder if I'm going deaf from how loud my other two kids are," Lana managed a small laugh. "It's definitely been said that my imagination is just a smidge overactive, so it could just be that, but it sometimes feels like my energy is being literally sucked out of my body. It's like there's this black hole following me around the house, and all my thoughts are just going straight into the void. I can't remember shit."

"Just in the house?" Tess asked.

"Just in the house."

"So this void isn't here now?"

"No, it's good here."

"Thanks, I do my best," Tess said, trying to inject some levity into the conversation. "That's a lie, I don't do my best. I do enough while accepting my limitations. Maybe I could have dusted."

"I'm so sorry to dump this on you," said Lana. "You know that thing where you keep stuff inside too long, and the longer you try not to say something, the more likely you are to blurt it out at weird times in conversations with people you barely know? Like, you're at the grocery store, you run into some lady from the kids' school, you're talking about the weather and suddenly you confess you're worried you might have irritable bowel syndrome?"

"That sounds about right," said Tess, trying to imagine this scenario. "But I don't think you can say that you and I barely know each other. I mean, not now. You've bestowed heirlooms upon me. I think that means we're friends now."

"Yeah. That sounds nice. I don't have many friends. Or actually I don't have any. My husband is my friend. That sounds so lame. It's nice to have a girlfriend... a friend who's a girl... a grown-up female friend. God, why can I not speak today?" Lana looked endearingly alarmed at her lack of control over her words, her mouth running automatically without input.

Lana was funny when she got to talking, Tess thought. She was chatty underneath. Maybe she held things in for fear of rambling, she thought. She had a particular way of talking, of acting her inner thoughts. Most people perform little expressions to compliment the things they said, for dramatic effect. But Lana acted out her own reactions to the things she was saying, like they were two separate things. It was fascinating to watch, and it made her so easy to read that Tess barely had to try at all. It was nice not to feel that she was prying. Lana was happy for her to know everything, at least subconsciously. She had no filter and she'd put up a wall around herself to make up for it. But once the wall came down, everything was on full display.

"I get it," said Tess. And she did.

"Hey would you mind putting my coffee in the microwave for a sec?" Lana asked, her fingers still curled around the cup, with its barely touched coffee. "Not literally a sec. Maybe like forty secs."

Tess took the cup from Lana, confused. She'd only just poured it. As soon as her fingers touched it, she realised it was stone cold. Lana was preoccupied removing a lock of her hair from Cody's mouth. Tess took a furtive sip from the cup. It was like ice water, and it was slightly sour, like buttermilk. She picked up her own cup, which was still hot, and tasted it. It was fine. Something was wrong.

She looked at Cody, bouncing happily on his mother's knee, and thought inexplicably of environmental toxins. She thought about forever chemicals and phthalates and diesel particulates and black mould. She thought about the things she needed to keep away from Steve. And she realised that she had categorised Lana as a hazard, as a pollutant.

Something was wrong with Lana. She really looked at her, looked hard. Lana was wearing two cardigans. Lana's lips were chapped and there was bruise darkness under her smiling eyes. There was darkness inside her eyes too. It was easy to wave these things away as tiredness, stress, as things a mother of three might be expected to have. But it was something else, Tess knew.

Tess made her a fresh cup, claiming the microwave was on the fritz. Maybe it was. It came with the house and she'd never turned it on. Lana drank it quickly, urgently.

They chatted about other things. Lana was quiet at first, preoccupied by difficult thoughts. Tess could see it in her eyes, something unpleasant being turned over and inspected from different angles. Tess knew how to fix it. She didn't need a lot of information to know how people worked.

She mentioned being worried about what to cook for Steve, when he started needing actual nutritious food. She said she wasn't much of a cook, but that she was weird about chemicals. She didn't say that she had only been weird about chemicals since Steve's very medicalised birth, since all the drugs and plastic packets of sterile swabs and IV fluids. Something about it had released an old fear she'd made peace with. A fear of artificial and harmful things. The whys and the wherefores could wait for another day. She was sure she would end up telling Lana these things. She seemed like she would listen.

But for now, she just set the stage, made a space in the

conversation for Lana to fill. And she did. The recipes came thick and fast, delivered with mounting enthusiasm as Lana forgot the unpleasant thing. Tess fetched a bill from the kitchen counter, still in its envelope, and scribbled down Lana's various tips and asides, of which there were many.

Lana had an interesting way of describing recipes, citing vegetables or seasonings that might compliment the target dish, rather than any exact measurements of anything. Occasionally an ingredient would actually be important, and she would make sure Tess wrote it down. The meals she suggested were defined more by their texture or vibe or speed of preparing, rather than by a recognisable name. She had instructions for 'sort-of falafels' and 'corn shapes'. She described 'sweet potato things' which could be baked or fried, and could include an egg or could just as easily not.

They played on the floor with the babies. Lana wiped Steve's nose with a tissue from her pocket, and with this gesture seemed to earn his undying admiration. She was the kind of person to have tissues, Tess thought, tissues in a packet rather than scrunched in a pocket.

Lana nursed Cody, sat on the floor with her back against the wall, one knee folded up, sunlight streaming across her outstretched leg. When she leaned over Cody to see if he was sleeping yet, the sunlight splashed her long hair, revealing its hidden colours. The silence was pleasant now, a shared silence without pressure. Tess felt a little lonely in that moment. She did want to share silence. She had been hoarding it.

Cody was fast asleep now, and Lana deftly reassembled her nursing bra, sliding the clip into place and fastening it. Tess held out her arms wordlessly to take Cody from her, to allow her to get up off the floor. Lana handed him over without question. He was small and warm and his sleeping face was astonishingly beautiful. Lana trusted her. And that was beautiful too. She handed him back, her arms feeling immediately cold and somehow sad. Cradling his head in her elbow, Lana announced in hushed tones that she had better be going.

A twinge of intuition pulled at Tess' eye sockets, trying to get her attention. There was something else to do. It came to her. She went into her bedroom and opened a drawer, taking out a small dark stone striped with caramel bands. She went back to Lana, who's arms were busy holding Cody. Tess put the stone in Lana's jeans pocket.

"You take this one with you," said Tess.

"What is it?"

"It's a tiger's eye. It's for protection, or that's what they say anyway. Maybe you could use some."

Tess had it with her when she'd gone into hospital with Steve. It hadn't helped her. Or maybe it had. She couldn't know. She hadn't got the outcome she'd been hoping for but it could certainly have gone worse. She didn't want to be ungrateful when coming home alive with a baby, also alive, was a better outcome than some people got. Either way, it felt like it would be useful to Lana now.

"Thanks," Lana smiled. Then she sighed deeply, the smile melting. "I need to go."

"Where do you need to go?" Tess hadn't really meant to say that out loud. She thought Lana might rebuke her, tell her to mind her own business, storm off. Except, of course, she didn't. Because she wanted Tess to ask her.

"Gotta get my Halloween things back to the house," said Lana, oddly expressionless. "Can you believe it's snowed so much before Halloween?"

"I don't know how things work around here. I don't know when it's supposed to snow. But a lot of people have asked me today if I can believe it or not. It's not like I can say I don't. It has snowed. It's apparent."

Lana mulled this over.

"Okay," Tess continued, "well get home safe, get your pumpkins on the porch, get your ghosts in the windows, or whatever it is that you do."

Lana let out a high-pitched laugh, hushed so as to not wake Cody, that could not have felt more inappropriate or more false. It was like nails on a chalkboard, but inside Tess' heart.

"Sorry, that was weird," said Lana. "I'll see you next week maybe? I think the group could be good for me. Structure, y'know."

"I'll be there," said Tess. "Because that's where I live."

Tess got the door for her, and Lana descended the stairs down to the street. She looked back up at Tess at the bottom door, to offer an awkward shrug and a half smile as a goodbye, as her hands were occupied. Tess raised a cordial hand, then retreated inside.

Chapter 20.

Allie knew Lana was faltering; maybe they both were. Things got a little hazy now and then, but perhaps it had always been like that. At first it had been difficult to climb inside Lana's body, nudge her consciousness to one side. Now it was easy. That had to be evidence of something. Evidence that Lana couldn't cope and didn't have the strength to resist her. Some people couldn't take the day-to-day stress of regular life. Maybe Lana was one of those people.

Allie used to think she was like that; one of the people for whom the world was too sharp and too dull all at once. Someone who didn't quite fit and couldn't muster the energy to keep on coping. Someone like her mother. But she'd found something in Lana's home, and in her family. There was purpose here and meaning. There were things Allie could hold onto here. But she wouldn't be able to hold on much longer.

There was only so much time, and she could feel it slipping away. Allie could see something strange in Lana's face when she looked at her, as if Allie didn't look quite right. It was the only kind of reflection she could create, and it wasn't a flattering one. She forgot things too. She forgot that she needed to let Lana be in control. It felt so natural having a physical form again, and she forgot it wasn't entirely hers. She wanted to touch and taste the world around her. She didn't want to share things.

But if Lana was having difficulties anyway, then maybe there was no problem. It would be better for her to rest. Better for her to sleep in the back seat. Allie could drive for a while. And if she never recovered, if her stress reached the point where it started to overflow, then it was a good thing there was someone else to take the wheel for good. Lana's mother had died when Lana was a teenager. It was the thing that set them apart from each other. It had obviously done something to Lana, something that hadn't been done to Allie. It had caused a structural weakness that Allie didn't have.

Allie knew Lana as well as she knew herself, so she knew that Lana wouldn't want that for her own kids. They didn't deserve to see her break down, or be taken away, or worse. They didn't deserve to see the things Lana must have seen. Allie wanted to be a person again, but it wasn't all selfishness. It might be better for everyone involved, if she shouldered Lana's burdens for her, if she bore her reality.

There was something else too. It was difficult for Allie to really remember her past. It felt so blurry, probably because those memories weren't entirely real in this reality. Allie had enough self-awareness to know that her memories were comprised of things that never actually happened, according to the material of Lana's world anyway. It was the same for her, she guessed. She was never a person here, so she wasn't now. It felt like maybe the atoms of her new reality were on the brink of figuring out there was an intruder present. The idea of being swept away, like a bead of condensation on a windowpane, was sickening. She tried not to think of it.

She tried to be practical, to find solutions. As difficult as it was to remember her past, she was sure there was something there to work with. A clue waiting in the darkness. It was the things that made them different that offered potential weaknesses. She didn't know everything about Lana.

Lana's parents had both died earlier. That was something. Lana had been alone for longer, until she had created her own family. And Lana's mother had died at a bad time. Allie had memories of that time, dark enough to make an impression even through the haze. She remembered plates thrown and screaming in the night. But her mother had hung on a few more years, time for the relationship to become a little less jagged. Lana's hadn't. There was something there. Lana's past was darker, people died earlier than they did in Allie's world. But every time Allie tried to pick at the thread, it slipped through her fingers and back below the surface.

Chapter 21.

Lana was taking a bath in her dream. She knew immediately that it was a dream, because she'd had the same one countless times. She had read an article online about coping with recurring nightmares. She to check for the signs. The water in the bath had no temperature, neither did the blood pouring from between her legs. It should have been warm and slick, but it wasn't anything. It didn't make it less frightening. *Here we go again.* She knew there was no choice but to strap in and ride the dream to its conclusion.

Magnus was there, squeezing her wet hand and shouting her name. It was the same as it had been in real life. Except then she had felt detached. It had been as if she was watching herself from a distance. In the dream, she was stuck inside her body unmoving and unmoved. That's why Magnus had shaken her and shouted in her face, she supposed. He wanted to make sure she was still in there. She wondered whether he had the same dream.

But it's not quite the same as always. Something's different. Allie was there too, standing in the corner, facing away. She sometimes did that, just stood in the corner like a piece of furniture. Lana thought maybe that was how she slept, or rested, or whatever it was that she was doing when she was switched off.

Lana felt her baby squirming inside her body, the baby that they didn't yet know was Cody. *That hadn't happened.* She hadn't been able to feel much at that point. There had been contractions, and they had felt like her body was tearing in two, her skeleton cracking down the centre to make way for the baby. *Like an egg.* And then she had fallen backwards into a different area of her brain, a private waiting room from which she could watch the whole process. That was when she had realised something was wrong. She was being shielded from something.

Her only remaining anchors to the moment had been

Magnus' increasingly frenzied voice – he was talking to someone on the phone then – and pain where her leg bones connected to her pelvis. That was too sharp to be knocked out. She completely forgot about the baby. She could feel him now though, in this dream. He tossed and turned like an eel. She had missed him, she realised. She had missed holding him inside of her, having a little creature all her own, who went everywhere with her. She had missed having him sleep under her heart. They had taken him away as soon as he was born. *It wasn't how it was supposed to be.* She worried he had been sad, that he had wondered where she'd gone.

She was bleeding profusely, but it didn't feel like a problem. It was just how the dream went. It would end when the ambulance came. She couldn't remember if she was supposed to do something. It felt like there was something to do. Magnus put his head against hers, holding her and breathing hard against her face. His breath was hot and urgent. She breathed in his smell, which seemed more real than anything in the room.

Lana was dimly aware that Allie had turned to face her. She caught the movement on the peripheries of her vision. *That's not important.* Magnus was fully clothed, bloody handprints on his flannel shirt, fresher blood on his hands and matted into the blonde hair on his forearms. Lana was wearing only a bra, and her tattoos. She felt self-conscious for a moment, then felt immediately ridiculous for thinking it. Things were getting sharper. *That means it's almost over.* She willed herself to wake up the rest of the way, to move her body in the reality she knew was only a hair's breadth away. And the dream started to peel away. Things became solid.

It was late, Lana knew instinctively. It was dark and the air felt like 3am. The familiar hiss of Cody's sound machine, simulated rain on a tin roof, filled her ears. *But something's still wrong.* She was awake but her body still felt damp still. There was a weight on top of her, pressing her chest and pelvis down into the bed. *Sleep paralysis?* She struggled against it for a moment, twisting her torso against the immovable something crushing her. It was futile. Her voice caught up with her consciousness and she called out.

"Crap. What's the matter? Did I hurt you?" Magnus half whispered, the way they always spoke to each other when Cody was sleeping beside them in his crib.

Lana figured out the space, things orienting themselves around her as she shook off the last fragments of the dream. Her eyes adjusted to the dark, enough to see Magnus' blonde beard in front of her, glinting faintly in the light of the single red LED blinking on Lana's laptop charger. He took some of his weight off her warily.

"What's happening? What are you doing?"

She could feel the semi-healed incision from her episiotomy, where the doctors had scalpel-nicked her vagina to get Cody out. It had faded recently to a persistent ache, with occasional papercut twinges. But now it was burning. She realised what was happening.

"Let me up!" she choked at Magnus, sounding so much more afraid and vulnerable than she meant to. He gingerly extricated himself from around her. Lana felt cold. She pulled her knees up to her chest and let out a pitiful trembling breath. It wasn't quite a sob, but it was enough like one for Magnus to feel something was wrong. He pulled on a pair of sweatpants in the total silence in which they had both become used to doing things. Lana couldn't bring herself to look around the room. She couldn't face the possibility that Allie was there somewhere, half hidden in the darkness. She didn't want to catch a glimpse of her semi-luminescent face. She was so much more disturbing in the dark. Lana knew she was there somewhere.

Magnus threw a blanket around Lana's shoulders and eased her to her feet, his arm around her, holding her close to his body. He opened the bedroom door silently. There was a particular way to do it, pulling the door while turning the handle so the latch didn't click. Lana allowed herself to be driven by Magnus' hand against her back. He guided her into the living room, to the sofa. It was brighter in here, with the curtains open and the moonlight streaming in through the window. The room looked weird in the pale light, all the things inside it were the wrong colour.

He sat next to her on the sofa. On the wrong side, Lana noted. He was usually on the other side.

"What happened?" he asked her, the anxiety on his face crushingly sad.

"You tell me," said Lana. But she knew what had happened. She knew Allie had pushed her out again. It seemed to happen when she was sleeping, when she couldn't see her coming. Her ghost had slipped inside her unattended body, a shadow crawling inside the shape that had cast it, a perfect fit. She knew it. It had happened before.

Allie would always hide from her afterwards, leaving hours or even days before returning to the scene of the crime, as if it was something that Lana might forget. The time didn't make it sting any less keenly. Sometimes she would half admit what had happened. She would tell Lana that she had wanted to let her sleep or do a few chores for her. She couldn't possibly think Lana would believe it. Or maybe she did.

Sometimes she tried to gaslight Lana, which had worked a little in the beginning, when Lana was lying to herself too. The self-delusion combined with Allie's lies and Magnus' suggestion that she was suffering from something understandable and normal. It made it something she could almost accept. Now Allie went back and forth between denial and justification. Lana wasn't sure if she was even aware of her inconsistency. That was the right word for her behaviour, Lana thought, inconsistent. She didn't blame Magnus. He had spoken to Lana while Allie was driving, she didn't know how many times. This was just another interaction. It did sting. But it wasn't his fault. *How could he know?*

"I don't know," he said. "We were having sex. I mean, you were there. You seemed like you wanted to. And then it was like all the breath went out of you, and you sort of froze up, and then you told me to stop. Fuck, I thought you might be having a seizure or something. I almost had a heart attack."

"I don't remember any of that. I'm pretty sure I was asleep. Did I say I wanted to? Did I say the actual words in the right order? Or did I say some crazy dream soup?" As soon as she said it, she realised it sounded like an accusation. She wanted to know if Allie had initiated it, whether she had directed the situation or just been swept along, and abandoned ship when things got too far.

"You said so," said Magnus, through gritted teeth, jaw clenched. "I'm sure of it. What's the matter with you? I don't mean to be harsh. But seriously, what's wrong? Why can't you remember anything properly?"

"I'm sure it's just stress," said Lana. "The others at the baby group said they had the same. It's the hormones going back to normal. It's like it leaves gaps that things fall out of. It'll get better. The gaps will close."

She was feeling better. She was the right temperature, and the feeling had come back to her limbs and face. She scrambled closer to Magnus and butted his shoulder with her face like a cat. It was something they did after an argument, when they wanted to make up without saying all the things, to just fall back into familiarity.

"I'm sorry I got scared. I genuinely think I was sleeping. Were my eyes open?"

"You were talking." He didn't warm to her embrace.

"I think that was just my subconscious or whatever. You know sometimes your brain wakes up before your body and you get a sleep paralysis? And sometimes your brain wakes up before your body and you reply out loud to something someone says in a dream? You sleep talk all the time. You asked me for a pecan quesadilla last week."

"I guess." His face said that he didn't quite buy it. But he was willing to accept the explanation to make Lana happy. He finally put his forehead against Lana's. She accepted his apology in the unspoken way that they could know what the other one was thinking. She breathed in the smell of his hair and wished she could fix herself for him. She looked at the digital clock on the TV unit. It was 5am. That felt about right.

"I can't go back to sleep. I'm too wired now. Too much talking. I think I'll just make some coffee and watch TV until Cody wakes up. You go back to bed," she said.

"I'll make the coffee," he said, standing up. "Is it too early for breakfast? I'll stay with you. If the kids are in another room, it counts as a date." That was the qualifier. It was so difficult to have a proper date night out that they'd decided one kid or fewer in the actual room with them, plus the provision of food or beverages, made it an official date. Magnus smiled as earnestly as he could manage and left the room.

Lana felt his absence immediately. She was glad he was staying with her. She felt vulnerable. She wasn't wired. She was afraid to sleep. And she felt violated. Too many people had too big a share of her. She had been glad of Allie in the beginning because they shared everything. They shared a past, a personality, a face. There were no barriers between them. But now the lack of dividing walls made her feel edgeless. Anyone or anything could strike at her exposed heart. Something flickered at the edge of her eyeline, and her eyes snapped to attention, to find the thing. There was nothing. Her eyes were tired and every moving shadow felt like a threat. Keep your distance, she thought, her pulse pounding in her throat. She couldn't live any longer in a haunted house.

Chapter 22.

Lana had a plan

Magnus was asleep by the time sunlight began to creep over the horizon, snoring and crumpled against the arm of the sofa. Cody was asleep too, still in his cot in their bedroom. Magnus had sneaked back downstairs to grab the monitor and Lana had to fight the impulse to cower under a blanket while he was gone. Cody was quiet as a mouse. *Maybe he preferred having the room to himself.*

She knew it was a long shot, but she needed to bring Tess into the situation. That meant getting her into the house. *Is that wrong? Deliberately involving another person in this mess so she can tell me what's going on? What else can I do though?* Lana had asked her about ghosts and she hadn't seemed particularly receptive. She didn't seem to think Lana was crazy, which was good, but she had opted for a more psychological interpretation of a haunting, which was not good. Understandable, certainly. And probably what Lana would have said to someone if they'd come to her a couple of months ago with a supernatural problem, but not what Lana was looking for.

It was time to lay it all out, tell her everything. She'd either be able to help or she wouldn't. It felt stupid to admit, even just to herself, that she was hoping Tess would be able to wave a magic wand and make the problem go away. The problem being Allie. Lana wanted an exorcism, plain and simple. And if she couldn't help, if Tess wasn't the kind of witch who could wave a magic wand and fix things . . . Lana wasn't sure what options she had left.

There was a last-ditch plan floating at the back of her mind behind all the things she'd forgotten to do. She didn't want to look at it too closely. *Burn it all down.* The thought came to her now and again, the clouds parting before it and then obscuring it again. It didn't feel like a good idea. She was sure, somehow, that Allie could not be separated from her. They were entwined in a way that made Lana sure she would die if Allie did. She couldn't explain it. But it felt like they had both gone too far down a path to turn back. There was only forward.

Lana heard Cody stirring finally around 6am. He wasn't outraged like he often was. He cooed happily, wondering where everyone was, what game was being played. Lana went to him and gathered him up in his blanket. She heard a flurry of footsteps behind Seb and Emmy's door. Seb always crept to the door and put his eye against the keyhole, which had never had a key, when he heard someone coming. He was a light sleeper and secretly very worried about nighttime monsters. He didn't like for Lana to acknowledge his concerns. He was like her in that way, she thought. So, she left him to his ritual, and didn't chide him for it. He did what he needed to do to reassure himself. Emmy was fast asleep, never disturbed by Seb's scuttling.

Cody's tiny fingers pinched and pulled at Lana's top as she settled back onto the sofa. She lifted her t-shirt and he latched onto her breast, drawing out the milk in long, drowsy swallows. He fell asleep again quickly. He was curled up, pet-like on her lap, his fingers tangled in her hair, his soft face stuck to her exposed breast with dried milk. She tucked the edges of his baby blanket underneath him, cocooning him.

The TV was on, and a man with outrageous hair was making a case for an alien super-government running the world from the shadows. At this point, it was difficult to call anything ridiculous, thought Lana. The sound was barely audible, and the auto-generated subtitles were patently incorrect. Magnus had the remote though, and he was still asleep. Of course, she thought suddenly, Tess might just think she had gone mad, that she was as mad as the guy on TV who was now gesturing wildly and beaming with righteous conviction. She needed to get Tess in the house, and let her breathe in that claustrophobic air, and maybe that would help her to understand.

She texted Tess, awkwardly with her left hand because Cody was cradled in the nook of her right elbow. She wondered if Tess would be awake. Lana typed out her message. It was long, and when she read it back, it seemed crazy. She started again, and edited and agonised for fifteen minutes until she had whittled it down to; "Want to come for dinner some evening this week? I'll make stuffed shells :) xx".

It took less than five minutes for Tess to reply. So, she was awake. "Friday night? I'll call the babysitter."

"See you at 7.30?" Lana shot back.

"It's a date x".

Chapter 23.

Friday night came. Lana sautéed spinach, pressed out the green water with paper towels and mixed it with ricotta. She added pepper and an egg with a bright sunshine yolk. She spooned the mixture into cooked, cooled pasta shells, one by one. The shells were a little warm and soft in her hand and she held them open with one thumb, like holding a page in a book, tenderly transferring teaspoons of ricotta mixture. She slid the little palm sized boats, laden with filling, to a glass dish, and blanketed them with homemade tomato sauce. The dish went into the oven. The dirty bowls went into the dishwasher with the kids' dinner plates. Lana washed her hands and surveyed the kitchen. The good plates were in place, the ones with 1970s brown and orange flower motifs that she didn't dare put in the dishwasher. The matching glasses were out. Lana would take the chipped one.

Magnus put the kids in bed, Lana put Cody in his cot and clipped the baby monitor to the waistband of her jeans. Cody was still mostly her responsibility. There was no discussion of how they should divide up the kids. Magnus took the other two. She took Cody, because she had to feed him, and because it seemed obvious that he was just so much more hers than anybody else's. Lana had to be the one to lay him down and say goodnight. Seb had tried once to put his little brother to bed. He had insisted. But Cody had screamed until he was red in the face and Lana was genuinely worried Seb might have some kind of panic attack. Seb had needed a quiet hour listening to audiobooks, nestled on his beanbag, to calm down. He was only a baby himself, Lana thought. It was only in comparison to Cody that he seemed grown up. He didn't like noise unless he was the cause of it, and he didn't like for the situation to leave his control. Although, Lana supposed, nobody really likes those things. He was not an unreasonable little boy. Lana wished she had more time with him. But he was at school, and when he was home Cody often created a distance between him and his mother. Then, at bedtime, it was more often Magnus who gave him a bath, read him a story and settled him into his bed. Because Lana was busy with the baby. Emmy went everywhere Seb went. They slept in the same room, so Lana was kept a little further away from Emmy too. But Emmy was tough, she was resilient. Seb was more delicate even though he was older. He was her first baby, so he was always a baby.

Lana finished putting Cody down, already milk-drunk and half asleep when his head touched the mattress, just as she heard the kids' bedroom door close softly. *Perfectly done.* There was a small part of her that was secretly hoping it would fall apart. *It wouldn't be the worst thing if someone came down with a cold, if Cody had another tooth coming, if I set the kitchen on fire. Maybe we don't need to do this.* She sighed, and returned to the kitchen to make sure the plates were where she had left them, to make sure everything was where it should be and that nothing was there that shouldn't be.

Except Allie was there.

Lana's heart dropped. She had been hiding since the last time she pushed Lana out. Lana didn't for a second think she had gone for good. She could still feel her in the house. Just because she couldn't be seen didn't mean she wasn't there, Lana had learned. Lana felt an ember burning deep inside her, she felt her mouth fighting to twist into a fierce expression. She knew she was starting to actually hate Allie. As much as she felt sorry for her, and as much as she knew she had no right to feel superior to her, she couldn't help but despise her at the same time.

Allie looked like a kicked dog, half crouched and sorry but inexplicably hopeful. Hopeful that she might be accepted back into the warm light of Lana's forgiveness. She looked worse than ever, her skin reflecting the warm lighting all wrong, a milky green tinge to her face, cataract scales in her eyes. She was crumbling, Lana thought, and the sharp edge of her rage dulled instantly. There was something about her that made Lana feel intensely guilty. *Survivor's guilt*, Lana thought.

Allie flitted around Lana as she busied herself with the last of the preparations, asking inconsequential questions, trying to start up a casual conversation, trying not to acknowledge what had happened. Lana didn't respond to her. She knew Allie would hate that, to be treated like she wasn't there. She asked about Tess. She knew her name. Knew she was coming to dinner. *So, she has been eavesdropping.* She was glad she had been careful not to mention that Tess was a witch. It wasn't intentional, at first. She merely neglected to mention it to Magnus. It hadn't felt like something he needed to know. And then Lana had got to thinking about what Allie would make of Tess and had decided it would be better for everyone if Tess was just a friend from the mother and baby group. That was non-threatening. Even though Allie had never expressed a violent thought, the nature of her being untouchable made Lana nervous. It didn't feel like a good idea to draw her ire. She could hurt Lana, after all. And potentially the children. She couldn't bear to think about it. She was sure Allie would never. *But just in case.* Bringing a witch home felt a lot like bringing a priest into a haunted house. There was no way Allie wouldn't read into that. And if she felt threatened, Lana didn't want to think about what might happen if Allie felt her already weak grip on this reality slipping.

Allie changed tactic.

"I get that you're ignoring me. It's not like I can't tell. It's actually very rude. Is this about the other night? You had some kind of nightmare or whatever? And Magnus had to take you to the living room and calm you down?" Her performative confusion was infuriating.

"Were you watching us?" Lana asked, although she was certain already that Allie had been.

"I don't know what you think happened," said Allie,

ignoring the question. "Are you sure you didn't just space out again? Like what happened before? Or it was sleepwalking, like that guy said, the sleep doctor you went to. Or not so much sleepwalking as sleep fucking, am I right? I guess you do what you need to to keep the magic alive when you've got three kids."

She laughed cruelly, then switched to a soft and sympathetic expression in a second.

"You're overstretched. I mean, two little kids and a baby. There's so much to do around the house. No wonder. You were just tired and you're not remembering it right. You fell asleep during sex and Magnus didn't notice. It happens. I can see why you'd be mad at him but it's really not that big a deal. If anything, he should be mad at you. You're the one who fell asleep. That's hardly an ego boost for him, is it?"

Often, Lana had noticed, Allie couldn't decide on an approach, a viewpoint. So she launched into every possible explanation and emotion, delivering them all in a confusing barrage, and letting Lana choose what she wanted from the assorted offerings. Lana guessed that Allie either didn't know that's what she was doing or didn't remember that wasn't how people spoke to one another. Either way, it didn't bode well. Lana put her back to the kitchen window. Tess would be there soon, and Lana didn't want her to see her arguing with nobody.

"That's not what happened. I was asleep the whole time," said Lana. She tried to speak simply to Allie these days. She didn't want to give her too much to work with.

"Well that's a pretty serious allegation. I'm sure he would never -"

"No. He was talking to me. We were mid conversation, when I woke up," Lana insisted. She wanted to raise her voice. It was straining in her throat, ready to stand her ground. But she kept her voice low and soft, the way she always spoke to Allie when someone else was home.

"You must have been talking in your sleep and he

misconstrued something. Things lead to other things and . . . y'know, it happens."

"It was you. I know it was you. Just like all the other times."

"You mean the times I let you sleep? The times I let you rest while I watched the kids? You know most people would kill to have a babysitter they could trust like you can trust me. We're literally the same person. We wouldn't be able to share a body if we weren't the same. I fit into your body as good as you do. It's not something we should be fighting against. Sisters shouldn't fight."

Lana wanted to scream. She wanted to call Allie a psychopath. She wanted to accuse her of trying to steal her body, trying to push Lana out for good and leave her soul out in the cold, as Allie's was. She wanted to accuse her of trying to have sex with her husband. She wanted to call her a bad sister. And then she felt sorry for her again. The pity was always there. Lana wasn't sure she had chosen to feel pity for Allie. It felt like something involuntary, like something Allie was doing to her. Something to do with them sharing molecules. She could only hope the feeling was mutual. That Allie's hand would be stayed by that same metaphysical kinship if she ever felt moved to hurt Lana.

Allie was unreadable, staring at her, waiting. Then Allie's milky eyes glowed bright white, reflecting a set of headlights beaming in through the kitchen window. It made Allie look disturbingly animal for a second, like a fox in a torch beam. Lana turned to look out of the window. Tess was in the driveway. When Lana turned back Allie was gone.

Chapter 24.

The front door opened, spilling orange light onto every mote of falling snow before it. It was delicate snow, barely hanging together, tentatively deciding not to be rain, collapsing into slush on the ground. Lana hurried through the snow, wrapped in a thick cardigan and wearing what Tess could only assume were her husband's slippers.

"You didn't need to come out here. It's cold. I can get to the front door just fine," Tess said, locking her car and pulling the hood of her coat up for the short walk. There was no sense getting her hair wet.

"Well I just wanted to say -" said Lana, trailing off. The snow was collecting on her eyelashes and shoulders. It didn't melt on contact, which was probably a bad sign, Tess thought. Lana touched Tess's arm lightly. Tess looked down at her freckled hand.

"I can't believe I forgot to mention it," Lana said, grinning at her own forgetfulness, so painfully and obviously a lie, "but my husband, Magnus, is pretty superstitious and I didn't tell him you're a witch. He doesn't know you run the witch store. You're just my friend from the baby group."

"Uh . . . Okay. Sure. Don't ask, don't tell," said Tess.

"It's not so much a lie as an omission. I told him you sell homewares which, also, is kind of true. Candles are a homeware. They're for the home." Lana was talking too quickly, her pitch too high, trying to sell the lie as a good thing for everyone.

"Well . . . that's actually very close. I'll keep my mouth shut, sure. Secret's safe with me. But what if he came into the store one day? It doesn't feel like a lie - I mean an omission - that's going to hold up in the long term. I'm not saying no. I'll do whatever makes you feel comfortable, but it seems a bit flimsy."

"Why would he come in? No offence to your business model but I don't know if he's really your demographic.

Anyway, it doesn't really matter. Let's just get through the evening. We can unpick it later."

Lana brushed the snow from her eyelashes and kicked it from the toes of her oversized slippers. The light refracted in the falling snow dimmed a little, as another figure appeared in the open doorway, a big blonde man with a beard. Magnus, Tess guessed.

"What the shit are you doing outside?" he called to them, his voice rough and soft at the same time. It felt from that single question, from just a few words, that Lana was mistaken. Tess could do a lot with someone's voice. It revealed so much about a person. And nothing about it read as paranoid or fearful or superstitious.

"We're coming," Lana called back up the drive. The house felt very far away, for some reason. It might have been all the snow in the air between them and the house, but the distance seemed to grow the more Tess considered it. Lana's husband in the doorway was only a stone's throw away from them, but it felt like she would need to shout to make him hear her. They started towards the warm light.

"Is he very Christian or something?" Tess whispered to Lana.

"Not as such," Lana smiled, leaving it at that. Follow up questions were impossible. They were within earshot now.

Magnus stepped aside to let them in and closed the door behind them. Tess had expected it to be stiflingly hot inside. It looked like it should be. But it was comfortably cool, like an office space or a show home. Tess scanned the hall and the adjacent living room. The pram sat in the hall, its wheels still dirty from the world outside, the floorboards dirty underneath it. In the living room there were two vast wicker hampers full of toys, both with their lids balanced on top of an overflowing hoard of plastic construction vehicles and naked Barbies and candy-coloured stuffed animals. The living room rug had a design of a little town with roads and mountains and shops, for the kids to put little people and cars on. The coffee table looked modern and stylish, but had the scratched patina of a misused antique, probably the result of moist fruit peels and scratchy crafts. Everything was slightly ruined, but it didn't detract from the aesthetic. It looked real.

She knew she was being nosey, but she couldn't help it. It definitely felt like Lana had invited her here to show her something. She was sure there was something she was supposed to be looking for. She thought about those pictures that test for colour-blindness, with a secret number in the middle of a field of static. This was like that, if the static was the colour of warm mood-lighting.

Now that she thought about it, there were a lot of lamps. Too many lamps. More lamps than she would advise for a family with three small children. Pools of light blended together and merged like infinite overlapping Venn diagrams, keeping the shadows at bay, pushing illumination into every corner. It was diffuse and not overly bright, but it was inescapable. No part of the room was permitted to sink into shadow. It felt unnecessary and odd. Tess thought about cleansing a space. She burned sage. Now and then she sprinkled rainwater she'd collected. Sometimes she left the rainwater outside in a silver dish under a full moon before sprinkling it. Although that felt a little excessive even to her. And more than once she'd found little birds frolicking in her moon water come the morning. She supposed maybe you could use light instead. It flowed like smoke, it covered everything, it was a strong and elemental concept. The symbolism held up. Was that what Lana was trying to do? Was there something in the shadows? The bad feeling Lana had been talking about?

Wary of disappearing into her own thoughts, Tess made an effort to bring her attention back to Lana, who was brushing the snow off her body onto the doormat. Tess didn't need to. It was already gone. There was that too. The fact that the natural laws were a little wonky around Lana. It wasn't just that she was cold, but that she had been flagged by the physics around her as something cold, something on which snow didn't melt. Tess removed her coat and handed it to Magnus, who was waiting with his hands out to take it. He hung it on a hook above a heating vent. She'd seen him before, she realised. But she couldn't quite place him.

The hardware store, she remembered. She'd been in to buy a few things for the shop and for her home when she'd first moved to town and realised she was responsible for things like shelves for the first time in her life. He had been beaming and effusive, not for any apparent reason, like someone who's never known a reason to be otherwise. He was someone for whom things worked out, and who wasn't driven to negativity by the life stuff that ground some people down. He had a bushy beard and thick blonde hair, treading the line between mountain man and teddy bear. He was too masculine to be cuddly, his beard too bristly and features too sharp, but his eyes crinkled at the corner when he smiled in the most genuinely friendly way. It was a face on which a lie would be plain. He had a quality that was difficult to pin down, thought Tess, trying to taste the aura around him. It was something to do with solidness and protection. He was part of the house, a homebody, a domestic animal, but still rough around the edges. He was not what she expected. And she knew she had been right straight away: he didn't seem like a superstitious person.

Tess was an awkward guest. She always had been. She was supposed to say "What a lovely home you have" or something to that effect, but she was struggling to find a way to say it that wouldn't sound disingenuous. She was just standing there, coatless, dissecting Lana's home and husband with her eyes. She realised she was clutching her handbag to her body like it might disappear. There was nothing inside it, so it wouldn't have mattered even if it did. She picked it up as she was leaving the house, feeling vaguely like it was the kind of thing and adult brought with them when they went places. She almost picked up her everyday backpack, the one full of wet wipes and loose banana chips and teething toys. The one covered in ketchup. What did people carry about with them when their baby is at home, she thought desperately? She had briefly contemplated whether she might need a change of clothes or a book.

Magnus broke the silence.

"How are those brackets working out for you?" he asked.

"Yeah, they're great. Not fallen down yet. Although I'm not the most competent handyman so give it time." She smiled.

"I'm Magnus," he said, holding out his hand for her to shake. Did people really shake hands? "I figured I'd just tell you, as I'm not wearing a name tag this time."

"I know. Lana told me. I'm Tess, as you probably also know." She took his hand. It was rough, and bigger than a hand had any right to be. Tess didn't have much experience holding men's hands. She wondered if that's what Steve's tiny little starfish hands would become one day.

"I was probably supposed to do the introductions," Lana said more to herself than to them. "Ah well. I'll check on the shells. Do you want to go sit down in the living room?" she asked Tess. "I'll bring you a drink? We have elderflower cordial. I made it myself. Do you like elderflower?"

"Sure," said Tess.

Tess perched on the sofa in the living room, which was too comfortable. It made her want to curl up into the armrest and maybe take a nap. Magnus sat down next to her, the sofa sagging under his weight. She tipped toward him awkwardly. He was a better host than Lana and carried the conversation, asking about various home-related issues Tess had run into since moving to town, and then describing the solutions at length.

Tess felt eyes on her and looked up in time to see a small boy staring at her from around a corner. Magnus followed her eyeline.

"Hey," said Magnus, "you're supposed to be in bed. Go on, get out of here." He made a shooing gesture.

The boy disappeared. But the feeling of being watched didn't subside. Magnus was explaining how to shave down doors so they don't stick in the frame, and Tess was nodding as if she fully intended to do that. But she still felt eyes on her. More than once her attention snapped back to the corner where she'd seen Lana's kid spying on her, but he wasn't there. She couldn't find the source of the feeling. And suddenly the light from all the lamps crowding the room felt insufficient. There was something in the air, a whisper she couldn't so much hear as feel.

Lana appeared and pulled a lounge chair closer to the sofa. The elderflower cordial was good. It was tart and smooth and served over ice in very outdated glassware that made it feel like some kind of interesting elixir. Tess liked glassware and bottles and little containers for storing and serving things in. She had never known any practising witch who didn't.

The three of them talked mostly about what to expect from the various seasons, when tourists were most abundant, when the roads were the most impassable, and interesting spots around town that made a good day out with kids. Magnus told her about the hardware store, which he turned out to be the owner of. He worked on the counter because he had become quickly bored by his administrative and accounting responsibilities. He had hired a manager, who worked entirely from home, to do the things he didn't want to do, essentially someone to trade places with. Magnus wanted to give unsolicited advice and hear local gossip. He hadn't exactly said this, but Tess could tell. There had been another hardware store in town, but the two-horse race had come to an end when the owner had died of old age, and now Magnus held the monopoly on door handles and drill bits.

Tess watched his moustache twitch as he spoke. His beard made it a little difficult to gage his expressions, but then his eyes were unmistakably affable. They sparkled like ice. She'd almost forgotten about Lana, who was quiet and seemed awkward even in her own home. Sometimes the appearance of a new person to figure out would push everything else out of her brain. Lana had told her not to mention witchcraft. Probably she was thinking that would simplify something, smooth something out that might have been difficult. But Tess could not think what that might be. It was a pity Lana didn't know her very well. She would have known it was a bad idea to set up a puzzle for her.

Music was playing, an inoffensive oldies playlist, wafting from a speaker on a high shelf. There was a second tier to the room, a complex of floating shelves, the top halves of bookcases, the mantle, on which everything breakable or expensive sat. Tess had only just noticed. It was a good idea. Lana and Magnus glanced up at the speaker at the same time, as a new song came on. Patsy Cline, Tess thought, or Loretta Lynn. One of those cool old country ladies. Magnus and Lana shared a little half smile, that was so painfully adorable that Tess smiled herself. And then the moment faded, and Lana's anxious energy returned.

Tess could swear the room grew colder. The watching feeling was back. It was something to do with Lana. Did she do that? Did she know she was doing it? Magnus was still talking, unaware of anything, totally at ease. He was rattling on about a new playground that was proposed for the piece of scrub land behind the post office, and about a rat he had seen there the size of a Yorkshire terrier. Tess nodded along on autopilot, but it felt like the air had gone out of her lungs. She looked at Lana, right in the eyes, and caught a little slice of meaning in the air between them.

There was something. Lana could feel it. She didn't know what was happening. She wanted Tess to tell her. Okay then, Tess decided. That was enough invitation for her. She was officially on the case now.

The oven timer beeped loudly. Lana almost fell off her chair and sprinted to the kitchen to shut it off.

"She thinks it'll wake the kids," Magnus explained. "It won't though. Cody's got his rain sounds and that blurs out mostly everything. The kids will be sleeping like logs by now. How could they not be? They literally spend the entire day running about. Jesus, I'd sleep for a week if I was that manic all day long." He grinned, and then the grin flickered slightly, a sad little expression flashing across his face for a second.

"What's wrong?" asked Tess. She knew he would tell her. He was easy to crack, she could tell. Not someone you wanted as a confident.

"It's nothing," he shrugged. He held out for a half second before continuing, "It's just Lana. She's a bit weird about little noises sometimes. More than sometimes. But she wasn't always. She went to a sleep doctor, you know? Maybe I shouldn't have told you that."

"No, I'm sure she'd be fine with it. I know that she's been a bit stressed out, a bit under the weather," Tess said. It wasn't untrue.

Magnus squinted at her suspiciously, like he was trying to decipher a code.

"I'm glad she told you. She's can be secretive about stuff. She's private. Self-contained, I guess. She's always taken care of herself. Her mother was a piece of work, from what I gather. She doesn't like to talk about it. I think they parted on bad terms. But she's tough, like I said. Anyway, lately it's like it's too much for her to take care of herself as well as the kids. I do what I can. But she can be prickly." He attempted another smile, but it was watery. Tess was a little worried he might cry. She wasn't sure what she would do if he started crying. And if Lana walked back in at the wrong moment it would look like she'd made him cry. He looked at the ceiling and blinked back his feelings. Tess could hear cutlery tapping against china. She could smell pasta sauce, tangy and salty and sharp.

Lana's face appeared in the doorway. Her face was pink from the heat of the oven. "It came out good," she beamed. Tess would have bet money that Lana's cooking always came out good.

"I'm just gonna go to the bathroom," said Tess. Lana pointed the way before scurrying back to the warmth of the ovenside.

Chapter 25.

The floorboards sagged in the bathroom, bending worryingly underneath the bottle green carpet. Damp, Tess supposed. A huge network of stains covered the carpet next to the bath, where she guessed something had leaked at some point. A rusty smell filled the air. It was surprising Magnus hadn't attended to this yet, given his area of expertise. Maybe plumbing was outside of his wheelhouse, Tess thought. She sat on the toilet and checked her phone.

She looked at a photo her babysitter, Hannah, had sent her, of Steve curled up in his pjs clutching a picture book about a duck and smiling in the weirdly stiff, self-conscious way he smiled whenever someone took a photo of him. She texted back, washed her hands and fixed her hair in the mirror, pushing some of the flyaway strands back inside their scruffy plaits. She rarely took it out of the braids. Sometimes she pinned them up, milkmaid style. That was the extent of her hairstyle repertoire. Her hair was long. She knew it was too long. It took forever to wash and forever to dry. It had sneaked up on her, gotten long while she wasn't looking. And then it was so long that it seemed a shame to cut it.

Tess threw the braids over her shoulders and tried to focus on the problem at hand. Something was wrong with Lana. With her friend. She was supposed to help her. Because nobody else could. Because the something was something not natural. She looked at her reflection and thought that the woman in front of her, with her small round face and untidy hair, didn't look like the kind of person who could do things like that. Maybe once. Not since the birth. She wasn't certain anymore. She had believed in magic and in her ability to restore balance, and now it all felt like something incomprehensibly big. So big that it would never notice her down on the ground. Magic had become something vast, and people had become small things fit only for getting chewed up in the cosmic mechanism.

The lighting was wrong in the room, she thought. The bulb was too orange, almost brown, and it flickered like an old dimmer turned to just the wrong point. Tess' eyes looked dark. She didn't know those eyes. She leaned in closer to the mirror. They were not her eyes.

She blinked rapidly. They were still not her eyes. And suddenly it was not her face at all. The hair was dark and long, the eyes tired, the face freckled. It was Lana's face. But there was something wrong with it. It had a greenish underwater hue and it glowed faintly. The face was looking at her, unmistakably, but in an unfocused hazy way. The mirror face could not see Tess seeing her back. Tess swallowed her fear and tried to look past the face, keeping it together, feeling her pulse pounding in her neck and praying it didn't show. She tucked a strand of hair behind her ear, just to do something, and stepped away from the face in the mirror.

It came to her in a second, now blindingly obvious. She felt so stupid for not realising. The smell in the air wasn't rust. The stain on the carpet wasn't from water damage. It was blood. It was Lana's blood. There was a blood curse on the house.

Her heart didn't slow for the remainder of the evening. She did her best to eat the pasta Lana had made, but it might as well have been a bowl of ash. She tried to talk and to be social, but every little sound, every draft, made her think she was having a heart attack. Her voice was high and too fast. She tried to pass it off as too much caffeine, and laughed and made a self-deprecating joke about her jittery hands when she spilled pasta sauce on her lap.

There was a weird energy in the air, a prickling on her skin that felt like she had cold sores brewing all over her body. Her sixth sense, as she sometimes thought of it, her way of knowing things, was going haywire. Everything felt like a threat. She checked her phone compulsively, hoping that whatever was happening here hadn't made its way along the invisible channels connecting her phone to the babysitter's phone. There was a poison here and she couldn't bear the thought of it contaminating her own home. She knew it couldn't. After all Lana had been in her house. Lana wasn't the problem, her home was. Still, she felt like a decontamination shower after dinner would put her mind at ease.

There was a protection charm in her coat, like the Tiger's Eye she had given Lana, which that now felt as woefully inadequate as a cocktail umbrella in a hurricane. Tess' charm was a piece of obsidian that she had bought at a market stall and put straight in her pocket. Tess had never thought to take it out. It's not like she had a shortage of small, tumbled rocks. Its place was in her pocket, for her fingers to brush whenever she looked for her keys, to be squeezed when she was anxious, occasionally to be mistaken for an old piece of liquorice. Her coat was hanging in the hall, and it felt very far away. She wanted her rock, as irrational as it felt to hope that a rock could fix anything. The butter on the table in its glass dish was perspiring slightly, and Tess realised she was staring at it intently, and had been for some time.

Something was taking her measure. Tess knew if she concentrated hard, she would be able to feel it touching her hair, smelling her neck, intruding. She concentrated on the opposite, on not feeling it. It was like having an eyelash on her face that she couldn't locate, she thought, ever present but minute.

Lana was peering at her over her glass. She could see Tess trying to feel out the formless thing in the air, and to hide from it. The strangest thing was how oblivious Magnus seemed. Tess hoped the children shared his temperament. It was awful to think of them, asleep in their bedrooms while something grotesque floated on the air just outside their doors. Or not outside. She didn't want to contemplate that.

Magnus talked about the price of pears at the grocery

store yesterday. He didn't so much talk about things, Tess decided, as use things as an excuse to talk. He'd become used to filling silence, she thought. He might not have felt the threat around them, the way Tess did, the way Lana seemed to. But he had adapted to it. His job was to counter it. To fill the house with chatter and warmth and life. Lana probably owed him a great deal, Tess thought. She was sure that Lana would be in a much worse position without him. He grounded her. That was his purpose, his difficult to pin down quality. He grounded the whole house, the whole family. He kept them from slipping into the abyss. And for a second Tess felt jealous and lonely. And then she saw the wet sheen of desperation in Lana's eye, even as she laughed at something Magnus said. She forgot her jealously.

Tess managed to white-knuckle her way through the rest of the dinner, excusing herself as soon as her leaving wouldn't seem unforgivably early. The babysitter had texted her, she said, and Steve was being irritable. Maybe another tooth was making its way through, she said. She didn't like to lie. She was starting to get a headache. She didn't say that though. It felt rude in some way.

Tess shrugged on her coat, her hand going straight to the smooth black stone in her pocket. She needed the bathroom but didn't even consider going back in that room.

"I'll walk you to your car," said Lana. And Magnus made a face, a little smile that took the place of a comment about them having secret conversations. He seemed to approve, like he wanted Lana to have little conspiracies.

"See ya, Tess," he said. "It's been fun. Maybe we should all get together with the kids some time? Like a playdate but also a grown-up date? Not a date, obviously. A casual gathering."

"A casual gathering," she repeated, instead of making a joke about swinging. She'd held back on saying a lot of things. Her response to fear was often to make strange jokes that were never well received.

"Like a picnic or something. Although it's winter," he added, as though he genuinely hadn't thought of that. "Sleds and Thermoses at the park then. How old's your little one again? Nearly one, right? Never too young for sledding."

"You bet," she said, feeling that actually you could be too young for sledding.

Magnus took off his cardigan and handed it to Lana. She hadn't asked for it. But she wrapped it around herself and thanked him with a little silent gesture. They were on the same wavelength, but there was something else there, interfering with their shared space. Something was intruding on their little spousal hive mind.

It had stopped snowing. Everything was pristine white, still slushy but frozen around the edges. The worst driving conditions. Tess didn't care. The air outside was the freshest air Tess had ever breathed. She filled her lungs like air might not ever be so good again.

"Oh my god. What the fuck?" was all she could think to say. "What's wrong with the air in there? It was fine when I went in, but now I'm actually outside it's like I was being strangled in there and I didn't notice or something."

"Yeah, or something," said Lana. "That's about the scope of it. I asked you about ghosts and you told me I was imagining it." She was different out here. She was sharper. She was more the person who'd shared cake and coffee in Tess' apartment, and less the fearful woman imprisoned in her own house.

"I did not say that." Tess felt terrible about that. She very much had said that.

"Well you implied it."

"That's fair," Tess admitted with a guilty sigh. "Although, I will say, ghost is a strong word. I don't know if ghost is exactly right."

"Can we talk about it tomorrow? Not here. Coffee shop? Do you know Sunny Side? Say, half nine?"

"Yeah, I know it. Sure. I don't open 'til 11 tomorrow." Tess paused to consider this. "I don't know why I said that. Obviously, I would meet up whenever. I think this takes precedence over the maintaining of normal business hours. This is some serious shit. Like some actual shit. This is very concerning. Are you seeing my face? The concern on my face? I'm having a hard time."

"Yeah, I get that," said Lana, so sadly that Tess stopped rambling.

Tess got into her car, closed the door and rolled down the window. She looked up at Lana, who was trembling slightly, hugging herself in her huge cardigan, but smiling hopefully. She was smiling because of her, Tess thought. She was smiling because she hoped Tess could help her. She turned the key and the sound of the ignition echoed in the frozen air.

"Okay, great to see you. Take care!" Tess shouted cheerily over the engine, for anyone or anything that might be listening.

"Take care," Lana said, with none of the theatrical timbre. Entirely earnestly. Divorced from its normal meaningless pleasantry, it wasn't a reassuring thing to hear.

Tess nodded back. No promises.

Chapter 26.

Sunny Side was the only cafe that remained safe from tourists when they descended on Castor twice a year for hiking and skiing. Its entrance was unassuming. It just looked like any other house aside from its yellow mailbox with the name painted on the side. Although the greasy sweet diner smell and chefs' curses that poured from the kitchen window were a slight giveaway. While the front entrance was unexceptional, the back door opened into a red and white covered walkway that had been there as long as anyone still living could remember. The walkway snaked downhill to the riverside, and little birds made their nests in the rafters in the spring. Lana had taken the kids there so many times she'd lost count, to watch the water, whatever the season.

Today it was cold. The planks of the covered walkway would be icy and treacherous. They had already been worn as smooth as glass with age, and the steps were perilously uneven, as old things tended to be.

Lana sat inside the cafe. She wasn't going down to the river today. It felt like a betrayal to be there without the kids. She would make it up to them later. Maybe she would take them to the park. Lana had fed Cody and put him back in his cot, and he had fallen asleep again while she got dressed. So she left the house with everyone inside it still asleep, which made her feel like some kind of reverse burglar. Seb didn't normally sleep in. She could only guess he had been up all-night listening to the grown-ups talking.

Lana chose a booth. A table for two was too intimate. She wanted a little bit of space to properly unpack everything, to air everything that needed to be aired. She wanted elbow room, though she wasn't entirely sure why. But it was busier than she had counted on, and Tess was late and now she seemed like narcissist who had insisted upon a huge table for one. Larger parties were narrowing their eyes at her from across the room.

179

The diner had been redecorated only once, the way Magnus told it, to a faux 50s theme, over a decade ago. But they hadn't bothered to get rid of the old rustic mountain lodge theme and the two co-existed awkwardly side by side. Baby blue Formica clashed with heavily stained shiplap boards. A taxidermy moose head stared out over the jukebox. Lana fidgeted with the Tiger's Eye stone Tess had given her, turning it over in her pocket. It didn't seem to do much good beyond being cool and smooth and something for her hand to do. *As usual, it's the thought that counts.*

The bell over the door jingled merrily as Tess walked inside. Lana waved her over to her booth.

"Where's Steve?" asked Lana.

"Hannah stayed over. That's my babysitter. She's watching cartoons with him. She's going paddleboarding today but not until later."

"Jeez, in this weather?" Lana was still wearing her scarf.

"She's crazy," said Tess.

Tess took off her coat, revealing an impressive array of crystal pendants.

"You hit it off with a gem miner?" asked Lana.

"Shut up," said Tess affectionately. "You can never have too many crystals. Or that's my hope anyway. I barely slept last night, you know? And I had to smudge the whole apartment, with sage. I basically stayed up all night consulting my books."

"Consulting your books?" repeated Lana.

"I did also consult Google," Tess admitted.

Their waitress appeared beside the booth, giving them both a thousand-watt smile. She was in her early twenties, Lana guessed, and looked like she'd never once been tired or ill or stressed.

Tess was looking hard at her menu. Lana had had plenty of time to think about what she wanted. She wanted coffee. She always wanted coffee, and scrambled eggs and tofu bacon. She wanted these things to be hot, screamingly hot. Hot enough to burn her. But they wouldn't be. They would be lukewarm like everything else. Things didn't stay hot for very long around her. It had taken her a long time to accept that because it seemed so profoundly strange and also like something she might easily have imagined. But it was real. She knew that now. She had accepted it. Orders scribbled down, the waitress pushed her pad back into her apron and flounced away joyfully.

"She's got a spring in her step," said Tess. "She makes me feel bad for feeling bad."

Lana laughed. "I know. I don't think I was ever like that. I've never been peppy. I feel like I missed out on something."

"Maybe she's just faking it. Although I've been a waitress and, if she's faking it, I'm impressed. That's worth a substantial tip if you ask me."

Their coffee arrived almost immediately - a latte for Tess, and black filter for Lana.

"Free re-fills," she explained, raising the cup.

"Okay. I have so many questions," said Tess, banging her cup down a little too hard on the table.

"Shoot," said Lana, cradling her coffee cup.

"So, the first thing is; what the shit happened in your bathroom? That was blood all over the carpet, right? It felt like blood."

"Why did you feel a stain on my carpet?" asked Lana.

"No, I mean I felt that's what it was. It seemed like blood. The air was metallic."

"Is that because you're magic, or do you think the average guest would be able to tell it was blood?"

"I'm not magic. But probably the average person wouldn't guess, no. I thought it was damp at first."

"Sounds like I need to remodel the bathroom," said Lana. "There's usually a rug over it but I guess it shifted."

"Forget the stain. It's what caused it that's the problem. I think. It's your blood, right?"

"You're good. It's from when I had Cody. You should

be a detective. A magic detective. I'm pretty sure I've seen that show."

"Again, not magic." Tess paused to sip her coffee. "I think it's a curse."

"Someone cursed me?" asked Lana, a little too loudly.

Lana realised that their waitress was standing behind her, a plate in each hand, unconvincingly pretending she hadn't heard them.

"Thanks, this looks great," Lana mumbled as the waitress set the plates down. She gave Lana a pitying smile and left them to it.

"She thinks I'm crazy," Lana said with disinterest, deciding what she wanted to eat first.

"Yeah," said Tess gently.

"What were we saying?" Lana took a bite of her tofu bacon. "Oh yeah, so I've been cursed?"

"Maybe. But that's not usually how these things work. I've never known a direct person-to-person curse to be even remotely successful. You can't really hex people like in the movies," Tess explained, pouring maple syrup on her pancakes. "Not that I've tried!" she added hastily. "I've just seen it attempted. Anyway, they're more often things, like, manifest naturally, over years, over decades sometimes. And then something happens, some catalyst that comes just at the exact worst moment, but the perfect moment, and - " she clapped her hands together, "you got a curse."

"So, the catalyst?"

"Could have been you nearly bleeding out in the bath. Like that must have been a serious amount of blood. Sounds fairly distressing." Tess forked up a wedge of maple drenched pancakes and shoved it into her mouth.

"I guess," said Lana dreamily. "I don't really remember it." She could still feel the warm, oil slickness of the blood on her legs sometimes. On her hands. "And what about the other bit? The part where it starts forming? Manifesting."

"Family trauma? Unnatural deaths? General strife? Take your pick. It can be as vague as something in the air. It can be a place with too many scars. That's why I said to you that a ghost is more likely to be a state of mind. That's how it can start out. From what I was reading, something like you're experiencing is much rarer. I mean, I actually saw it." Lana saw that Tess's hands were trembling. "I actually saw a manifestation. In your house. In the mirror. It looked like you but so so fucked up." Her voice was trembling too.

"You saw her?"

"*You've* seen her?" asked Tess, the trembling subsiding immediately in favour of bewilderment.

"Her name is Allie."

"You've spoken to her!?"

"Hey, come on ladies, use your indoor voices," said a tired looking man in a trucker hat at a nearby table. "Some of us are trying to chase away a hangover."

"Sorry," said Tess, before turning back to Lana.

"Lana that is not good. You can't speak to it. Or her. Whatever. That'll give her more purchase."

"Oh."

"Oh!?"

"I wish I knew that sooner. Because we have talked, a lot. We've had literally hours and hours of conversation. She knows everything about me. Except that I'm now really scared of her. I try not to let her know that." Lana tried not to let even herself know that. "It was fine at the beginning, but she's turned . . . strange. She used to look just like me and now she looks . . ."

"Like a monster."

"Yeah," Lana whispered.

"It's not your fault," said Tess. "You don't owe her anything. She's not even really real. She's most likely just some projection from inside your brain."

"But she's not," Lana insisted. "She's separate from me. We're not the same. We have slightly different

183

memories. Our pasts happened in different orders. We got out of step at some point. She doesn't have kids or a husband or – Why are you making that face?"

Tess looked equally alarmed and reluctant, like she was trying to keep back an even worse expression.

"That's really not good. If she's more than a projection . . . if she's a shadow . . . I'm out of my depth on this one. If she's autonomous, an actual self-governing intelligence . . . That's really not good. Did she say why she's here?"

"No. I asked a bunch and she kept giving me non-answers so I gave up."

Tess stared into her coffee, swirling it with a long spoon. They sat in silence for a moment. Lana wondered if it would seem strange if she resumed eating her breakfast. It was only half finished, but it didn't feel like a good time to eat scrambled eggs. She flagged down a passing waitress for a coffee re-fill and sipped it while it was still hot. Tess said nothing. She didn't even look up. Lana was a little worried she'd broken her somehow. She tentatively returned to her scrambled eggs.

"It's the divergence," said Tess, so suddenly that Lana dropped her forkful of eggs. Tess drained the last of her coffee, looking triumphant. "That's the curse. The divergence. The moment you two split. There's always a clue with these things. Find that point. I'll bet money that's when this thing spawned. And it fermented on its own until your traumatic and bloody labour pushed it into this world, creating your doppelganger." Tess grinned triumphantly and returned to her pancakes.

It made sense. Even though Lana didn't want it to. She had a feeling she knew what the divergence was. The worst thing that had ever happened to her. The worst thing she'd done. *Time to pay the piper.*

"Except she says she's from another reality. She wasn't created. I didn't create her."

"If she's from another reality, where's the rest of her?" asked Tess.

Chapter 27

Talking to Tess made Lana feel better. Tess made her feel the opposite of the way Allie made her feel, which was guilty and miserable and like she was going slowly insane. She tried to keep that strength with her as she entered her home. She envisioned the positive energy circulating around her body even as the cold flooded through her at the threshold, like stepping into an industrial freezer. She envisioned the energy as warm and sunshine yellow, sparkling in her veins, protecting her.

Seb immediately barrelled into her knees, almost knocking them out from under her, and launched into a report about how his father had set off the smoke alarm and burnt the waffles.

"I looked away for a second, ya little nark!" came Magnus' voice from the kitchen. Lana ruffled Seb's hair. He smoothed it back down and grinned at his mother.

"We watched cartoons. And Emmy put Legos in the toilet," he said. "I got them out with a spatula. We put the Legos in the dishwasher. Will they be okay in the dishwasher? Dad says they will, but I think they will melt." He didn't seem particularly concerned whether they melted, merely curious. That was his way. He liked to air his hypotheses so that he could say "I told you so" later, and everyone would know he was the first to suspect.

"I guess we'll see," said Lana. "My spatula better be in the dishwasher too."

"Dad said you went to Sunny Side with your friend. Did you have ice cream sundaes without me?" He looked suddenly horrified.

"No, kid. We didn't have ice cream sundaes for breakfast. We had grown up food and coffees."

Seb was suddenly profoundly uninterested and walked away abruptly. Emmy appeared, wearing Magnus' rubber boots, which reached up to her thighs. She was shirtless and had a pair of Seb's underpants around her neck like a cravat.

"I'm pirate," said Emmy, beaming. She clomped away unsteadily.

Lana found Magnus hunched over the kitchen counter, chipping burnt batter out of the waffle maker with a butter knife.

"You'll scratch the Teflon off," said Lana, taking the knife from him.

He straightened up and cracked his back.

"Why don't the plates come out of this? It's impossible to clean. How hard would it be to make something with detachable plates? I hate these stupid counter-top appliances that only make one thing and can't be cleaned," he complained.

"You hate the waffle maker, but you like the waffles," said Lana.

"True," he said graciously. "I got some good ones before it went to shit. The kids don't really care if the waffles are burnt or raw. Some of them were burnt on the outside and raw in the middle so that they tore in half when I opened the thing. They liked those best, I think." He glowered at the waffle maker. "I thought they'd make a good ice cream sandwich, but I figured that was too luxurious for breakfast."

Magnus folded his arms over his chest and leaned back against the kitchen counter. Lana plugged in the waffle iron and poured a little water in it, to steam off the scraps of charred batter.

"I'm sure Seb would have been happy," said Lana.

"Did you have a nice time? What did you guys talk about? Did something happen last night? There was a weird vibe. And Tess just rushed off. Was her little boy okay? Steve? I can't get over him being called Steve. Who calls a baby Steve? Not Stephen. Stephen's fine. Steve," Magnus laughed.

"I think it's so cute. Little baby Steve. He was fine. I guess he had a hot tooth or something. We just had more stuff to talk about. Girl stuff."

"You guys got a secret project?"

"She's just still kind of new in town. And still kind of new to motherhood."

"Ah, showing her the ropes, eh? You're a good friend. She's lucky. I can tell she's sharp though. She seems like someone who learns fast. Assimilates fast."

Allie was there. Lana hadn't noticed her. It wasn't so much that she appeared from nowhere in a flash, like something popping suddenly into existence. It was more that Lana's awareness of her suddenly appeared. As if she'd been there the whole time but camouflaged against the wall, so still that she was imperceptible. And then she would move, and Lana would notice her. Allie's arms were folded. She was smirking conspiratorially. It was the expression of a schoolgirl waiting for the teacher to turn away so she could share a joke with a friend. It was supposed to be her and Allie against Tess, Lana guessed. For now, raised eyebrows would have to do, because Magnus was still around.

Lana wafted the bad smelling steam away from the waffle iron and unplugged it again.

"Just leave that to cool down," she said. "That crap should come right off."

"We should have people over more often," said Magnus. "Like maybe more than once a decade, and maybe more than one person. It's good for you to have some friends. You need friends."

"Rude. Do you not need friends?"

"I have friends," he insisted, pretending to be wounded by her accusation. "The guys at the store. My accountant. I sometimes talk to this one kid's dad at Emmy's daycare drop-off. His name's like Dan or John or something."

"Is that the dad's name or the kid's name?" Lana moved over to Magnus, still leaning on the counter. She wrapped her arms around him, pressing her body into his and resting her head on his shoulder. Allie made a smug face and Lana closed her eyes. She knew that Allie wanted him. She'd known for a while. She couldn't have him. And she wouldn't let Allie's presence stop her from enjoying him.

"The dad. The kid's called Willow or Whippoorwill or Windmill or some crap like that," Magnus said to the top of Lana's head.

"I like Willow. Y'know I actually kind of like Windmill too," she smirked to herself.

"Well we can name our next kid Windmill," said Magnus. His body stiffened instantly. He knew he'd said the wrong thing.

Lana let it slide. She gently exhaled the breath that had caught in her throat. She didn't want Allie to see her rattled by the comment. She didn't want to think about that. She didn't want to think about giving birth again or being pregnant again. Especially with Allie in the house. There wouldn't be another one.

Magnus cleared his throat. Lana was glad she couldn't see his face. He would be making that guilty face that she hated. "Anyway, friends are good. That's what I'm trying to say. I can tell you like her. They say women . . . mothers . . . mothers with little kids . . ." he floundered. "They say it's good to have a support circle."

"Support network?" asked Lana.

"That's the one. That's what they say," he insisted.

"Do they?"

"And Tess is a tough cookie, like you. I can tell. You'll support the shit out of each other," he concluded.

"I'm not a tough cookie," said Lana. "I'm like one of those cookies that gets lost at the back of the cabinet and when you find it it's all bendy. Fit only for the trash." She was smiling, despite everything, relishing the melodrama.

"No way," said Magnus, and she could hear in his voice that he was smiling too. "You're tough. You're like those fancy almond cookies for with coffee. The ones that are too hard for kids to eat. You're just having a soft cookie time right now because Cody needs you, and because you almost bled out in the bath. You'll find your way back."

He buried his face in her hair and kissed her head. She held him close and said nothing and kept her eyes screwed tight.

***

Lana didn't find herself alone with Allie until much later that day. It happened like that sometimes, mostly at the weekend. Allie almost never tried to talk with Lana when people were within earshot. Lana wasn't sure if this was because she didn't want Lana to seem mad talking to nobody, or because Allie knew she would be ignored, and that was the thing she hated more than anything else.

Lana was alone in her bedroom, folding bedsheets hot from the dryer. There were always more sheets to wash. She was standing on top of the bed so that she could hold up the sheets at their full length. It was easier that way.

"I wish I could give you a hand," said Allie, announcing her arrival.

"Yeah, me too," said Lana, jumping down to put the neatly folded parcel into the laundry basket.

"I wanted to talk to you about your friend. The one that came over last night," said Allie, as if Lana had another friend she could be talking about.

"Well, I could see you making a face earlier, when Magnus was talking about her. You didn't like her," said Lana, selecting another sheet and climbing up onto the bed to shake it out.

"I didn't say anything," said Allie, looking up at her.

"No but you're wearing a very sour expression. You didn't fuck around with her, did you? You didn't try and scare her or something?"

"Rude. I'm not a fucking poltergeist. I'm a person. I wouldn't try and ruin your evening for no reason. And I couldn't do even if I wanted to. Only you can see me. Or did you forget?"

"I didn't forget," said Lana, folding the sheet in half.

"I'm going to be honest with you now -" started Allie.

"Are you not normally honest with me?"

"Christ. Just listen. It feels to me like, of the two of us, I'm probably the better judge of character. It's something I've always been good at. And you seem . . . not great at it. No offence. So, we're not exactly the same, right? We've got different strengths and weaknesses. My strength is taking the measure of people. Your strength is . . . something else. Let's look at the people you've chosen to have in your life. One; our father, who was a drunk and a conspiracy weirdo. Two; Magnus, who is just not very perceptive. Three -"

"Hey!" said Lana, louder than she had meant to. "Magnus is very perceptive. He's just not very meddlesome. That's one of the things I like about him. He doesn't stick his nose in."

"What else do you like about him?" asked Allie, seemingly forgetting her previous train of thought. "What are the other things?"

"I don't know," said Lana, shrugging. She dropped the sheet and sat down on the bed, cross-legged. Allie drifted closer. "He's nice. It sounds dumb but he's just nice. He's kind and he smells good and we like all the same movies. And he's big and when he holds me really tight it's like I can't hear the shit in my own head. I just melt away, and all I can hear is his heartbeat."

Allie wrinkled her nose. "You're a sap. That's another difference between you and me. You're describing a security blanket, not a husband. This morning he got maple syrup on the sleeve of his bathrobe and he licked it off, like a dog. I don't know if he's anything special."

Lana knew Allie was lying. She did think Magnus was something special. The fact that she was lying about it was suspicious.

"Which bring me to number three; Tessa," Allie

concluded triumphantly.

"It's just Tess."

"What's that even short for?" asked Allie. "Do you know?"

"No. I don't know that it's short for anything. I think it's just Tess."

"My point exactly," Allie continued smugly.

"What point? What are you talking about?" asked Lana, too loudly again. She could feel her nerves becoming frazzled.

"You don't know her. You shouldn't let someone you don't know into your house."

The door handle rattled loudly, and Magnus walked into the room. Allie didn't trouble herself to disappear, and just stood there looking at him, waiting for him to speak, as if he might speak to her.

"Who are you talking to?" he asked Lana. He stared at her hard, but his eyes twitched around the room involuntarily, following the direction Lana's body was angled toward. "And before you say 'nobody', I one hundred percent heard you talking to someone."

Allie rolled her eyes. "What, was he listening at the door?" she scoffed.

"What, were you listening at the door?" Lana said.

"No, I was coming to ask you if Seb's allowed to watch the X-Files? It's on tv and he says he wants to watch it."

"No, I don't think so. Well, it depends which episode -"

"But now I'm more interested in who you were just talking to."

Allie leaned in towards Lana. "Tell him you were on the phone."

"I was on the phone," said Lana without thinking.

"This phone?" asked Magnus, pulling Lana's phone out of his back pocket.

"God! I was talking to myself, okay? I sometimes say things out loud. It's not so unusual. I see you talking to yourself all the time, making little faces and gestures like you're talking to someone. I know you have little imaginary arguments with your parents because you always do it when we come back from their house."

Seb appeared behind Magnus, frowning performatively. He clung to his father's leg and stared a sad stare up at him.

"What's the matter bud?" asked Magnus.

"I saw a scary thing on TV," he said flatly. Turning his attention to his mother, he continued, "Dad let me watch a scary thing on TV."

Seb wandered over to his mother and curled up on the bed next to her. He looked so small, wearing pyjama shorts, odd socks and the top half of a Spiderman costume. He put his head on Lana's lap, and she stroked his hair. Emmy didn't need her like Seb did. She knew she'd not given him the attention he wanted, needed, recently. He was still a baby; Emmy was still a baby. They needed her as much as Cody did. But her attention was split between Cody and Allie. Allie, who was still staring at her, her awful pale eyes boring through Lana's body, seeding ice crystals in her blood.

"I'm fine, okay?" she said to Magnus, keeping her tone casual for Seb's sake, and for her own. She knew he wouldn't argue in front of Seb. Lana clung to him.

Chapter 28.

Tess was busy. She figured that would be the case in the run-up to Halloween. This was her busy season, she supposed. Still, her turnover in candles had taken her by surprise.

She had made a cosy corner in the shop, with sheepskin throws arranged artfully on the reading sofa, and fairy lights and stacks of books. She'd learned about hygge, the Danish art of cosiness, and she credited hygge with her recently boom in candle sales. She was selling considerably more homewares than witchcraft paraphernalia, but she had known that would probably be the case. She'd contracted a local craftswoman to make a vaguely pagan festive window display, with garlands of dried orange slices and cinnamon sticks hanging from the ceiling. When the light hit the slivers of orange just right, they were like tiny stained-glass windows. Every time she looked at them, she was reminded of how amazing and beautiful nature could be. Every time Steve looked at them, he was reminded of how much he liked oranges. Tess watched him straining to reach them. He couldn't fully comprehend distances yet. There were only things he could reach, and things he could not.

The door opened and closed, and Tess did not look up from her book. She was reading a dusty old tome she'd bought online, promising practical advice regarding hauntings, if a haunting was even the right word for Lana's predicament. The book wasn't helping at all. It was just some old Victorian nonsense, the kind of book written by charlatans who ran spiritualist parties for the upper crust. Most people who claimed expertise in the supernatural were liars, Tess had learned. People who admitted their limitations were more likely to be telling the truth but unfortunately, they were no more helpful.

"Good book?" said a voice. A male voice. She didn't get a lot of male customers. Men were much less interested in candles, as a general rule. She looked up. It was Magnus.

"Oh," was all she could think to say. She closed the book hastily. "Not so much, no. It's about ghosts. Hauntings, spiritual infestations, that kind of thing. But no, it's not very good."

"Spooky," he said, non-committally.

Tess slid the book under the counter. Magnus looked around, making an expression somewhere between confusion and amusement. His eyes settled on Steve, sitting in a collapsible playpen next to the counter. Steve stared up at him, fascinated. He had never seen someone with a beard before, Tess realised.

Magnus crouched down next to the playpen and made small talk with Steve, the kind of meaningless chit-chat people usually save for acquaintances at the bus stop. Steve beamed, loving, as always, to be the centre of attention. Tess liked Magnus. He was the kind of person to take the time to acknowledge a baby. She wanted to keep Magnus safe, him and Lana. It was ridiculous, she knew. He was twice her size, and the flannel shirt stretched across his broad shoulders made him look not unlike a retired lumberjack. But no amount of brawn could keep someone safe from the creature in his house. The creature he still didn't know about. She fought against the urge to just tell him, just blurt it all out. He wouldn't believe her, she told herself. But, then again, he just might.

Magnus straightened up.

"I like your oranges," he said. "I was looking at them, thinking how you might make something like this. Do you need a dehydrator or do you just air dry them?"

"I don't make them. The lady from the craft store made them. Opposite the place that sells ski stuff? I don't know the street names yet. I've always been bad with street names," said Tess.

He nodded. "Anyway, I was looking at them and I saw you and I thought I'd come say hi. It's different than I thought it'd be. Lana said it was homewares."

"There's homewares," Tess pointed to her cozy corner.

"Yeah, and there's also that," he gestured to a piece of wall art, an enormous five-pointed star constructed from sage, lilac, lavender, and whatever other dried leaves and sticks Tess was able to hot glue to the wall. It looked good, she thought. Maybe a tad Wicker Man. But it had taken too long to put up, and had much such a terrible mess that she wasn't about to take it down any time soon.

"Do you have a problem with it?" she asked. She knew he didn't, but it came out a little more confrontational than she'd meant it.

Magnus put his hands up in surrender and smiled disarmingly. "No problem. Just curious. I would have thought Lana would have mentioned something like that. It's interesting is all. I feel like she doesn't tell me things sometimes." He shrugged but made no effort to move the conversation away from the subject of Lana.

"What kinds of things?" asked Tess. He wanted her to ask. It was fine.

"It's like sometimes she's just walking around on autopilot. She'll sometimes sing a song for Cody and it's not any song I've ever heard. And anyway, she never used to sing songs. She mostly sort of spoken-words her way through them, like William Shatner."

He smiled to himself, then the smile fell. "I ask her questions and she's just so absent minded. We've been talking about painting the front door yellow. We had multiple discussions about it. We don't get out much. But I showed her some swatches a couple of days ago and she did not remember at all. And she made Emmy a tuna sandwich for daycare, even though it's a cold hard fact that Emmy hates tuna. It's other things too. It's just a lot of little things. And ..." he paused, waiting for a signal to keep going, worried that he should stop.

"What?" asked Tess. He hardly needed permission.

"There's this mirror in the bathroom."

Tess's blood went cold. The face in the mirror

appeared in her mind, crystal clear.

"She said she wanted to get rid of it, then she totally forgot about it. Then she wants me to put it in the car, then she wants me to put it back on the wall. I see her just staring at it sometimes, like there's something wrong with it, like it's a broken tv or something. It freaks me out." He glanced around the shop again, instinctively. He's looking for help, Tess thought. He's looking for something here to help him, just like Lana was when she first met her. The spousal hive mind again.

"Can you help her?" he asked, looking right through her suddenly. The way Tess looked right through other people. It wasn't a pleasant feeling. She felt that he could see her failures, her shortcomings. He could see the limits of her power. He could see that the universe didn't care about her. That she was forsaken.

"I can try," she said.

"That's all we can do, right?" He gave her a lopsided smile. "Well, I gotta split. See ya around, Tess. Bye little Steve." He left, brow creased with deep anxiety.

Tess took the book back out, opened it, closed it again. It was useless. She needed to get through this one on pure intuition. That was the case with most things. Or at least anything besides putting up shelves or doing taxes. Those things required detailed, step-by-step instructions. This wasn't like that. There was no IKEA manual with handy little pictograms for getting a ghost out of a house, out of a reality. It wasn't like assembling furniture. The idea of furniture hung around in her head, settling in. The ghost was in the fibres of the house, like mould, like a lingering smell, like sickness. Was there a treatment? A medicine? No, that wasn't it. The idea stayed, amorphous, like something recently forgotten. Something important.

She closed her eyes, resting her palms on the counter to orient herself. Steve's babbling, the sound of people chatting outside, her spatial awareness, all faded to nothing. She held on to the vanishing smoke trail of the idea, the important thing. The thing about the furniture. Shelves. The house. Lana. The mirror. *Mirror, mirror on the wall, who doesn't belong on this plane of existence at all?* She opened her eyes. She had to get that mirror.

Chapter 29.

Allie had always known darkness. There was a hole deep in her heart and there always had been. Had it been carved out over the years or had she built herself around it? Which came first?

It was the source of everything bad, and Lana had it too, she was certain. The well of poison. Everything awful became condensed into a black droplet of some corrosive substance, and into the well it went. And eventually it would brim over. That's what happened to their mother. That's what happened to Allie. Lana hadn't reached that tipping point yet. It was strange, Allie thought. She would have thought Lana had suffered more than she had. She endured their mother's when she was just a teenager. That felt like something that would make the well brim over. But apparently it hadn't. Maybe it had saved her. Maybe their mother was her own kind of poison. Maybe she was down there at the bottom of the well.

Maybe it was the kids that made Lana different. She had something to live for. They were so cute and so funny, even when they were red faced and screaming about something that really didn't matter at all. They were spoiled children, Allie thought, but that's the way it needed to be. If they were hers, and in a way, they already were, she would give them anything and everything. They had gentle lives, they had gentle souls, and it felt like the most important thing in the world to keep it that way.

She did worry about Lana though. She didn't seem well. She didn't seem completely sane. She worried about how close Lana was to her breaking point. Everybody had one. Everyone in their bloodline anyway.

Allie couldn't remember much of her own reality. It worried her sometimes how quickly it had faded to a tiny distant point. Then again, what did it matter? She preferred to look forwards. If it wasn't for that cursed mirror in the bathroom, she would never have to think about it at all.

She would never have to think about her own version of the house, with its white walls and stale air and blood on the floor.

She remembered she'd been lonely, and it had caused a profound unwellness. Allie thought it was self-indulgent to be upset by loneliness, so she never looked at it. She left it alone and it festered beneath the surface, turning hope to dust. And slowly the acid from all her old wounds rose right up to her throat, choking her. That feeling had been everything. All-consuming flames. Now it was nothing. It was good, she supposed. It was better.

Everything in this reality was fresh. Her old life was just a dream and now she was awake. The problem was that everything had the same clarity. Lana looked at her sometimes like she'd said something strange, like she'd forgotten something. But it wasn't that. It was that everything had the same freshness. It was difficult to remember the sequence of things when the memory of something months prior was just as bright as something unfolding before her eyes.

The concept of 'now' was difficult. Sometimes she was invisible, and Lana didn't see her. And she couldn't be sure which things she had observed in secret. There was a time, when she had first broken through to Lana's world, that Lana hadn't been able to see her at all. She thought it would probably be best if Lana didn't know about that time.

She hadn't had the house long, her own version of the house, before she visited Lana. She got a phone call to say her father had died. She had been in a meeting, or some other room with people gathered around a big table. She didn't even know he'd been alive. She had hardly known him, so she couldn't say she was sad. But there was a feeling of something. Like all the people before her had died. Like someone was calling her number. A feeling like she was next. Allie had become the last of her line. A child is supposed to know the death of their parents. It was the right way around. But it was also wrong. It wasn't supposed to be like this. The only thing she had known about her father was that he was gone, and then the only thing she knew about him was that he was dead.

She had inherited his house, if she wanted it. She hired people to empty it before she got there. She didn't want to know him. She didn't go to his funeral. And when she arrived to look at the house, to see what the resale value might be, every wall was smooth and white. They had only painted inside the house. They left the front door as it was. It was red and scratched and Allie hated it.

Allie took a little time off work and drove up from the city. It was spring and the flowers were in bloom, but she barely noticed them. She made a series of appointments with realtors over the coming weekend. She brought a camp bed with her and put it in one corner of what she assumed was the living room. Allie didn't want to stay in a hotel, didn't want to get to know Castor. She brought her laptop, some clothes, not much else. She couldn't say why she'd even gone there, or what she was hoping to find. There was nothing. It was empty. She had requested that it be that way.

On the first night, staring up at the ceiling from the creaky camp bed, she became convinced the house was haunted. The way the light moved through the house felt strange. The mirrors had all been left on the walls for the listing photos. It made an empty house seem more saleable, made it seem bigger. But it was too big. The mirrors had been polished so professionally that they looked more like windows, and Allie found that her eyes started to avoid them.

It was too quiet. In the daytime, hikers passed by the window, heading for the mountain trail, their boots crunching on gravel. But in the nighttime, it was eerie. She was used to the ambient noise of the street outside. Her ears whined, making up sound to keep her brain engaged, to keep her thoughts at bay. It was too quiet and too dark.

She was sure there were mice under the floor. She could hear things scratching. It was so quiet that she had no choice but to dwell on every little sound, every whisper of a leaf blowing across the deck outside. Odd crackings and whistlings from up the mountain. And all the little creaks and scratches and whispers bled into each other, and they began to sound like voices.

She thought about her parents, and the misfortune that had followed them. Allie remembered realising the house was a spider's web, that it stuck more the more she struggled. And she didn't remember much after that, except that she'd followed the whispers down a hole and ended up in front of the bathroom mirror. Something warm and bright was vibrating inside it. She thought it was the white light she'd heard about.

But it was a different side of the coin, a shinier side.

There was blood on this side too, and red water running over the side of the bathtub.

She could probably have left the way she came. She could feel the window closing behind her as she watched Lana labouring and Magnus shouting hysterically. She didn't feel like leaving. There was nothing back there, just a room growing cold. It was warm here.

She stayed in new place, the new reality. She blew around the hallways and in between rooms like so much dust, just watching, with no particular aim to be seen or to interact. It was nice. There was no pressure. It was like a vacation from the demands of being anything at all. She was just a dream that had become conscious. The sharp things from her reality were nothing here. She watched Lana and the kids going about their business and came to know them. She learned that Lana liked to read when it was quiet enough, when she had a minute. She would read just a few lines of a book, or half an article on her phone. Allie didn't know how she could keep things straight in her mind, taking in tiny little fragments like that.

She read stories to the children. The middle one,

Emmy, would get up halfway through the story to play a game. The eldest, Seb, was more patient. He would until the end of the story, then asked for another. Lana remembered everything the kids did during the day, anything that was funny or noteworthy. She remembered every drawing or Lego creation they were proud of, and then relayed this to her husband when he got home. And she baked a lot. She liked to make special little cookies for occasions. Lana didn't seem to get on especially well with anybody, but she left the house with trays of baked treats cocooned in plastic wrap for Seb's school functions. If there was a fair or a party, Lana would contribute something. That was her way of interacting. She gave people her time, rather than her actual presence.

Allie watched the children too. She didn't really like children, as a rule, but it was different with these particular children. She wouldn't have minded having a kid like Seb. He had focus, and he was smart. He would go places, she knew, so long as he didn't get sidetracked by anxiety. She could see the seeds of anxiousness in him. He liked things to be a certain way. Emmy wasn't like that, she was messy and loud and she didn't care who knew it. Cody wasn't like anything at all. He cried sometimes and puked and pooped and laughed and slept. Allie was glad sometimes that she couldn't smell. She would bet money that the house did not smell good, and probably hadn't for a long time. People with kids didn't realise how bad their homes smelled, she had noticed.

She tried to be charitable though. She tried to cut Lana some slack. It looked tough, balancing everything. The older kids drew pictures, they chattered to themselves and to each other. Sometimes Allie watched them when they were asleep. She had found that whatever she was now, she didn't sleep. She lay down on the bed when everyone was out, staring at the ceiling in the bright sunlight. She closed her eyes even, but she didn't sleep.

She came around to Magnus quickly. She didn't initially

understand him, or why Lana had chosen him. Allie wouldn't have. She wouldn't have looked at him twice. She hadn't had many good relationships. A couple that had lasted more than a year. But she found it hard to share herself. She liked to maintain equilibrium and jumping headfirst into a relationship on nothing more than hope felt like a bad idea. She hadn't found anyone worth upending her life for. She had immersed herself in her work and in curating a beautiful apartment. Except the longer she spent in Lana's reality, the less she remembered about her career. It had involved diagrams on unmanageably large sheets of paper, and little grey models of buildings. She was sure she gave presentations. She was sure she had worn a suit, that had maybe been blue. She remembered nothing at all about her apartment, except that it contained the same diagrams and little grey models. But she remembered going out for drinks after work, wearing red, to cool night spots in the city, with men who also wore suits and worked in tall buildings. They merged in her head into one man with shiny hair and crisp edges, holding a glass with one huge ice cube in, and laughing in a way that showed a lot of teeth.

Magnus read books, watched movies, read books about movies and watched movie adaptations of books. He listened to records with huge headphones, the kind with thick, coiled wires. He had a desk in the corner where he occasionally sat, sometimes with a slice of cold strudel, looking at receipts. He seemed at home in the suburbs. He had his space, he had his things, and his family. He was not the kind of man to visit cool night spots in the city. Allie went to touch his shoulder sometimes. Occasionally she thought he almost responded. He would pull a face like someone trying not to yawn. She watched him lying in bed with Lana on Sunday mornings, chatting and giggling about stupid things until the children ran in to jump on him. Together they were annoying, and hokey, like most married couples.

But she came to like Magnus. He had a quality. Lana felt like the heart of the household, but Magnus was the pulse that kept it alive. He brought life and warmth and reassurance. Allie wanted to touch that pulse, that heartbeat. She wanted it to breathe life into her, to give her substance.

Chapter 30.

Lana hoisted the mirror up onto one hip and pressed Tess's doorbell. The mirror was wrapped in a blanket. *So it doesn't break. No other reason.* Tess had asked her to bring it. Allie had asked her to get rid of it: she'd gently suggested it, then firmly suggested it, then taken control of Lana's body and tried to put it in Lana's car.

Tess was onto something. *So maybe it's not just about it breaking.* It was something like not wanting the mirror to see where it was. Lana worried slightly that Allie might be able to see her through it. Although if that were the case, why would she want it put in the storage unit? Allie didn't want the mirror. It made her uneasy. Allie had been pleased when Lana told her that she'd decided to get rid of it after all. Lana felt guilty, like the worst kind of double-crosser. But lying to Allie felt like a small confirmation that at least Allie didn't seem to be able to read her mind. She had no idea what Lana was going to do. Then again, neither did Lana. Not really. She just knew that Tess had asked for the mirror, and she had brought it.

She felt ridiculous, standing outside Tess's building, at the mercy of the intercom, worried somebody would see her with the mirror and think … *what?* Nobody knew what was going on, least of all Lana herself. She wanted to get inside. She didn't want to be holding the mirror anymore. She didn't want to hold the thing that scared the person that scared her.

Tess's crackling voice filtered through the speaker, just the end part of something.

"-lo? Can you hear me?"

"Yeah, it's me," Lana replied.

"-never works right. Come in."

The was a buzz and a click as the lock released.

Lana heaved the mirror up the stairs to Tess's apartment. It was heavier than she remembered it being. Or she was weaker. Either option felt portentous.

Tess opened her door. She was always dressed the same, Lana thought, more or less. She was wearing mismatched socks, different shades of black, and one of her shapeless black dresses. Combined with her long, splintered braids, she looked like a child wearing her mother's t-shirt. There was a comforting aspect to her sameness, her predictability. In a world where it was possible for people to slowly transform into luminous green monsters, Lana liked when people were reliably the same. She liked that about Magnus. He was always dressed like it was autumn and his hair always looked like he'd come in from the wind. Tess was similar. She always looked like she had got dressed in a rush, with her scant makeup and slept-in pigtails. But she exuded a vibe of easiness, like she'd never actually rushed in her life.

Lana shuffled past her into the narrow hall, turning her parcel sideways. She didn't want to bump it, didn't want to disturb it.

"You brought the mirror?" asked Tess.

"Uh... yes. That's what this is." Lana held up the rectangular object wrapped in a blanket patterned with cartoon sea-lions. "What did you think this was? Did you think I'd commissioned a portrait for you?" Lana felt her heart pounding in her throat, squeezing her words as she spoke.

"I don't know. I was just checking. I'm on edge."

"Me too. By the way, this is Emmy's blanket, and she very much wants it back. I just didn't want it breaking in my car. That's all I need. Seven years bad luck on top of the bad luck I'm already suffering. Is it seven years?"

They were distracted by Steve suddenly hurtling into the hall, clinging onto a baby walker, and crashing it straight into the wall. He let go and tumbled onto his backside, looking distressed.

"God damn that thing!" shouted Tess. "Someone from the baby group gave it to me. I have no idea why. I didn't ask for it. They thought Steve should get started with learning to walk and they had it laying around and . . . I don't know, somehow I ended up with it here. There's no room! I don't need him cannonballing around on that thing. And it's not even helping him to walk. He's not learning to walk, he's just learning to smash into walls and cupboards."

Steve stared at Lana, blankly. He was deciding whether he was supposed to cry, searching her face for a cue. Lana kept her gaze stony. She had played this game many times. He eventually peeled his eyes away from her and turned to his mother. Tess affected a sympathetic frown. That was what he was looking for. He burst into tears.

Tess scooped him up, gently shushing him. She balanced him on one hip, one hand supporting his back, and he buried his face in her neck.

"It's okay, bud. It's too fast for you, huh?" With her free hand she opened the door to what Lana guessed was a broom closet, and threw the walker inside. It tumbled loudly over metal buckets and cans of paint and settled somewhere amongst seldom-used things. Tess walked through to the kitchen, beckoning Lana to follow.

Coffee was already set out. Lana leaned the mirror against the wall and took a seat opposite Tess. Steve, bored with sympathy, eased himself onto the floor and started army crawling in no particular direction, a little bit forward, a little bit back, barely moving but absorbed with the task of trying.

"Should he be able to walk?" asked Tess. "Or crawl? He kind of just does this. This wriggling thing. If I stand him up and put his hands on something he'll sort of stand in place for a while. And he can fall over in a direction with the walker. I don't know if I'd call it walking. It runs away with him and he can hang on for a while."

Lana shrugged. "They say they're either walkers or talkers. Like they can either walk early and take longer to learn to talk, or vice versa. I don't know if that's true though. I've had all early walkers and it's nothing to aspire to. It just means more things get broken sooner. He seems happy. Just let him learn in his own time. He'll be fine."

Tess poured coffee and they sipped it in silence.

"Where are your kids?" Tess asked, suddenly realising Cody's absence.

"They are all at the in-laws' with Magnus." Lana grimaced. "It's fine. I'm making a face but it's fine. It's just they don't really get kids. They don't really understand their ways. It's a very clean house and it's very tidy and kids are just . . . the opposite of those things. Plus, I'm pretty sure they think I'm having an emotional breakdown. I try really hard to look like I'm keeping it together, but then my eyes get all wet. I say it's dust mites but there's not a single particle of dust in that house. Sometimes Magnus tells them things. I really wish he wouldn't."

"Well, he told me about the mirror," said Tess.

"What did he tell you?" Lana felt a cold stab of something like betrayal.

"That you do weird things sometimes and you don't seem like yourself. That you've tried to get rid of that particular mirror, the mirror I saw her in. The ghost. He's just looking out for you," said Tess, realising as she said it that she wished someone would look out for her. If she was in Lana's situation, there'd be nobody to support her, to help watch over Steve. She missed Emily again, irrationally, because she would be less than useless in this situation. She'd already abandoned Tess; she'd already abandoned Steve. That was an emotion to shelve, she decided. It wasn't the time.

"Allie," Lana reminded her. "I don't think she wants to be thought of a ghost. She's not really a ghost. She's just a something. But I think she was a person at some point."

"Yeah, like a ghost. You've defined a ghost," said Tess flatly.

"Maybe," said Lana. It was time to tell her the rest. *Or some of the rest. It's now or never.*

"That thing Magnus said about me being not myself?

Well, that's because I'm actually *not* myself. Those are the times when she's driving."

She knew Tess was right about Magnus. As much as it annoyed her, he was just trying to help. He told Tess what was going on, even if it seemed weird, even though he knew it would annoy Lana, in the chance that she might know what to do. She should do the same. It was embarrassing somehow. Tess had told her not to speak with Allie, not to tell her things, not to let her get purchase. She'd given her the ultimate purchase. She'd let Allie live inside her body. She was supposed to keep a safe distance, stop Allie from getting everything. But she had failed. There must have been something she could have done differently. Tess would have done things differently. Still, it was done, and there was nothing to gain from keeping it a secret.

"Driving? What do you mean?" asked Tess. But Lana could tell from the hard glint in her eyes that she already knew what she meant.

"Driving my body. Walking around inside my skin, talking to people, doing stuff." Lana couldn't quite meet Tess's eyes. She looked into her coffee instead.

"And where are you?" Tess asked, no emotion in her voice. "You're a passenger?"

"More like I'm unconscious in the back seat. It only happens when I'm already asleep. I'm not sure. I just wake up and I'm somewhere random. Often I'm in the middle of a conversation or..." she trailed off, clenched her jaw. *She doesn't need to know absolutely everything.* "And I think she actually pushed me out one time when I was awake. I passed out. But she says she didn't do anything."

"You believe her?" Steve looked back at Tess, puzzled..

"I don't know," Lana said, quietly. "Why would she lie? It's not like I can do anything about it anyway. I know that she knows that I know she's slipping in now and then. Sometimes she says she's just letting me rest."

"That is bullshit," said Tess bluntly. She picked up her

cup, hand shaking, eyes blazing, then set it down again. "It's bullshit. She's not trying to help you. She's trying to replace you. I thought the worst thing she could do was drive you crazy. Maybe hurt you. Maybe. If she found a way to directly engage. But this is so much worse than that. You're being remarkably calm. That's freaking me out more than anything else. Aren't you scared?"

"Of course I'm scared, but I'm used to it. I'm scared all the time. But it's not sustainable. It's at a point where it's hard to escalate. I'm scared for the kids mostly. I can resign myself to whatever's going to happen to me. But I'm worried for the kids, and for Magnus."

It was true. Lana had made her peace with mortality the night she'd gone into labour with Cody. She knew there was too much blood. She knew it would end badly. It hadn't happened. She hadn't died. But the feelings she'd gone through had been real. She had made her peace. She had bargained with whatever higher power would accept her, that she could tolerate her own death, as long as her kids and her husband were okay.

It felt like she wasn't supposed to be here anyway. Her number had come up. *But maybe Allie's hadn't.* She knew it was dangerous to think like that. She knew it was defeatist and miserable. But there are rational thoughts, and there are base feelings. The idea that maybe Allie deserved a place at the table, and maybe she didn't – that was a feeling. The idea that it should be otherwise, that Allie should disappear, and Lana should continue – that was a rational thought.

"You're crazy," said Tess, snapping Lana back to reality.

"What?"

"That ghost has melted your brain or something. You'd really let a malignant spirit just scratch you out? You don't owe her shit. Sure, you're worried about your kids. I get it. But what about you? You exist too."

"I guess." Lana sipped her coffee and tried not to cry.

She couldn't untangle her feelings. They were unresolvable and building, mounting and threatening to spill over.

Tess was vibrating with righteous anger and bewilderment. She kept fussing with her coffee cup, with her saucer, with the splintered edge of the table, with the frayed ends of her hair. Then suddenly, having no further distractions, pushed herself up from the table. She skirted around the table and clamped Lana to her body in a rough, awkward hug.

Lana turned her face slightly to breathe past Tess's arm, and smelled spicy, botanical things. Tess felt warm, and she knew that she must feel as cold as stone. Tess held her close, with an almost panicked tightness, not knowing how to climb down from the situation or how to make things better, just holding on because it was easier than letting go. Lana's head swam with an empty calm, and she thought she might fall asleep. She would fall out of Tess's embrace, and off her chair and through the floor and just keep falling forever. She pulled away and blinked in the brightness.

"Thanks," was all she could think to say.

Tess looked at the mirror leaned against the wall, still wrapped in its blanket.

Lana coughed and blinked and switched gears. "So what do we do with this then? Do we break it?"

"I'm not sure," said Tess, still looking at it like something might happen. "She's tied to the house, not the mirror. I mean, I'm guessing. You can't see her here right?" It hadn't occurred to Lana until then that the ghost might actually leave her house, might follow the mirror. *Was it a mistake to bring this here?* Tess looked as though she was having the same thought.

"No, she's not here. I can't always see her, you know. She's invisible a lot of the time. But I can always feel her. I think recently she's not as in control of it, the appearing and disappearing. She's started wandering about in an aimless way, appearing suddenly and walking through walls, which she never did before. It's like she's not limited by the normal human pathways through the house. A closed door or a wall used to stop her. Now it doesn't. And she repeats things. We have little bits of conversations again and again, with the exact same intonation. I don't know if she doesn't remember, or she doesn't think I remember. It's become very vague. It's become not like talking to a person," said Lana, making sense of things she hadn't really confronted in her own head. The act of forming sentences around her unformed suspicions made it feel real. It was strange to say these things out loud, outside of her head, and outside of the house.

"You can't let her win, you know. What you said before, about resigning yourself to whatever happens. You can't do that," said Tess, suddenly looking from the mirror back to Lana.

Lana was caught off guard by tracking back to the conversation she thought had ended. She had already drawn a line under that. She didn't want to talk about it, but her mouth started moving before she knew what she was going to say.

"What I think I find hardest is not looking at her. She's always wandering about, and sometimes she's looking at me, and sometimes she's just staring at nothing. But when Magnus is home, or even Seb, I can't look at her. I have to move my eyes away, or look through her, not jump when she surprises me and not follow her to see where she's going. It's hard pretending all the time not to be crazy."

"But you're not crazy. I saw her," said Tess in her softest and most reassuring voice.

"But I don't want to *seem* crazy, and I don't want to infect my family with this crap," said Lana. "And sometimes I start to think it would be easier not to. It would be easier if I never had to see her. If I never opened my eyes. I sometimes wonder if there's a time limit on how long a person can live in that fight-or-flight zone. I worry I'll have a heart attack and die and that she'll take over my body and nobody will even know what happened. Sometimes I kind of hope that will actually happen because at least then it would all be over, you know?"

"I'd know what happened," said Tess, still in her calm voice, so song-like in its gentle cadence that it felt like it had come from inside Lana's own head.

Tess didn't argue with her this time though. She didn't insist Lana deserved to triumph. Lana was glad. She didn't want to have that conversation. *We don't need to get into that, into who deserves what.* The fact that Lana had this life first didn't seem to hold up under her own scrutiny.

"Let's see what we can do about this mirror then," was all Tess said. She hauled it up onto the table, and told Lana to back away into the corner, in case her entangled energy got in the way of whatever she had planned. Lana dragged her chair over to the space between the refrigerator and the trash can and sat down, still holding a now cold cup of coffee.

Tess located Steve, on the floor outside the closet that contained his walker, and placed him in his crib in their bedroom. Lana heard her shushing him, suggesting that he take a little nap with his bear and his blanket. And then she reappeared, her expression set, all business.

"What are you going to do?" Lana asked, taking a sip of her cold coffee out of habit.

"I'm not sure," Tess admitted warily. "This may shock you but I'm very much making this up as I go along. Maybe scrying. Maybe I'll cast some stones on it. That'll scratch it though. I don't know how much that matters. Tarot. You want to do a tarot reading? I know that's not specific to the mirror but I just feel it's good to have it here with us. There's something about it."

She threw the blanket off the mirror and her face went blank.

Chapter 31.

If she was being honest with herself, Tess hadn't expected to see anything. She wasn't sure what she was going to do, but she knew Lana would probably have to leave the mirror with her overnight. Letting herself fall into a trance and staring into the reflection of her own pupils in a darkened room felt like a solid option. That had the potential to become very eerie and abstract though, she remembered. But it might have thrown up something; some lightning bolt of inspiration, a whisper that came from somewhere inside her own head. That was the kind of thing she usually did. But it had been a while since she felt the pull of such practices.

She felt forsaken, and a little afraid. Afraid that nothing would happen. Afraid of emptiness and aloneness. She hadn't even meditated in a long time. There was a pressure, having not tried for so long. And there was a feeling that, if it didn't work, if nothing happened, that her worst fears were confirmed. That there had been nothing special about her or about the universe this whole time. That she was just another cliché. Even after everything she had seen to the contrary. It was strangely easy to forget the terror of seeing the ghost face hiding under her own the last time she looked into this mirror. She was much more afraid that she was wrong than that she was right, about the lurking darkness in Lana's house.

Lana's haunting was a difficult thing to reconcile. It was terrifying in an almost incomprehensible way. It was impossible to touch or to fight. But, on the other hand, the ghost was definitely not of this world. If the ghost was real, magic could be real too. Tess felt oddly grateful to Lana, and to the ghost, just for existing. For giving her purpose, for forcing her to reconcile with her beliefs. But she forgot this gratitude in an instant, as soon as she looked into the mirror.

Tess expected her own reflection. But it wasn't there.

There was a sensation of falling forward, like her own image wasn't there to catch her, and her gaze fell past where it had expected to land. She thought for a moment that Lana had brought a painting instead, to trick her. Except the frame was the same as the mirror she had seen in Lana's bathroom, and the image wasn't something flat and made up of tangible daubs of paint. It had depth and clarity and a living texture. It was a window. She looked down into it, and straight into Lana's bathroom, the view from the mirror in its original position.

"What is it?" Lana asked, so quietly and so far away, almost from another dimension. Tess ignored her. It wasn't important, and she was so far away.

The mirror pulled her down, she could feel it sucking something from inside her heart, extruding her essence. She felt her body sway, her knees buckle. She managed to stay upright, her hands gripping the table hard even as they fought to tremble. The focal point of the view in front of her was difficult to fully see, like a detail from a dream that becomes hazier the harder you try to comprehend it. The strange perspective of looking down at something close, but also looking across at something distant made Tess feel sick, and her perception seemed to circle the bathtub, landing on firmer details around the perimeter of the room.

It was not the same, she realised blearily. The room was different. It was decorated differently. Lana's bathroom didn't have white tiles, didn't have white painted walls, didn't have splashes of red water on the floor, didn't have blood dripping. Lana's bathroom didn't have a fully clothed mannequin in the bathtub. That was odd, Tess managed to comprehend, through the distracting pounding of her own heart, through the competing urges to pass out and throw up. She allowed herself to fall a little further into the scene.

She needed to get just deep enough, and stay conscious just long enough, to figure it out, to really see. She knew the window was temporary, the kind of fleeting thing that she wouldn't get a second chance to see. She wasn't even really sure if she was seeing it now. Tess almost forgot about her body again, about her kitchen and Lana. Her knees buckled again to remind her. She steadied herself. It felt like she was getting far away from her body, like her face had become something long and snake-like and descended through the frame of the mirror. Her lungs, now very far from her, were crackling. She could hear them struggling. She made a last stab at the scene in front of her, opened her eyes as best as she could and willed the fog to clear.

It wasn't a mannequin. And she felt ridiculous for thinking that it was. It was Lana, and she was definitely dead. Her body was purplish and pale and her face was like a wax carving of Lana's real face, with her dark hair plastered spiderlike across her neck. The face was the worst of it, blank and mottled and inhuman.

Tess pulled herself away from the sight in front of her, moving further backwards and upwards than seemed possible, back to her body. She merged back with herself and felt her essence orient itself inside her body. It was not a pleasant feeling. Coolness and clarity and oxygen returned, and she realised how keenly she had felt the absence of these things. Lana was talking loudly.

"What are you doing? Is this supposed to be happening?" Lana sounded frantic, but she hadn't moved from her chair. Tess had told her not to, she remembered. Lana did what she was told. Her knees buckled again and this time she didn't manage to catch herself. She crashed to the floor. Lana was beside her in an instant. It felt very strange to Tess that it was still daytime. It felt like a long time had passed. It felt like it should be later, like coming out of a movie theatre and it's still mid-afternoon.

Tess found she was not immediately able to talk. She nodded and made little sounds to let Lana know she was okay. Tess's hands shook, her legs felt like she'd run a marathon. Lana helped her up and she took another look into the mirror. There was nothing but her own face, her own ceiling.

Lana helped her into the tiny living room, and she collapsed onto the sofa. Tess swallowed a stale taste. Lana's wide, dark eyes were fixed anxiously on her. Tess couldn't help but see the woman in the bathtub when she looked at Lana. The same dark hair. Although it hadn't really been Lana. It was the other one, Allie. That was the body she'd had before, a copy of the one she now had designs on. She'd been right, Tess thought, she was a ghost. A ghost who'd transported herself across to another dimension. It was something to do with the blood. The blood on both sides, in the same place, it had created a pathway. Or that was her best theory anyway. She couldn't be sure. How could she be?

"That was awful," said Lana, carefully positioning herself next to Tess on the sofa. "I've never seen anybody do that before. I've never seen anyone do magic."

"Yeah, me neither," said Tess thickly. She'd never felt anything like that. She'd heard people talk about trances, about seeing the future, about hearing truths from disembodied voices. She always figured those people were probably overselling it a little. Turning something vague into something people would understand. Maybe an idea came to someone, Tess supposed, seemingly from nowhere, like thoughts sometimes do when your mind is very clear. And maybe in the re-telling, this random idea becomes an actual voice belonging to a separate entity. Gives it a bit more gravitas, makes it a bit more witchy. Tess could understand the impulse, although she was more likely to dismiss her own unexplainable 'knowings' as run of the mill intuition. Still, she had her store, she did tarot readings. She understood that there was a certain amount of showmanship required.

But now she wasn't sure what she knew. Certainly, whatever had just happened didn't require any added theatricality. It wasn't performance. It was just something really horrible that had happened to her. Exactly half of her was reeling in horror. The other half was elated. However awful it was that the image of Lana's waterlogged corpse seemed to live permanently behind her eyelids, there was no more questioning in her heart, no more doubt. She knew what was real.

Everything.

"So, what happened? Did you figure it out?" asked Lana.

Tess didn't want to tell her. It felt like something she wouldn't want to hear, something nobody would want to hear. Still, it was what Lana had come there to be told. This is what Lana had been waiting for Tess to tell her since they first met. This was her mission. Her duty.

"It was your bathroom. Her bathroom. I won't paint you a picture or anything, but she was dead. One hundred percent."

Lana nodded.

"In the bathtub," she said. It wasn't a question. Lana spoke in a monotone, but her eyes were shining. "I thought maybe she was . . . *fine*. That she was fine somewhere else. Or maybe I didn't think that. I *wanted* to think that. I wanted to think there was a chance she could just go back where she came from, and everything would be okay again."

Tess jumped to an unkind conclusion, that Lana was an idiot who couldn't see what was right in front of her, and for failing to react to a danger that was threatening her whole family. Then she realised Lana wasn't an idiot. She was being honest. She actually wanted to believe that everything could go back to how it was. She was afraid of having ruined something beyond repair. Not that it was even her fault at all. She just wanted everything back in its place, and for nobody to have been hurt. Except maybe herself. She was willing to sacrifice herself to make things right. And Tess understood Lana's words from earlier, that she sometimes thought she could disappear, and Allie could take her place and everything would look alright on the outside. It was desperately sad, but Tess understood her.

"Lana, didn't you think . . .?" Tess began.

"I don't know what I thought. She said she was just visiting. I thought maybe she could go back," said Lana, suddenly frantic. Tess kept her cool, kept her voice even.

"She can't go back, Lana. There's nothing to go back to. We need to think of a plan. She needs to go."

"Maybe she could just-"

"What? Hang around your house forever until you go insane?"

"I could move. I could just move out?"

"If she knows you're going, it'll escalate things. You do not want that. That's basic hostage negotiation," said Tess.

"I could just wait a little while and -"

"No," Tess said as firmly as she could. There was no room for negotiation. "No, Lana. She needs to go. She's degrading. And then she'll get violent. And then you'll be so deep in the shit I don't know how you'll be able to fix it."

Tess didn't know that this was true. But she felt it. She had felt it as soon as she had looked into Allie's face in the mirror, the night she had dinner at Lana's. She had felt the precariousness of Allie's mind, no longer a working brain responding to the world around her, but a tangle of half-formed ideas and drives. She knew then that something had to be done and fast.

Chapter 32.

Lana was back home before anybody else. The house was empty and looming, more imposing somehow than the mountain ridge that shadowed it. She sent Magnus a text from the lawn.

He'd stopped at the library on the way home, as a treat, because the kids had been well behaved at lunch. Better him than me. The library seemed to incite some anarchist streak in Emmy. Seb was happy to sit on a beanbag and work through a little curated pile of books. Emmy felt insulted by an establishment that depended on its customers' ability to read. She raised hell, yelled and climbed up the shelves. She made steps and obstacle courses out of all the books within reach and kicked the beanbags around the room. Lana had given up on the library, which was a pity because Seb liked it. She guessed he'd had his choice of treat for some reason. Emmy would have chosen the park.

Lana thought for a minute, pretending to look at her phone in case Allie was looking at her from one of the windows. She could just head back into town. Then again, Magnus wouldn't be long. She could wait in the house for a while. It would be just her and Allie. Not even Cody to be a buffer. And she felt a pang of guilt for thinking of her baby as someone who could or should protect her from her demons. *No, she's my problem. I'll deal with her, like Tess said*

Allie wasn't there. She was usually behind the door, waiting for Lana to get home like a golden retriever. But she was nowhere to be seen.

Lana walked around the house, tidying up a little as she went, half-heartedly acting out a reason to walk in and out of rooms, acting for someone who may not even be able to see her. With most of the toys returned to their various baskets and a load of laundry tumbling heavily in the washing machine, Lana made herself a latte, using the

220

coffee machine that she almost never used. It was terrifyingly loud and it never failed to wake Cody or make Emmy scream with displeasure, so she never used it. Now was her chance, and she couldn't help grinning at the small pleasure of using the milk-frother. The thing for compressing the ground coffee in the filter had been missing when they'd bought the machine, at a yard sale years before. She'd found that the end of the rolling pin was a good enough substitute. Lana didn't know the names of any of the parts and had only a cursory understanding of the machine. But it didn't really matter. She would have bet money that Allie knew what the squashing thing was called, and the handle thing with the filter on the end that Lana thought of secretly as 'the candle snuffer'.

Allie was still nowhere.

Lana sat down with her coffee and turned on the TV. She connected it to her phone and queued a few birthday cake tutorial videos. Emmy changed her mind daily on what kind of birthday cake she wanted. Lana put her coffee down on a coaster, let her spine melt into the sofa cushions, and exhaled a breath that she felt she'd been holding in for years.

She fell asleep almost instantly.

When she woke up, only moments later, Allie was an inch from her face.

Run!

Lana screamed and scrambled away from her, falling over the back of the sofa and landing hard on her shoulder. Her arm went numb, but she could feel bruises already blooming on the bony areas that had contacted the floor. She hurried to her feet, almost falling again. A rib began worrying at her too. She scanned the room frantically, back against the wall. Allie was nowhere again.

Was that real? Was she there? Fuck! Why did I scream?

Steam was still rising from her untouched coffee. She can't have been asleep for more than a minute. Which meant that Allie had been following her the whole time, fully invisible, just waiting for her moment.

That face.

It had been Allie but it hadn't. It was more discoloured than ever, and sharp somehow. The eyes had a laser focus and they had been staring right through her, right through reality to something Lana couldn't see. Of course, Lana knew things about Allie now. She knew she had nowhere to go back to. She knew she was dead. She knew that the something in the mirror that caught Allie's attention so often was her own decaying body. Seeing that all the time, just over her shoulder whenever she lingered in the bathroom to talk to Lana . . . well, it would have been a miracle if Allie's sanity had remained intact. Lana understood, empathised, in the way that she had taught herself to do after her mother had died. But she knew that her understanding made her vulnerable. She knew there was something to fear here. And she supposed she was afraid. She had screamed.

Lana couldn't move. She couldn't do anything but swallow dryly and let her eyes roll over the room, waiting for something to jump out at her. She saw something, a flicker in the corridor, something the gauzy colour of Allie's hair, which was no longer black like Lana's, but something between dark grey and oil-spill green, reflecting light in random ways like crumpled vinyl. Lana swallowed her fear and followed.

The door of her bedroom moved minutely in a breeze that wasn't there. Lana pushed open the door cautiously just in time to see Allie's back disappear though the wall separating hers and the kids' bedroom. Lana ran back out of the room and into the kids' room next door, trying to cut Allie off. It was empty. Seb's night light was still on though the room was filled with sunlight. A little glowing blue moon with a sleeping monkey nestled inside the crescent. Lana turned it off gently. Allie shouldn't be in here, she thought vaguely.

"Where did you go today?" asked Allie's voice, so

suddenly that Lana should have jumped. But she didn't. Because she had known Allie was there, hiding.

"I went into town to see a friend," said Lana, turning on the spot, her eyes scanning the room, scrutinising every stuffed animal and Lego skyscraper and laundry basket.

"Tess," said the disembodied voice. "You took my mirror."

"You hated that mirror," said Lana, trying hard not to oversell it. "You said I should get rid of it. That it was ugly. I took it to a thrift store. I decided, when I really looked at it, I didn't much like it either." The mirror was still at Tess's house, still wrapped in Emmy's blanket, while Tess decided what to do with it.

There was no reply for a moment. The silence rang in Lana's ears. She hated it. She hated the silence, and she hated the sinking feeling of lying to Allie and she hated walking on eggshells, trying to avoid an argument. She thought of her mother. Allie was so much like her; she couldn't believe she hadn't seen it sooner. But she wasn't sure what that meant. They were the same. Both were adversarial and self-destructive and Lana had just wanted to be left alone to live a peaceful life. Lana just wanted freedom. And both of them had died. Except she couldn't move away and pretend it didn't happen this time. It had caught up with her. Her mind spiralled. That was the way her thoughts went now and then. When she really thought about what happened to her mother, and about their relationship and about that time, she was in danger of being sucked down. Sucked down the drain with her mother. She pulled herself back up. Her ears whined.

"WHY DID YOU SCREAM!?" the voice thundered, right in Lana's left ear, louder than anything Lana had ever heard in her life, louder than a passenger jet taking off, louder than anything, totally obliterating her own thoughts and reason. Lana whirled around, totally on instinct, her left ear ringing, and hurled her fist at the space she expected Allie to occupy. She didn't consider the fact that

Allie was a ghost, or that she wasn't sure where she was, or that it wasn't a good idea to antagonise her. She didn't think anything at all. It was just a motor response. It was all she had, and it was fuelled by weeks of claustrophobic pent-up fear and anxiety and guilt.

She put everything into the punch. She saw the faint glimmer of her doppelganger as she slithered away from her, melting into the cowboy wallpaper. Her fist hit the wall. And Lana had a split second to think about crash-testing, about cars crumpling against concrete walls in slow motion, about metal hoods folding like paper fans. Then she heard a pop like an empty milk carton being stomped flat. A sick feeling followed the pop. Lana doubled over, dry heaving, head spinning.

The feeling subsided, leaving being a cold shakiness and a growing white-hot pain in the first knuckle of her little finger. Lana thought of every time she'd idly snapped a twig in half. She forced herself to look at her hand. It looked okay, better than she's thought it would. But there was a horrible feeling of confusion brewing in her fingers, like they'd been put on the wrong way around. The pain continued to build. She held her damaged hand gently with her other, like it was an injured bird, and held it to her chest. She ran from the room, threw herself out of the front door and slammed it behind her.

***

She sat on the front lawn. The sun was still shining, although there was a chilly breeze ruffling the few remaining leaves on the trees. She had grabbed the blanket from Seb's bed to wrap around her shoulders as she fled his bedroom. It smelled like Seb. Like the children that Allie would never hurt. *A literal security blanket.* Lana breathed in the smell. Her hand was swelling up now, the skin darkening, bleeding beneath the skin. She didn't look at it, just kept it safely nestled behind her other arm, like she could keep it from getting worse if she just kept the air off it.

It's just not my day. Why are some days so much longer than others? I've never known a day so long. How the hell is it still the same day as it was this morning?

She just wanted it to be over. She wanted to go to bed. Not long ago, she prayed for it to be morning, she thought. She wanted the nights to be over just because they were sad and because Cody was irritable. And she had a horrible, intrusive thought, that if she were to be dead, if she were to kill herself, then there would be no more nights and no more days to wish away. They would all be over forever, at the end of everything.

She looked back at the house. A curtain twitched.

Fuck you.

She took out her phone, awkwardly navigating her left hand around her broken – and she was certain now that it was broken – right hand to retrieve it from her right-side pocket. She called Magnus and told him she'd had an accident. She needed him to drive her to the emergency room. And she needed him not to scare the kids, and if they were having a good time, she was happy to wait. She wasn't going anywhere.

Chapter 33.

Tess was aware of a buzzing – a small bothersome interference that came and went. Like a little loose something vibrating its way off the top of the dryer. And then it was gone again. She shrugged, turning her attention back to the only customer in the store. Tess didn't want to make her feel watched, but she wanted to watch her, nonetheless. She just had to be surreptitious, her speciality. The customer was a pretty redhead, thumbing through a dense volume about astrology.

The buzzing returned. It sounded to her now like a wasp spinning on its back in some dusty corner. She looked at Steve, who was licking the mesh side of his playpen and guilelessly staring at the redhead. The sound wasn't troubling him. Tess searched among the shelves behind the counter, opening drawers and shifting papers.

It was her phone. Of course it was, she chided herself. Tess's phone was only ever on vibrate, which was fine when it was in her pocket, and the pocket was on something she was currently wearing. But often her phone was lost in the folds of her duvet or left in a tote bag among the crumbs and emergency ketchup packets. She missed most calls.

Luckily, most of the time it wasn't important. Tess could tell from the several missed calls, seconds apart, that this was not one of those times. Lana's name flashed on the screen and Tess jabbed the 'accept call' button.

"Hey, how's it going?" Tess asked, knowing it wouldn't be good.

"Hey . . . It's good. It's good, yeah." Lana swallowed dryly. "No, it's not. I don't know why I said that. So, here's the thing. I broke my hand."

"You broke your hand? When? You were just at my house," said Tess.

The red-headed customer made a face but didn't look up from the book she was idly flipping through. Tess

226

could tell she was eavesdropping, and that she was a practised eavesdropper. They had that in common.

"When I got home. Nobody was there and Allie freaked me out somehow. I'm not even really sure. I think she tricked me. Anyway, I put my fist through a wall," said Lana, with a strange mix of calmness and apologetic self-effacement. She spoke like she was telling Tess about how she'd remembered someone's name wrong, or accidentally put salt in her coffee.

"Actually *through* the wall!?" exclaimed Tess, forgetting about the redhead.

"Well, not through it. Not literally," said Lana. "I guess my hand broke so it's more like the wall went through me. Anyway, it's called a 'boxer's fracture' apparently. My metacarpal snapped. Or metatarsal. Whichever one is the one in a hand. The doctor said she'd never seen this happen to a female. It's mostly young guys with anger issues. I told her I tried to punch a wasp and I missed. I don't think she believed me. I don't think Magnus believed me either. I'm in the bathroom at the moment, at the ER."

Tess decided that Lana didn't sound okay. She looked at Steve. He was in his playpen, near the front window of the store so he could watch people walking by. It was supposed to snow later. He would want to see that. Right now he was licking the bottom of his foot. He was so much safer than Lana's kids. They were in danger. It made Tess feel queasy. She felt bad for Lana herself, of course, but she was a grown woman and aware of the danger. The kids didn't know what was floating around their house. Like asbestos in the ceiling, drifting down like poison snow when the rafters shifted. It was better not to know, but it was also worse.

"Does it hurt?"

"Not as much as you'd think. It hurt when it happened. I thought I'd throw up. But it's mainly aching now, and my fingers feel kind of backwards. There's a bruise coming on both sides of my hand. It goes all the way through."

"That's awful," said Tess, unable to avoid the image of a human hand cut in half, with a bruise all the way through like a spoiled fruit.

"They're going to put a cast on it. How am I going to nurse Cody with a cast on my hand? Have you ever had a cast?" Lana asked, a little despair creeping into her voice now.

"Sure. I broke my leg when I was a kid. Fell out of a tree. Just your classic childhood capers. People signed it. I guess that's not much of a consolation prize at this point. For what it's worth, I'll sign your cast if you want me to," said Tess.

The redhead smiled to herself. It was a private smile but full of warmth, like she'd remembered something wholesome and sustaining. She should talk to her, Tess thought. No, she told herself, forget her. You're supposed to help Lana.

"We're going to sleep at Magnus' parents tonight. I pretended it hurt more than it does. I said I wanted to be closer to the hospital. I made a fuss." Lana spat the word 'fuss' like it was a curse word. "I don't want to go home. It's bad. I know this is a big ask, but can you come by? Like, come to the hospital? Magnus is here but the kids are not having a good time. Emmy keeps running away and Cody's really tired. Magnus is going to take them to his parents', then go home and get their stuff. She won't hurt him. He's safe there. But I'm still waiting for some meds. If you could pick me up maybe and drive me back to Magnus' parents' place after …" Lana trailed off.

"No problem. I'll come get you. See you soon." Tess hung up.

Tess approached the redhead.

"Hi there. I'm really sorry about this but I have to go pick up a friend from the hospital. It's kind of an emergency. Would you mind coming back another time?" Tess said, as politely as she could manage.

"Oh, yeah, totally. I understand," she said, smiling a

smile like a summer's day. The kind of day that was dwindling to nothingness in the rear-view mirror. The kind of day that wouldn't be back for months to come. She had preserved something fresh and vital to see her through the winter. Tess cursed herself for falling into that smile. There was work to do. Her brain was trying to distract her from Lana, finding something sweet and safe to explore instead.

The customer closed the book and gently placed it back on the table. Tess knew she probably hadn't meant to buy anything, she was just idling away the time. It was fine. Tess had created a nice space for idling away time. This was its intended purpose.

They both shrugged on their jackets in awkward silence. Tess scooped up Steve and stuffed him into a puffy winter onesie that made him look like a giant starfish. Then, with Steve balanced on one hip, keys clenched between her teeth, Tess flipped the sign on the door from open to closed, killed the lights and held the door open for the customer. The bell jingled behind them. Stay safe out there Tess, it seemed to say.

On the sidewalk outside, Tess fumbled the keys and dropped them. She felt a keen embarrassment that hadn't troubled her in a long time, and realised she couldn't retrieve them without putting Steve down. She stood still, staring stupidly at the keys as if she could convince them to jump up into her hand, hoping the redhead had gone away.

"It's cool. I got 'em," said the woman, stooping to pick up the keys. She dropped them into Tess' hand. "What's this little guy's name?" she asked, grinning at the baby.

For a horrible moment, Tess couldn't remember. Mercifully, it came to her.

"Steve," she said.

The woman laughed.

"That's the cutest. See you around, little Steve. And you, too." She gave a small wave and walked away in the dwindling light.

229

It was a pity the snow hadn't arrived yet, Tess thought. That would have been nice. Tess realised she had forgotten to ask her name, and she forgot to say her own name, and she actually didn't say anything at all except to ask her to leave. And, more importantly, she was supposed to be meeting Lana.

***

Tess found Lana in a waiting room at the hospital, the kind for bruised and bandaged people who couldn't leave just yet. Lana was holding a paper cone of water and staring into the distance. She looked pale and sad, but her clenched teeth made Tess hopeful that there was a shred of something like determination left underneath everything else. Her hand and forearm were encased in a hard plaster cast that looked to Tess like a white fur muff at first.

Tess sat down next to her, on a chair that was bolted to the floor. It had a cracked orange vinyl seat that looked like an old leathery tangerine. Steve was strapped to her chest, sleeping in the carrier. It was awkward to lower herself into the chair without the straps riding up, but she made it work.

"How's it going?" she said, leaning back in the chair so Steve could rest his head against her shoulder.

"Really crap," said Lana. "I hate this." She rapped her cast against the metal arm of the chair. It sounded hollow. "And Magnus is mad at me, I think."

"He's mad at you because you broke your hand?"

"He's mad at me because everything's going wrong. And he thinks it's something I could fix if I chose to. He thinks I'm sabotaging things because I won't admit there's a problem. Or something like that. He thinks I'm crazy." Lana blinked back tears and took a sudden, shuddering breath. "Which is why I need this fixed. I'm scared to go home. I can admit that. I'm scared of her. I thought it was just that I felt sorry for her, or guilty about what happened to her, but I'm scared. I'll admit to that."

"Lana, I'm sorry but I'm not sure what to do. There's not a textbook for something like this. I've never heard of anything like it before. I don't know any more than you. Honestly, I'm leaning towards burning the house down. Magnus and the kids are at your in-laws', right? So maybe that's a sign. Maybe that's your permission to go back there with a gas can and torch the place?" said Tess, aware that the reassuring tone she'd aimed for was slightly at odds with her advice. But she didn't know what else to do, or what else she could suggest.

"It's my house," said Lana, quietly. "It's the only thing I got from my dad. It's where all my kids were little babies, and where I got married. And if I burn it down, I'll have to leave town, or else be that crazy woman who burned down her own house."

She paused and then continued, quietly.

"I like this place. I moved here after what happened with my mother, and I felt safe here for the first time in my life. I'd like to stay here. And what would Magnus think? It's not like I could hide it. The fire department would figure it out. That would just confirm to him that I actually have gone insane. What about the kids? All their stuff, their bedrooms, their home, would just be a smouldering pile of bricks.

If it even worked! If it even got rid of her! What if she just got free? What if she followed me?" Lana was babbling, eyes wide and terrified.

"Okay, okay, I hear you," said Tess.

They sat quietly for a while, listening to the distant beeping of some machine.

Tess hated the hospital. She hated the smell and the memories that came floating back to her, the one where her body was gone from the waist down. She hadn't been able to leave her hospital bed to visit Steve in his little plastic box one floor above her. A nurse had suggested that her partner, and she'd put emphasis on the word partner, would be able to see him, would be able to video call her. But there was nobody. She supposed Lana had some unpleasant hospital memories too. Most people did, in her experience. It was a place where bad things happened. Steve snored against her chest, mouth open, drool soaking into her t-shirt. She felt his snores and snuffles in her breastbone. Good things happened in hospitals sometimes. It was just more emotional baggage, a term she hadn't really understood until recently. The longer she spent on earth, the heavier she felt her heart getting. It wasn't bad. It was just something that happened. Pages behind the bookmark.

"Unfinished business," Tess said aloud, without really meaning to.

"Huh?" said Lana.

"There's no textbook for this, like I said. But there's a million movies, right?" said Tess. "We're overthinking this. Why do ghosts show up in the movies?"

"Because developers built a family home on a mass grave?" hazarded Lana.

"No. Not a poltergeist. A regular ghost. Think Sixth Sense, think Ghost. The classics."

"Unfinished business," said Lana, nodding.

"Bingo. It's something unresolved. Something she didn't do in life, but something she meant to. I'll bet money it's the divergence point. It's the thing between you that's different. Whatever that thing is, that's the thing she was fated to do, and she didn't. That's why you're you and she's her. That's why you're alive and she's dead."

"You're saying this thing, whatever it is . . . You're saying there was a right and a wrong thing to do? Like a good action and a bad action? And you think I did the right thing?"

Lana wasn't looking at Tess at all. It was like a wall had slammed down between them. Something invisible and impenetrable.

She knows what it was, Tess thought. Lana knew what

the thing was, the right and the wrong decision, and she wasn't telling Tess. Lana was turning it over in her mind. Deciding what to do with the information. She didn't trust Tess, even after everything.

"I don't know that it's like that exactly. I don't want to ascribe a moral significance to the thing, whatever it might be" Tess said. "It's just a thing that happened and a thing that didn't happen. I think you know what it is. I would stake my life on it, in fact. See, I wouldn't say I can read minds, but I can sure as shit read people, Lana. You're holding something back."

It felt bad to push her, to try and intimidate an answer out of Lana. Tess, with a baby strapped to her chest, with drool on her top, felt bad about it. She didn't like being the bad cop. But she needed to know, for no reason other than she needed to. It felt like the last piece of the puzzle. The reason everything was happening, and the reason it was happening to Lana. She had to have it.

"See," said Lana slowly, eyes fixed on her cast, "the problem is... the problem this whole time has been that there *is* a moral significance to it. I know the diversion point. I've known it for a long time. But the thing is . . . the problem is . . . that *I'm* the bad twin." She was almost whispering.

"No, I'm not saying there's a bad twin -" Tess started.

"You don't need to say it," Lana cut in. "Because I know there is. And I know that it's me. The divergence point is the day my mother died. The day I let her die. She drowned in the bathtub and I let her."

Lana's shining eyes finally overflowed. She hung her head and covered her face awkwardly with her unbroken hand. Tess could see the tears running down her palm and into her sleeve.

Tess squeezed her shoulder.

"Tell me," she said. It was all she had to say. Lana had already cracked. Tess had already broken her.

"She had this nerve condition," said Lana, between

233

quiet shuddering sobs, muffled by her hand. "It's supposed to be one of the most painful things a person can have. It caused these intense shooting pains in her face, and she'd had it for years. The pain, for so long, it made her really depressed and she lashed out at me all the time. We had these epic fights . . . I don't know how much of it was this condition and how much was her. I don't know if she knew either.

She took all these anticonvulsant drugs for it. But they made her sleepy. And when she took a lot of them, and the painkillers, they knocked her out cold."

Lana straightened up and wiped her eyes. She looked straight at the opposite wall and spoke robotically, like she was delivering a prepared statement. A confession, Tess thought.

"She told me all the time she wished she was dead. That there was no reason for her to be alive. The medication had an increased risk of suicide. I read the piece of paper that came with the box one time. Plus, an increased risk of everything else.

So, one day I came home to pick up some things - I'd been staying with a friend, just to get a bit of breathing space – and she didn't answer the door. Not unusual. I let myself in. The bathroom door was closed, a light under the door, and I remember the whole apartment felt damp somehow. The air was too thick. I figured she was soaking in the tub, wet towel over her face to help the headaches, so I didn't bother her. I thought I'd just get my stuff and leave again.

But there were empty boxes, and empty bottles. I saw them here and there even thought I tried not to notice. I stuffed my clothes in a bag, and a few other things. It was so quiet that I tried not to move things around too loudly, or even breathe too loudly.

I was half out the door again when I saw the note on the coffee table. I don't know how I didn't see it before. A piece of printer paper, folded in half and propped up, like the world's worst homemade birthday card. Alana, it said. Her handwriting.

I was going to take it, but I knew it was a trap. I knew it would close around my hand and I'd never be free, I knew it. Whatever was in there, I didn't want it. So I just left. And I locked the door behind me, and I never went back."

Lana stared out of the window and away into the distance, eyes glassy and face as still as a waxwork.

"Of course she was dead. And probably there was nothing I could have done. I mean, maybe there was. Maybe if I'd called an ambulance. Maybe if... maybe... but I didn't take the note. I never saw it again. Not even after. It was just gone, and so was she."

Tess knew it was bad. She knew it was a fucked-up, awful thing to do.

But she couldn't hold it against Lana.

Tess knew her. She knew she was a good person. The last piece of the puzzle had clicked into place so satisfyingly, like she'd known it would do. That last piece was Lana's guilt.

It was the reason she had been so slow to suspect Allie, so reluctant to do anything about it. She carried the guilt of that day. She was sure Lana was right, that there wasn't anything she could have done. But the what-ifs had stuck with Lana. What if she'd stayed, or come back sooner, or taken the note? What if the note had fixed everything? The note *had* been a trap, Tess thought. Lana thought she'd escaped it, but it was already sprung. It had trapped Lana with everything it might have said, with its infinite contents. It had cursed her forever, to be followed around by the memory of the worst decision she ever made, her weakest moment. And the long-smouldering guilt of that incident blazed to life again when Allie appeared. She was the oxygen it needed to consume Lana. Here was the person she should have been, the better person, the person who didn't do what Lana had done. How could she not feel lesser than her? How could she not think Allie was the light, and she the shadow?

"My mother died when I was nineteen," Lana said. "Allie's mother lived for years more. She saved her."

"It didn't help though, not in the long term," said Tess. "Sure, she lived a little longer. But Allie took her own life. You can't argue that she made the right decision."

Lana turned to her, two long streaks of mascara running down her face. It made her look like a sad clown and Tess almost laughed before realising how inappropriate that would be.

"What?"

"Anyway, it doesn't fucking matter. The decision you made was the best for you. And for your father, maybe? You had a relationship with him, Allie didn't. You wouldn't have met Magnus if you hadn't moved to Castor after your mother died. Your kids wouldn't exist.

There's no good twin, no bad twin. There's just you, who deserves to live and be happy and thrive, and some asshole ghost who's trying to kill you. She's actually trying to kill you. So if anyone's the bad twin, and I don't sanction that interpretation, then it's her. Because I know, without a doubt, that you're a good person. Despite what happened. Maybe *because* of what happened.

Ergo, she's the inversion, she's the intruder. You're Lana, and she's just an echo of someone who's already dead. We just need to make it permanent."

The thought occurred to Tess, quite suddenly, that the ghost in Lana's house was Allie's suicide note. Allie was her own final thoughts, regrets, recollections, addressed to Lana and sent between dimensions. But this time the content was impossible to ignore.

Tess didn't say it. If Lana hadn't seen that herself, there was no need to tell her.

Lana smiled, just a little, the mascara-blackened tears falling from her chin onto her plaster cast. The droplets soaked into the fabric, making little grey starbursts.

"Thanks," she said.

"No problem. I just tell it like it is," said Tess, feeling her face redden. She'd never been good at taking compliments. Tess rummaged in her backpack on the seat beside her and produced a packet of baby wipes. She handed one to Lana.

"Wipe your eyes. You look like that guy from The Crow."

"That guy? Pretty sure his name is The Crow."

But Lana did as she was told and they sat quietly, Tess cycling through scenarios in her head.

"I've got a plan," she said eventually. "You might not like it, but I think we need to go for broke. It's a risky play but... And, I mean, we can always keep the 'burning down the house' plan in reserve..."

"I'm in," said Lana. "Whatever you're thinking, I'm in."

Chapter 34.

Allie sat alone in the house, lights off, darkness outside, floating six inches above a kitchen chair. It wasn't usually this still when it was dark outside. That meant that it was late, even with the days getting shorter. Or did they just seem shorter? And when it was late, everyone was home. Or they should be.

Something bad had happened. A memory snaked, smoke-like and elusive, just behind her, just over her shoulder. She had done something bad to Lana. Or it might have been that Lana had done something bad to her. There was bad blood anyway. There had been a fight and Lana had been hurt. She wasn't sure how she had hurt Lana. It might have been that Lana had hurt herself. That seemed like something Lana would do. She was fragile like that. She was fragile in her bones and fragile in her mind. She wouldn't last long. Her body wouldn't last long without Allie's help. Of that much, Allie was certain. As certain as she could be, anyway.

Lana was always getting hurt. She was always tired and pale and rubbing parts of her body that harboured cold-sharp pains. She didn't listen to music anymore. She wasn't well. Allie was here to help her, after all, wasn't she? Yes, that's why she was here. Things were hard to remember. Things kept dancing away from her, right before she remembered them. She just had to get through it. Just keep going. Focus on why she was here. Here to help Lana. Here to fix her. Replace the parts that weren't working any more.

Allie sat in the room with the stove in it, with the big table in it. The breakfast and dinner room. It was still dark, the dark from the same night as it was before. Was it still that same night? She heard the front door and hurried to see who it was. Except she came into the bathroom with its missing mirror. Wrong. She tried again. She found the hallway.

It was Magnus. He was scowling, a hard sulky frown twisting his usually warm face into something formidable. Lana must have upset him, Allie thought. Why else would he be sad? Or was he angry? She couldn't quite tell. Lana was like a lightning rod for unhappiness. It followed her. It coiled around her and unspooled randomly, contaminating everything. Magnus didn't deserve it.

He moved through the house with slow determination, occasionally sighing hugely and making exasperated expressions like he was having fruitless conversations in his mind. He collected clothes from the cabinet in the kids' room, little neat squares that unfolded into t-shirts and shorts. Clothes Lana had folded. He put them in a duffel bag, along with Cody's little sleeping bag, the fluffy sheep whose name was Sheepie, the little blanket whose name was Blankie. Cody's essential items. Cody didn't name these things himself though. Who was it?

Magnus moved into his and Lana's room, grabbed some of Lana's clothes from the closet and added them to the bag. He squashed everything down, then lay down on the bed, still wearing his boots. Allie watched him. He had one burly arm thrown across his face, shielding his eyes from the ceiling light. His belly rose and fell with deep, rhythmic breaths. She couldn't tell if he was sleeping. Were they going somewhere? Were they going on a trip? She'd fought with Lana, she remembered. She'd hurt Lana. Or Lana had hurt herself. That seemed more like it.

Magnus' phone rang. He groaned and heaved himself to his feet. He rubbed his eyes roughly and answered it.

"Hi," he said, affecting a cheery manner. "Yeah, I'm just there. Just picking up some things. Why? Are they misbehaving?"

He paused and grinned at the response.

"No, they do that sometimes. Tell them they have to keep their own clothes on. Tell them I'll bring cookies from home if they can behave 'til I get back. Okay. I'll try and hurry. Thanks again for letting us stay."

He hung up and shoved the phone back into his jeans' pocket.

He hoisted the bag onto one shoulder. Allie followed him up the stairs, without her foot touching a single step, and into the kitchen.

He was staying somewhere else. He didn't say "I love you" so it wasn't Lana. Allie decided it was his parents maybe. Grandma and Grandpa. She couldn't remember their names. If they even had names. She supposed they did. But nobody had ever told her them. Or she forgot. Sometimes she forgot names.

Magnus opened the fridge and flicked open the clasps on a big Tupperware box of home-made cookies. Lana had made them before, big chewy cookies with pecans and chocolate chips. The kids had half each after dinner. Maybe that was yesterday. Maybe that was a different time Lana made cookies. Maybe she made the same ones again, just to confuse Allie. To trick her. Magnus put two of the cookies between his teeth, snapped the box shut and threw it into the bag. He flicked off the lights and walked back to the front door, eating the cookies sandwiched together like a giant Oreo with no filling.

Then he was gone, and Allie was alone in the dark again, the same dark from the same night. She stood still, trying to remember what happened. Trying to remember if she had fought with Lana, and how and why. Trying to remember if Lana told her where she was going. Probably Lana had done something stupid or desperate. Maybe she'd been in an accident. Had there been an accident? Allie hoped she was okay. Or she hoped her body was okay anyway. Because she had a use for that. And she thought of all the ways Lana's body could be useful to her, because that was the daydream that kept her sane in the long hours of the night. She thought about all the things she could do with Lana's body. All the things she and Magnus could do with Lana's body.

And gradually the light changed, and the day became

the next day, and Allie was still standing in the kitchen, still thinking. Making plans.

A key turned in the lock again, quieter this time. Lana and her small, careful hands. It was light now. A different day. Allie made a note of it. How long had it been since Magnus was there? Was it one day or two?

The door opened and this time Allie made it to the hallway in time to see Lana push the door open with her shoulder and tumble awkwardly through. Lana's eyes scanned the room anxiously but didn't land on Allie. She hadn't chosen exactly to be invisible. Sometimes the situation chose for her. So, she was invisible again. She could always reappear if she needed to. Or she hoped she would be able to. A slimy, creeping feeling of disgust filled her stomach, or where her stomach had been. She hated feeling Lana's eyes slide over her body, failing to latch, failing to notice her. Lana was mean sometimes. And then she remembered that she was invisible. Although maybe that was somehow Lana's fault too. Maybe Lana chose not to see her. It was the sort of thing she would do. Lana was mean sometimes.

Allie noticed something amiss, something different. There was a cast on Lana's right hand, already dirty and frayed. She held the hand close to her body so it looked at first like she was holding a roll of paper towels. What had she done?

Allie remembered the fight. Lana had taken a swing at her, and she had sidestepped it just in time. That seemed right. And now she'd come back to . . . what? To apologise. She should. Allie wasn't sure if she had it in her to forgive Lana. It was a pretty crappy thing that Lana had done, to try and hit her own sister. If she thought nothing of resorting to physical violence with her own twin, who's to say she wouldn't do the same to the kids? It was a distressing thought. It was an emotion strong enough to catch, to hang onto. Most things faded in an instant, like a grain of sherbet on her tongue, leaving behind the vague impression that there had been something. Some things were stronger. Some things allowed her purchase.

"I know you're here," said Lana.

Allie willed herself to be real.

Lana's eyes found her. Her eyes looked scared. Or maybe angry. It was hard to tell. Lana didn't like to let her emotions onto her face. It was suspicious, now that she thought about it. Lana was secretive, and what for? Lana's face was ashy, her eyes ringed with bruise-purple. Her lips were cracked and the same colour as her ashen face. She looked terrible. If anybody was a ghost, it was Lana. The whites of her eyes weren't white, they were grey, and there was a bright red mark in one of them. Blood in an egg is a bad omen, Allie thought, the idea spilling into her brain from somewhere very distant. Her mother had said so.

"Hi," said Lana, unsurprised by Allie's sudden appearance.

"Hi," Allie replied. "Where did you go? Everyone's gone. Where are the kids?"

Her voice sounded funny in her own ears. There was an echo. Emmy had a toy microphone that made her voice distorted and weird. She sometimes laughed hysterically into it, and the laugh was loud and bizarre and made her laugh all the harder until somebody, usually Seb, took it away from her. Allie's voice sounded like that.

"They're at Magnus' parents' house. You landed me in the ER, and now Magnus thinks I'm crazy," said Lana sadly.

"Maybe you are."

"Maybe so are you," said Lana.

She wasn't making sense, thought Allie. It was like arguing with a child.

"I found a way to make you go," said Lana, quickly, almost frantically. Allie looked back at her. Lana's jaw was set. She took a tentative step toward Allie, and another more determined one, until they were almost nose to nose.

"Tess and I found a way. She knows things. She knows

things about ghosts," Lana continued.

"I AM NOT A GHOST!" Allie screamed. She didn't mean to scream. She couldn't control the volume of her own voice. She couldn't rein it in. Her thoughts just exploded outward like there was nothing between the feeling of them and the expression of them. Lana had never said that before. She shouldn't say that.

Lana had her good hand and her cast pressed over her ears, her face turned away, eyes screwed shut. She was too fragile to even talk to.

Lana opened her eyes and stared Allie down, eyes wet and mouth pulled into a sad, grim shape.

"I just came by to tell you. To serve you an eviction notice. Tess is waiting in the car now, just outside. We're going back to her place and we're going to pull the plug on this fucked up situation. For what it's worth, I'm sorry it ended up like this. I'm sorry any of this ever happened," said Lana, "but you shouldn't have come here."

Her chin quivered and she seemed to be fighting to keep her eyes open, like if she blinked, she'd cry. But her words were hard. They hurt.

Allie thought about the kids: she'd never see them again. She'd be alone in the house. Again. And then she'd be gone. Again. Nobody to hold her hand. Nobody to miss her. Again. And it had been within her grasp to fix everything. Lana was so close to the end of her rope. She was so pale and so tired and pushing her out was becoming such a smooth and natural thing. There was hardly even any resistance anymore because the fight was going out of Lana. If Allie had the chance now, she was sure she could push Lana to one side like a sheet hung out to dry. Lana would blow away.

If only she had the chance.

Lana turned her back. It was her chance.

Allie threw herself at Lana, pure instinct and hatred pushing her forward. She rode the crest of a wave made up of every dark feeling, of envy and jealousy and regret. It buzzed and scratched and whirled like a tornado inside Allie's being. It was her, she realised with an unusual clarity. The engine roar of her own directionless rage was her. That screaming void was the sound of her own heart.

And then the sound was gone. And the frantic, crawling vibration inside her was gone. Because she was Lana. Her hold was firm. She fitted better into the space than she ever had before. Things aligned in a way they never had. There had been no fight, none of the warring between electrons or whatever it was that usually caused feedback, static, always threatening to push Allie back out. They were fully one: Allie's brain; Lana's body.

And the other part of Lana, the leftover part, the shadow part, wasn't in there with her.

Allie looked around, savouring the bright clarity of her physical eyes. Things had weight, temporal significance, dimension. The dreamlike, tv-show quality was gone. This was overwhelming and glorious. It was like seeing around her for the first time, seeing the places she had come to know so well, suddenly made real.

She could feel the fear Lana had felt, the physical remnants of her last thoughts. Her heart was racing but slowing; skin clammy but warming. The adrenaline rush of fight-or-flight was fading. She almost felt bad for Lana in that instant, but the joy of feeling anything at all was so sublime that she forgot her compassion almost immediately.

As if a mist was dispersing, things seemed to be growing clearer. The situation had seemed irreconcilable. There had been no other way. But now that she was able to look back on what had happened, it felt so unnecessary somehow. How had things become so fraught? Still, there was nowhere to go but forward, she reasoned. Allie could not allow herself to feel grief about Lana, for the sake of her new family. She needed to be for them everything that Lana had. It was the only way to properly honour her. Then again, she thought, fully realising a thought that had come to her only fleetingly in the past, Lana wasn't really gone. They were the same person. Allie was Lana.

There were no fewer people than there had been before she arrived. No empty bodies. Nothing lost. Only a few memories between them. What did it matter? Nobody would notice. Perhaps Magnus would sense something was amiss, but what could he reasonably assume? Lana had been suffering when Allie got there. She had cried and fretted and forgotten things and avoided difficult discussions. Allie would be happy for him, and Magnus would be grateful. And he would overlook little things, little inconsistencies.

Her hand hurt. Everything about her new body felt smooth and right, except the hand. It felt caught, like a twisted glove. There was a sharp pain when she flexed her fingers, both painful and delicious in its novelty. She thought about the bones inside the hand inside the cast. Her cast, her hand, her bones. She imagined the little bones fanned out from wrist to fingers. One was broken. And she envisioned it snapped in half like a popsicle stick. Lana was ridiculous to try and punch a ghost, for she saw now that's what she had been. She thought about Lana taking a swing at a brick wall, and couldn't help but laugh, a short, cynical bark.

Now Lana was nowhere. There was a poetic justice to it, Allie thought. Wherever Lana was now, she was invisible and silent. She was gone.

Chapter 35.

It happened just like Tess said it would.

She'd told her to provoke Allie, to push her so she would push back; and she'd push Lana right out of her body. It was the only way, Tess had said. How could they do anything about someone who couldn't be touched, couldn't even be seen except by Lana? They had to get the physical laws to notice Allie. So, Lana had pushed her. It felt awful. It felt like driving at breakneck speed in the pitch darkness. Lana had been so preoccupied with protecting herself, keeping Allie at a distance, keeping the relationship cordial. And she'd thrown it away in an instant, on a gamble. On the advice of someone she'd known for a shorter time than she'd known Allie.

When the push came, she wasn't ready. Even though she was anticipating it. It was like the bottom dropped out of her reality. She was suddenly swimming, directionless and numb. And then she was standing in her living room. She couldn't feel her face, or much of anything. Her own body was beside her. Allie was inside it.

Lana felt ill. Every fibre of her being, of whatever stuff she was made of now, rebelled against itself. The cognitive dissonance of looking at her own face was too much. She was glad when Allie turned her back on her. Glad she couldn't see her. Yet there was something terrifying about it, too, about being so wholly ignored. She reached out her hand to touch a lampshade on an end-table beside her. She could see the delicate criss-cross of the linen material, interlocking and elaborate like bismuth crystal. But she couldn't feel it. The texture was gone. Her hand slipped through the shade without troubling it. Her cast was gone, she noted distantly. She felt insignificant. The whole physical world had its back to her.

Lana followed Allie through the house, watching her touch things and smile to herself. Allie dived onto Lana's bed and breathed in the scent from the pillows. She stood in the doorway of the kids' room and stared in at their things. She didn't cross the threshold. Some things required a bigger step. Lana wondered if she might have reservations about becoming their mother. She was happy to take Lana's body and home and husband. But the children were a little more difficult. They knew Lana in ways other people didn't. They were her. Seb and Emmy and Cody were more Lana than Allie was. They would surely recognise that Allie wasn't one of them, wasn't part of them. Lana prayed they wouldn't have to.

When things had gotten unbearable with her mother, she thought her need for freedom was the most powerful thing she had ever felt. The way the need made her into a tool to execute it, just a vessel to hold a feeling, made her feel even less free, made the feeling stronger until it was everything she was. The want filling her up now was greater than that. It made her want to run and scream. What she wanted, with a desperation she had never felt, was for Tess to save her.

Chapter 36.

Allie wandered back into Lana's bedroom. Her bedroom. She wasn't sure what to do. It was enough to just breathe in the house, the house she hadn't wanted in her own reality. She remembered that now, remembered her version of the house. She'd had everything painted over and cleaned away. She couldn't get away from the idea that she'd done the same to Lana. She pushed the thought away.

These things were hers now. All the walls and floors and ceilings. All the furniture and all the scratches and marks on the furniture. These were her things. There was a deep dent on the corner of the closet. What had happened there? Maybe Magnus bumped into it, carrying some other piece of furniture. Maybe they bought it like that. She didn't know. She couldn't ask Magnus, in case it was some closely guarded anecdote, a special memory. She took a deep breath and exhaled, feeling some creeping thing, knowing it wasn't the end of it. It was a feeling poised to grow into something pervasive.

Somewhere outside, a car honked its horn. She wasn't ready to comprehend the outside world yet.

She changed her clothes. That was something people did, something Lana did. She was wearing a tank top with a picture of a frog on it, underneath one of Magnus' cardigans. Why were all of Lana's t-shirts so ridiculous? They somehow went right past whimsical and straight to perplexing. Allie would get rid of them all.

In removing the cardigan, she realised Lana had chosen it because it was just about possible to get her cast through the sleeve. It took a lot of skilful manoeuvring. Every time she moved her little finger, another sickening stab of pain and confusion flew along her nerves. Feeling things was quickly becoming less delightful. She had broken Lana. She had broken her in a lot of ways.

Allie put on a black, button down blouse with puff sleeves that were just a bit too milkmaid-esque. She wasn't sure why Lana would buy something like that. Still, it was the least absurd top she could find and she could fit her cast through the cuff. She would buy new things, classy things that were appropriate and professional. Except, she thought, Lana wasn't a professional. She had been a cake decorator in a bakery, then she was a mother, and some kind of typist or something on the side. Allie wasn't quite sure. She hadn't looked at Lana's resume. She didn't need to own professional clothes. Because Lana wasn't her. But she was Lana. Or she was now. She needed to acclimatise, and preferably before she needed to speak with anyone who knew Lana. It was lucky that Lana didn't have any friends.

She looked at herself in the mirror. Allie had missed having a reflection. It had only added to her feeling of alienation. Even mirrors ignored her. Except the one in the bathroom. She had wished that one would forget her. But looking into her reflection in the closet door, she was not especially comforted. It wasn't her. Things were wrong. There was the cast, for one. The tattoos. And her hair was too long, and dry and unkept. She took it down from its bun. It curled all one way. She ran her good hand through it. Loose hairs wrapped themselves around her fingers and she shook them onto the floor.

The car in the street outside honked loudly again, longer this time. This time it annoyed her. She was busy. She didn't want to be bothered.

The next few days would be challenging, no doubt about it, Allie conceded. She sat down on the bed, eyes still warily fixed on her reflection. She wanted to keep it in sight. She would need to go to Magnus' parents' house, except she had no idea where it was. She could figure it out. She would need to apologise to Magnus, tell him things were going to be okay now. Maybe she could manage to cry a little. He couldn't argue with her if she was crying. She would pull the kids into a huge hug, squashing them together and being ever so careful not to bang their heads with her cast. She would breathe them in, feel their hair on her face, kiss them and pray they didn't notice she wasn't their mother.

Hopefully in time they would forget she was ever someone else, that there was ever someone else who tucked them in at night. Their memories would amend eventually. Everything would smooth out in time. It was just the next few days. Maybe she could distract them with a surprise, she thought. She could come back home with her family in tow, put the kids to bed, swaddle Cody up like a burrito and set him down, ever so gently, in his bassinet.

Then she could sit on the sofa next to Magnus. She was embarrassed to admit to herself that it gave her a little thrill, something like first date jitters. Except the body that was now hers had known Magnus for a decade, slept naked beside him, borne his babies and held his hopes for the future. Still, Allie was as nervy as a teenager about to speak to their crush for the first time. She'd known him too. She knew him better than Lana, because she saw him when he was sure he was alone. She knew how to be around him. She would sit next to him in the same casual, proprietary way she'd seen Lana do. She'd lean up against him, wrap one arm around his body, drift in the warmth and security he provided.

And then she'd say that she'd been thinking about a family vacation. She'd say she needed fresh air and fresh vistas to get over the blue period she'd been floundering in. She'd got a handle on it now, she'd say. It just needed a little something more and she'd be free. He'd buy it. He'd ask what she had in mind. Allie had always wanted to stay in a cute little lodge in the Rockies. In the wintertime when she could ski and drink hot chocolate on the porch. It was hokey, but it was perfect in her mind, like a scene from inside a snow globe. She'd always wanted to do it. It was a childhood fantasy that had never left her. She wondered if Lana had the same fantasy. If she'd shared it with Magnus. It felt like something he'd like too. She imagined him with snow in his beard and she felt herself blush. That was new. A cabin might be too much hassle, she decided, with the kids. She was already modifying her plans for them, she noted with a smile. Maybe a hotel in Banff would be fine. The kids could toboggan and ride the gondolas. And – her reverie was cut off by the doorbell.

She'd forgotten about Tess. She was outside. Just outside in the car, the whole time.

Allie ran to the door, taking the stairs two at a time, and opened it just a crack, keeping it braced against her foot. There was nothing Tess could do now. Nothing. She couldn't tell anyone what had happened, if she even had the whole story herself. She would just seem like a lunatic.

"Hi," said Tess, peering through the gap, trying to see into the room beyond. "Are you done? Are you coming?" Her eyes searched Allie's face.

"Uh, no. I'm actually not," said Allie, hearing Lana's voice coming from her mouth. "Sorry. I've decided I don't want to go ahead and do . . . you know."

Allie didn't know what they had planned, or how much of anything Tess knew.

"My hand really hurts, and it's been a really long day. I think I'm just going to have a nap, and then I'll head over to the in-laws' later. Maybe we can catch up another time?" Allie had no intention of catching up another time.

"Okay," said Tess, scrutinising her face through the opening. "But how are you going to get there?"

"I'll drive," said Allie, noticing Lana's car behind Tess. Lana had left it there and Magnus had driven her to the hospital because -

"You have a broken hand," said Tess flatly.

"Look, I'll figure it out, okay?" Allie insisted. She was sure Tess wasn't buying it, but maybe she could intimidate her into accepting the situation. Maybe she could will her into going away. She just needed her to disappear.

"I thought you couldn't wait to get out of this house," said Tess. Allie knew that she knew. She was trying to provoke her. She looked hard at Tess. Her long, frayed braids were extremely annoying. They were so unkept. Why did she not just take them out and do them again? Or, better yet, brush out her hair and leave it alone? It felt juvenile somehow. But Tess's stare was hard and uncompromising. It cut through Allie. She could feel it.

"What are your in-laws' names?" asked Tess.

"Fuck you," said Allie, suddenly full of rage. "Just fuck off and leave me alone."

Tess couldn't do anything anyway. Why play games with her?

"Oh, that's how it is? So, you are her? You basically admitted it. Lana would never -"

"I don't care what Lana would or wouldn't do. You can't reverse it. It's me now. She's gone. I don't know where and I don't care," said Allie.

She tried to close the door, but Tess jammed her foot against it.

"Lana cared about you, though," said Tess. "She cared about where you might go if you moved on. That's why she never tried anything."

"What could she try?" shouted Allie, forgetting about the door, letting it slide open a few more inches so that she could more easily berate Tess.

"Magic," said Tess.

And for a second Allie thought she'd misheard her. It was so ridiculous that it knocked the spite out of her completely. She opened and closed her mouth twice before finding her voice.

"What the fuck are you talking about?"

"I'm a witch," said Tess.

Again, Allie thought she must have said something else. She couldn't be serious. "I used magic to look into that evil mirror. The one from the bathroom. I know what happened to you and I told Lana."

It made sense now. Lana had been scared of her, Allie remembered. She had felt something was different, but she didn't know what. She'd been blocked by the fog of uncertainly that had plagued her. Things would have been so different if only she'd been able to think properly. It was like she had been possessed. Little bits and pieces of her interactions with Lana were coming back. She didn't feel good about them.

Tess took advantage of this sudden attack of conscience to push the door open all the way. She snatched up a huge square parcel from where it leaned against the wall, something flat and wrapped in a bedsheet. Preoccupied with what this item might be, Allie failed to react to Tess's invasion, failed to slam her whole body against the door.

She let Tess in.

"There's nothing you can do," said Allie. It's what she kept telling herself. "There's no such thing as witches. There's no such thing as magic. And there's nothing you can do."

Tess looked like she might laugh.

"What are you then? How are you here? Explain it to me," Tess asked. She clearly expected no reply and Allie had none to give.

Tess walked past her into the kitchen and leaned the object against the leg of the kitchen table. Allie closed the front door and followed her. Tess sat at the table. Allie did the same. It was difficult to remember how to be flesh and blood. She stared at the chair a second too long before she remembered what to do

"What are you going to do now?" asked Tess, strangely calmly.

"I don't know," admitted Allie. She was in uncharted territory.

"Do you want to have a cup of coffee? I'll make it if you can't remember how. I know where things are," said

Tess.

She knew Allie wouldn't be able to make coffee. She could barely sit on a chair. Tess was an enemy, but there was an automatic empathy to her. She considered other perspectives. She noticed things.

Chapter 37.

Tess had only been to Lana's house once before, but she remembered where things were. Things she didn't know, like where the spoons were kept, she guessed. All kitchens were basically the same. They couldn't talk over the sound of the coffee machine percolating, but soon it would be done.

There was part of a blueberry pie in the refrigerator, Saran-wrapped to a serving plate shaped like a strawberry. Tess slid it out carefully, closed the fridge, paused to look at the drawings stuck to the door. Seb's drawings had his name in the corner, in neat block letters. He drew his family mostly, and animals, and fantasy creatures, all very small and meticulous, floating in a vast white nothingness. Other drawings, Tess guessed Emmy's, were more abstract. Just blobs of colour, with the occasional slightly creepy face. There was one little handprint on a small cardboard disc. Cody's, Tess thought.

She could feel Allie behind her, staring at her back. Tess had waited in the car the appropriate amount of time, enough time for Lana to provoke Allie. It wasn't a sure thing. They didn't know that Allie would do what they expected, not for sure. But when Lana's face appeared at the door, Tess knew it had happened. She was good at predicting what people would do, even ghosts, even in very specific and unusual circumstances.

Tess had a can of mace in her pocket, and she hadn't taken her hand off it until she was inside the house, until Allie was seated across from her at the kitchen table. It didn't seem like she was about to attack her. If anything, she was a lot more controlled than Tess had expected, like the victory had thawed her.

Tess returned to the table with two plates of pie, two cups of coffee, wondering vaguely if Lana was there too. Was she watching them sit at her table, eating her baked goods and using her cups? It was neither Tess's house nor

255

was it Allie's. It felt odd, like they had rented the space, like they were on vacation.

Allie forked at the pie with her left hand, sending pastry crumbs across the table.

"Ugh, stupid hand," she said, putting her cast down heavily onto the table.

Tess leaned over and roughly broke the pie into pieces with a butter knife. She didn't want to risk introducing a weapon to the situation, so a butter knife would have to suffice.

"Thanks," said Allie.

She impaled a chunk on her fork and quickly transferred it to her mouth.

She made a face like she'd taken a bite out of a lemon. A face somewhere between sensory overload and fascination. Tess took a bite of her own pie. It was good. It was normal. Nothing strange there. Maybe Allie wasn't used to tasting things. Maybe it was all too much.

Allie sipped her coffee and the face subsided.

"There are blackberries in this. They're from the garden," said Allie eventually, perfectly casually. "I saw the kids pick them and Lana washed them and froze them for later. That was before I ever spoke to her though, so I guess they've been in the freezer a long time."

"They taste fine to me."

"I didn't say they tasted bad. It's just weird to think about. A blackberry grows in the sunshine, then you put it on ice and it just stays the same, and when you get around to eating it, blackberries aren't anywhere. It's not blackberry season anymore. It's just weird," said Allie, staring into space.

Tess had the distinct impression she wasn't okay. Her mind hadn't quite made it through unscathed. Or maybe it was more that it had gone back to exactly how it had been, Tess thought darkly, the mental image of the bloody bathtub blooming behind her eyes.

"It's weird, sure," said Tess.

"Lana said you were going to get rid of me," said Allie, her eyes flashing dangerously for a second before falling quiet again. "How exactly were you going to do that?"

"Doesn't matter," said Tess. "Like you said, it's too late now, right? Lana's gone?"

"I think so," said Allie.

"Poor Lana. She really went through it, you know?"

"I know. I'm sorry for all that. It's like I wasn't myself. It wasn't even really me doing that. I mean, following her around her own home, following her around when she didn't know I was there. Other things too. Worse things," said Allie, still not meeting Tess's eye.

"You made her think she'd be better off dead. You made her give up. I'd think that someone in your position would think twice before doing something like that, playing with the mental state of someone already in a bad place. She was pretty ground down from having Cody -"

"I know. I saw," said Allie.

"- And then you whispered in her ear and pushed her and made her afraid to go to sleep."

"I said I was sorry!" Allie shouted, finally looking Tess in the eyes. There was fear there, more than Tess had expected. She looked like a cornered animal.

"You chose to end your life. I know all about it. It was a horrible thing to see, just so you know. That'll be with me forever. You wanted out. No judgement. It is what it is. I'm not going to say that was good or bad or whatever. This isn't A Christmas Carol. Or the other Christmas one where the guy tries to kill himself. I hated that movie."

"Me too," said Allie, grinning just a little. "What an asshole that guy was."

Tess smiled. Maybe Allie wasn't so bad. But she was still wrong. Whether she deserved to live, whether she deserved it more than Lana, wasn't really important. She'd taken something that wasn't hers. She'd tried to fix a suicide with a murder. It was just more death, even if it didn't look like anything at all from the outside.

Tess took another bite of pie. There had been powdered sugar on it once, she thought, but the condensation under the plastic wrap had melted it.

"What I'm saying is, you chose. A person is only made up of their choices, if you think about it." Tess had considered her argument carefully the night before, rehearsed it in the car while she watched the seconds tick by. She had considered the task at hand, of convincing a ghost to give up a second chance at living. Not an easy thing to do. She could only hope that Allie was similar enough to Lana that Tess could use the things she'd learned about her. She understood Lana. Hopefully she understood Allie.

"Sometimes you choose wrong, and it follows you," Tess continued. "You're always wondering if that was the right thing to do. Always thinking 'what if?' And that's why Lana and you aren't the same. Because you made different choices."

"Did she tell you the choice she made? The thing that makes us different?" said Allie ominously.

"She did," said Tess.

"I called an ambulance, you know? I saved her. I got there in time, and I saved our mother. Not in the long run, I guess. But I did the best I could."

"You don't even know if that was the same time. You don't know that the time Lana failed was the time you didn't," said Tess. "It's important to you, I get it. It was important to Lana too. She thought she was the bad twin, because she was haunted by what happened. She let you win because she thought you deserved it.

But, here's the problem. You chose to die. And then you wanted it not to be true. I get it. But you stole from Lana. You stole her ability to recover, and you stole her choice to keep living. You made your decision hers. That's not right. You can see that's not right."

A tear rolled down Allie's face. She wiped it away with the back of her cast and looked at it in bewilderment, at the small patch of moisture soaking into the fabric, already stained with the grey teardrops Lana had shed in the emergency room.

"Well, it's too late anyway," said Allie, her voice breaking.

"It's not," said Tess.

And this was the point that things would go either way, she knew. She put her hand back into her pocket, wrapping her fingers around the cool cylindrical mace can. It clinked against the obsidian gem. If Allie leapt across the table, she would spray her right in the face, and run to the car and drive back into Castor and lock her front door. Allie didn't know where she lived, so she'd be safe, for a while at least.

"This was the plan," said Tess. "I told Lana to let you push her out. I told her to step back and let you in. She's still around here somewhere. Or that's what I'm hoping anyway. Otherwise, I'll be left standing over a dead body when —"

"When I leave?" said Allie. The dangerous glint was back in her eyes, and she was throwing suspicious glances around the room.

"When you leave," said Tess firmly. "Lana's not dead. She's just stuck. Like you were. You can't get rid of her. She'll always be here, always looking at you, even though you can't see her. And she'll degrade, like you did. And then you'll be the one always looking over your shoulder. The body you've stolen is weak.

You feel it, right? Your teeth hurt? You feel woozy, bloodless? Your bones hurt. They're not just painful, they're weak. Lana told me the doctor at the hospital said so. That's why your hand is broken. You're cold, right? And I'll bet good money that coffee in your hand is stone cold too.

You're ill. And you'll never get better. I'm sure of it. Even if you move away. Because what's wrong is that reality has splintered. It'll never fix itself while you're here.

Because you being here is wrong.

This building around us isn't the haunted house, you are. Your body is the haunted house."

Tess paused, letting Allie consider it. She wasn't totally sure Allie had even heard her. She was staring into her coffee, like it was unknowably deep, like a well without end.

Tess picked up the parcel leaning against the table leg. She uncovered it and placed it on the kitchen table, sliding the plates and cups to one side to accommodate it.

"I knew that's what it was," said Allie, with a heavy sigh, as if resigning herself to the fact that the mirror had defeated her. She had not been able to get away from it, or to get it away from her.

"Time to make a choice," said Tess. "It's like the world's worst gameshow. But there is a right answer. And maybe something like redemption. There's a chance to make it better for Lana. I don't know about you."

Allie's eyes darted to the front door and her body tensed almost imperceptibly. Tess hand went back to the pepper spray. But the fight went out of Allie's eyes quickly. Her posture softened. She slumped forward in her chair.

"I'll go."

Relief hit Tess like a wave, and she thought for a moment she might throw up. She kept her face calm, though, compassionate, reassuring Allie that her choice was right. She only had to keep it together for a moment more.

"I'm not doing it for you," Allie said. "Your speech was actually very sanctimonious and patronising."

That caught Tess off guard. She almost decided to pick a fight with Allie before she remembered she was supposed to be compassionate. She set her expression and said nothing.

"I'll do it for Lana. I thought she was too fragile to keep going. I thought she wouldn't make it, that she was going to go out the same way I did. We're the same, after all. So, I thought, what's the difference if I'm here to take over from her? It'd be better for the kids. She got weaker and sadder and less able to cope with stuff.

I didn't realise I was doing that to her. I thought I was watching it happen, not making it happen. I didn't realise the universe, or whatever you want to call it, knew I was here."

"The universe always knows," said Tess.

Allie stood slowly and looked into the mirror. She let go of a single sudden sob she hadn't quite been able to hold back. Tess looked in too. There was nothing there but Lana's reflection. But Allie's gaze was long and deep, seeing past the glass, seeing something Tess couldn't. Tess fought not to feel bad for Allie, not to muddy the situation. She just had to get through it, just finish the task. She could feel Lana's encouragement. She could feel her watching the situation.

Save me.

Allie looked back up at Tess for a second, then her eyes broke away suddenly as Lana's body fell to the floor. The chair was knocked over, Lana's limbs crumpled, the cast banged hard against the tabletop and then the floor.

There was silence. It was up to Lana now.

Chapter 38.

Lana watched the conversation unfold. She knew the bare bones of what Tess planned to say. She knew she would try and convince Allie that Lana's body wouldn't hold in the long run, that two people were doomed if she stayed, but only one if she left.

Lana was not prepared to feel bad for Allie though. Every shuddering intake of breath, every tear, every numb stare, hurt Lana. It wasn't just because she was watching her own self fall to pieces. She felt something for Allie, something she'd never felt for her mother. *We're part of each other.*

Allie had tried to kill her, but it had been justified in her incorporeal brain. Lana could feel the beginnings of that now. It was a little more difficult to hang on to thoughts. There was a sense of having walked into a room to find something, only to have forgotten the thing. There was always something she wasn't remembering, just a hole where the thing should be. She couldn't imagine how bad it had been for Allie, how little of herself she'd had left, how lost she'd been. The weight of empathy was crushing.

Lana realised she hadn't been following their conversation. *This is important. Everything depends on this, on right now.* But she had just zoned out for no reason. She tried to focus in on the two people sitting at the table. Allie stood and stared down into the mirror, down a long, long way. Lana could feel the pull of the mirror, at the centre of an invisible vortex. And suddenly Allie was on the floor.

Except she was also standing next to Lana. *That's my body on the floor.* And the Allie next to her was made of the same stuff as her. They were both disembodied, floating on a secret plane that Tess obviously couldn't see, as she whirled around calling Lana's name. *That's not important right now. I'll deal with all that later.*

Lana realised that Allie was not the haunting green colour she usually was, nor did she look exactly like Lana, as she had a moment earlier. She was herself, the way she was when she had first appeared in Lana's house a lifetime ago.

"I'm sorry I tried to kill you," said Allie. "That's not really what it was though. You know that, right? Did you hear any of that?" she gestured toward Tess.

"Yeah, I got it. More or less," said Lana graciously.

"I know I don't deserve forgiveness. I'm not going to ask," said Allie with a little self-conscious shrug.

"No, you can have it. I forgive you," said Lana.

And she meant it. She found that she had no room inside her for animosity. She was too tired and too distant for grudges. And now that they were truly the same, more the same than they'd ever been, the line between Allie and herself felt remarkably arbitrary. They could so easily be switched. They were just souls; in the shape of the people they'd been. Two equivalent quantities of something unquantifiable. It was the easiest thing to forgive her.

Without deciding to, Lana stepped toward Allie, arms open. She pulled her in tight, their ghost bodies acting the way normal flesh and blood should. Lana held her for a time and stroked her hair and was grateful that the situation felt a little vague. She was sure she would be crying if she possibly could.

"I'm glad I got to know you," said Lana.

"You shouldn't be," said Allie.

"Maybe. I am though. I'd rather it went like this than just never knowing you existed."

Allie nodded. "I'm glad you know I existed."

Allie held her a little tighter, like she couldn't quite summon up the courage to look at Lana.

"Take care of those little nuggets," Allie mumbled into Lana's shoulder, "those little peanuts."

"I always do," said Lana.

Allie pulled away and gave her a look that held all the hours and days they'd been together. It had eternity in it. It was terrifying and sad and a hundred other things Lana couldn't quite feel. But the look made her soul feel old.

"I know you do. I'm going to go," said Allie. "I'm overdue."

"Good luck… y'know, with whatever comes now. Maybe I'll see you again some time."

Lana felt that she would. That look, the infinite distance in Allie's eyes when she'd given her that look, made her sure of it. It was something deeper and weirder than anything Lana had felt. It was a truth beyond her plane of existence, beyond Allie's, beyond anyone's.

Allie nodded, and smiled, knowing the same.

The mirror on the table exploded suddenly, without warning. Tess covered her face and dropped to her knees. Jagged fingers of glass skittered across the kitchen tiles, bouncing off the cabinets and sliding underneath the refrigerator. Little gravel-like chunks rolled along the floor, ringing faintly against the ceramic surface. When everything had come to a halt, Tess stood up and shook the glass from her clothing and hair. She picked a shard out of the side of her hand and flicked the bloody splinter across the room.

Lana lay on the floor, back in her body, covered in little stinging cuts. Her hand screamed in pain. She remembered the cast banging against the floor when Allie dropped. *Looks like it's back to the ER.*

"Lana?" Tess called, seeing her stir.

Lana felt right. Moving past the distraction of her broken hand, she explored the other sensations of her body. It felt warm, finally warm, and uncontested. Not a battleground anymore, just a home. She was okay, and blessedly alone.

Chapter 39.

Halloween felt different this year. Tess couldn't quite look at the little trick-or-treaters in their ghostly bedsheets in the same way. She couldn't not think about Allie. The Looking Glass was heaving with costumed guests. Some had made a huge effort, people for whom Halloween was a big deal. Some people had made do with plastic devil horns or cat ears. Tess was a witch, her pointy hat worn proudly. Steve was a newt. Tess had taken a great many photographs of him.

Lana and Magnus were in the category of people for whom Halloween was a major event. It felt to Tess sometimes like she didn't know Lana very well at all, because she had only gotten to know the haunted Lana. She only knew her to be overwhelmed and pressed, struggling to keep her head above water. She hadn't seen her in her element until now, enjoying a holiday she could somehow still find whimsical and fun even after what had happened. She turned out to be fantastic at compartmentalising things, as Tess had been sure she would be. Maybe that wasn't the best, thought Tess. It was her way though.

Lana was dressed as a mermaid, but a bloodthirsty mermaid with long tangled hair and eerie pale blue makeup. The cast was still there, frayed and battered, with silver paper scales glued on for the occasion. Even under the makeup and dark eyeshadow, she looked more alive than she had done. Her eyes were no longer flat and off-colour. They were alive.

Magnus appeared at Lana's side, dressed as the whaler to Lana's mermaid, complete with aluminium foil harpoon. He wrapped an arm around her waist, his sweater catching on the sequins of Lana's dress. He disentangled himself, scowling but not really scowling. He tried again, and held her tight. He laughed at something Lana said, and she laughed because he was laughing, like people without real problems. Just the regular amount of problems. The normal amount of regrets and bad choices.

The kids were there too. Tess felt her mouth quirk involuntarily at the idea that she thought of hers and Lana's collective kids as 'the kids'. Cody, wearing a hand-me-down pumpkin onesie, shared the playpen with Steve. Emmy was around somewhere. Tess saw her small hand appear over the snacks table now and then, to sneak a handful of chips and drag them back to the depths of her little den underneath the table. She had sulked at first, apparently because she'd not been able to bring her new bicycle to the party. Tess couldn't imagine the scale of the devastation if she'd been allowed to do so. She was spirited, Tess thought charitably, pushing other, less kind descriptors to the side.

Emmy was a girl cowboy. She had told Tess several times. Not a cowgirl. Lana had explained that Emmy was currently riding the crest of a cowboy mania that was showing no signs of slowing down. Lana had room in her mind for things like that now. Things that were objectively not important at all, but also the most precious random things. Things Lana would remember in a couple of years and cry at. Those things must feel all the more precious now, Tess thought, because Allie had wanted them so desperately. Lana had fought for those things.

Lana made her way over to Tess, a can of ginger beer in her hand looking very incongruous with her costume. Tess tipped the brim of her witch's hat. It was barely a costume at all, because she felt more like herself than ever. It was a shame that it wasn't an acceptable hat to wear daily.

"You're not mixing," said Lana. "Aren't you supposed to be mixing? It's your party. There's a redhead around here somewhere. She's dressed like a sexy demon, or sexy devil or sexy lobster. Something red with cleavage anyway. I caught her looking your way a couple of times." Lana winked like she barely understood how to wink, raising her opposite eyebrow ridiculously.

Tess almost choked on her drink.

"What?" said Lana. "I can notice things too."

"You're not mixing either. You're just hanging onto your husband. You can talk to him any time," said Tess, grinning.

"Yeah, I know," said Lana, shrugging in a way that made her starfish bra seem quite precarious. "Feels like there's a lot to catch up on though. Actually, I've got something for you. I just remembered."

Lana scurried away as quickly as her fishtail skirt would allow and returned with a purse shaped like a shell.

"I never get a chance to use this," Lana explained, prying the clasp open.

"Are you a mermaid just so you could use that bag?" asked Tess.

"Maybe. Anyway, this is for your collection." Lana reached into the bag and produced a small, dagger-like shard of mirror. She pressed it carefully into Tess's open palm.

"I'm still finding pieces, now and again. I swear if you put them all together you'd have more than one mirror's worth," said Lana.

"I'm not going to put them all together," said Tess.

Lana nodded sagely.

Tess had swept the pieces up, the ones she could find, after the mirror had broken. Lana had slumped on the sofa like a wet rag, sipping ice water and watching an infomercial about a mop on tv. She had worn a critical expression that was almost funny, despite everything. Tess had looked down at the mirror pieces in the dustpan, poised to tip them into the trash. And she hadn't been able to do it. She put them in an empty detergent container and took them home with her. She had transferred them to the walnut jewellery box Lana had given her. Then she had put the box inside another box, and put it on a high shelf, in the store, not in her house. If it was bad luck to break a mirror, throwing away the pieces felt even worse. She couldn't really say why. But trying to dispose of the evidence felt like it would invite further trouble. The pieces were fine up on the shelf. Her eye went to it now, just to make sure it was where she left it. It was fine. Of course it was fine.

Tess wrapped the new fragment in a napkin from the snack table, careful not to look into the mirror shard, just in case. She thought horribly about paramedics lifting Allie's wet and bloodless body from the bath. Probably not paramedics. Paramedics wouldn't do her much good. Who then? Who dealt with things like that? She hoped she never needed to know. Would the flesh fall off the bone? The thought came out of nowhere. No, the thought came from holding the glass in her hand. Is that what happened to dead bodies? From having been in water so long? Is that what happened? She put the piece of glass, in its paper shroud, into a drawer. The thoughts wafted away.

"I'm a bat," said a voice from near her elbow, making her jump. It was Seb, demonstrating the wingspan of his costume. She had asked him if he was Batman when he first came in. The look he had given her had caused genuine embarrassment. Now he felt the need to remind her, like she was an idiot.

"Bats use echolocation to see the world around them," he continued. "And they're pollinators, like bees."

"I know. Bats are cool, huh?" said Tess. She didn't have much experience talking to kids of his age. She hoped she figured it out before Steve was six.

Lana had warned her that he might corner her with his bat facts. Tess liked that he had researched his costume. He wanted Halloween to be an informative experience, which felt like a refreshing interpretation of the holiday.

"I wanted to tell you something," he said earnestly.

"Sure, shoot. Is it something about bats?" asked Tess.

He narrowed his eyes, noting the sarcasm Tess had done her best to avoid.

"No. I want to say that I'm glad you're friends with my mom," he said.

"That's so nice. Thanks, bud," said Tess, genuinely moved.

He nodded impatiently, like he'd been told enough times how nice and polite and well-mannered a little boy he was.

"My mom doesn't have many friends," he continued. "She's happy by herself, like me. My dad says me and her are a lot alike. We're not shy. But we're not loud. Dad is like Emmy. And I'm like mom."

Tess nodded and let him go on.

"And then, a while ago, she did get a friend. Only it was an imaginary friend. I used to have one of those, but then I got too old to play that. Plus I got Emmy and she's my real friend," he said.

Tess forgot to breathe.

"And then she got sad. I think maybe her imaginary friend was pretty mean. I sometimes hear what people say, through the door and stuff. But don't tell her I told you!" He suddenly looked very fierce and very much like Lana. The anger faded in a second.

"So I don't know for sure," he continued, "for one hundred percent, why she would even imagine a mean friend. You're supposed to imagine someone fun, but maybe she couldn't remember how to do that. But anyway," he exhaled wearily, "now you're her friend and the imaginary friend has gone away, because that's what happens when you get a real friend. Like with me and Emmy.

So I wanted to say thanks. And I was going to give you a sticker but I can't find it. Sometimes I put them inside my shoes so Emmy doesn't get them, but these aren't my regular shoes y'know. They're my bat shoes.

I gotta give you one another time. I'll remember."

He nodded very formally, his speech concluded, and walked away without saying anything else.

Tess watched him grab a handful of mini crackers from the snack table, spilling several, and scramble underneath the table to join his sister.

The End

RED on the INSIDE

ACKNOWLEDGEMENTS

This book would not exist without the support of some special people.

First, a heartfelt thank you to Richard at Burton Mayers Books for giving me the confidence I needed to get *Red On The Inside* into a publishable state. Thank you for having faith in my writing.

To my mum—thank you for reading drafts, offering feedback, and pushing me to dig deeper. Your thoughts were invaluable in shaping this novel.

A massive thank you to my family, especially my husband and children, for their patience and understanding during the writing process. Your love and support gave me the strength to keep going, even on the toughest days.

Lastly, to the writers whose work I've long admired—Stephen King, among others—thank you for showing me the joy in the strange and the dark.

ABOUT THE AUTHOR

Elizabeth Kuligowski is a writer of speculative fiction, horror, and magical realism. Her work has been shortlisted for the Curtis Brown Discoveries Prize and the Mslexia Children's & YA Novel Competition. With a degree in Classics from King's College London, she weaves ancient myths and narratives into eerie, contemporary settings.

Originally from the UK, she now lives in Sweden with her husband and two children. When she's not writing, she enjoys long walks in the forest and arguing about old movies.

OTHER TITLES FROM
BURTON MAYERS BOOKS:

Some truths are best left buried...

FOR RYE

GAVIN GARDINER

www.ingramcontent.com/pod-product-compliance
Lightning Source LLC
Chambersburg PA
CBHW022029240626
47154CB00007B/2327